BEFORE

What Reviewers Say About KE Payne's Work

365 Days

"One of the most real books I've ever read. It frequently made me giggle out loud to myself while muttering, "OMG, RIGHT?" —*AfterEllen.com*

me@you.com

"A wonderful, thought-provoking novel of a teenager discovering who she truly is."—*Fresh Fiction*

Another 365 Days

"Funny, engaging, and accessible."—*Kirkus Reviews*

The Road to Her

"An excellent piece of young adult fiction. I truly enjoyed it."—*All Things Lesbian*

Because of Her

"A must-read."—*Lesbian Fiction Reviews*

Once the Clouds Have Gone

"Delightful and heart-warming, this sweet romance was everything a good romance should be."—*Prism Book Alliance*

When I Knew You

"Extremely sweet and heartwarming, the heartbreak and missed opportunities between the two jumped off the page and pulled at my heartstrings."—*Fantastic Book Reviews*

By the Author

365 Days

me@you.com

Another 365 Days

The Road to Her

Because of Her

Once The Clouds Have Gone

When I Knew You

Before

Before

by

KE Payne

2016

BEFORE

ISBN 13: 978-1-62639-677-7

This Trade Paperback Original Is Published By
Bold Strokes Books, Inc.
P.O. Box 249
Valley Falls, NY 12185

First Edition: September 2016

Credits
Editor: Ruth Sternglantz
Production Design: Susan Ramundo
Cover Design By Sheri (graphicartist2020@hotmail.com)

Acknowledgments

My sincere thanks to Ruth Sternglantz and Stacia Seaman for making all my books look so wonderful, and to Cindy Cresap, Connie Ward, Sandy Lowe, and all the other wonderful people at BSB who work so tirelessly behind the scenes for us all. Also to Sheri for taking my picture idea and turning it into the amazing work of art you see on the front cover.

Continued thanks to both Sarah Martin and Mrs D for all their support and friendship.

To BJ for tirelessly reading and rereading endless drafts with me, but mostly for all the love, laughs and support.

Finally, a massive thank you to all the readers who continue to buy my books, and who take the time to contact me. I truly appreciate every email, Facebook comment, and Tweet that you send me. Your continued support is immensely important to me—thank you all so much.

PROLOGUE

The first time I met Alex Brody I had a headache. And I mean a real bitch of a headache. Bordering on a migraine, it was the type that made me hate everything and everyone, and made me just want to go home, pull the duvet up over my head, and sleep until it went away. Except I couldn't do any of those things. And that made me dislike Alex even more, which was really unfair of me, considering it was her first day with us, and ironic, bearing in mind everything that happened afterwards.

I guess there was another reason I initially disliked her, though. She wasn't Nicole. She was Alex, and she'd rocked up at the studio full of confidence and giving it all this couldn't-give-a-damn shit, and acting like she was our best friend. Which in hindsight I can see was her way of coping with her first-day nerves. Back then, though, I thought she was an idiot.

And, yeah. She wasn't Nicole.

Nicole Kelly had been a damned good singer, and I knew whoever replaced her would have to be something really special. Alex sure thought she was special. I thought differently, but that could have been because I wasn't acting like my normal self. But then, everyone else had been acting weird since it happened too. Since Nicole left. Since our manager called me and my bandmates into the studio to tell us. He'd wanted, he'd said, to let us be the first to know. Before the press got hold of it. Before Nicole's downward spiral had the chance to kill off Be4 just when we'd finally started to get somewhere.

But we'd had no time to stress about any of that, because Alex was brought in the very next day.

And that's when my life really started to change.

Chapter One

The tall, slender girl sitting on the edge of the mixing desk talking with the music tech guys when I arrived at the studio looked exactly as she had when I'd last seen her on the TV, just a few weeks before. Seventeen, like the rest of us, Alex Brody had a crop of dark, sleek hair and an air of easy confidence which I could sense even from behind the door of the studio as I watched her laughing and joking with the guys inside. I was apprehensive straight away.

"She's here already?" my bandmate Robyn whispered in my ear. "And why the fuck is Nate looking at her like that when he's supposed to be dating *me*?"

I looked at Robyn. She looked mad. Pretty much typical Robyn then.

I followed her gaze through the small window in the studio door, scrunching my eyes up against the harsh lights inside the studio, which were making my head hurt even more than it already was. Robyn was right; from where I was standing, it looked like her boyfriend was hanging on to Alex's every word. As were the two other music tech guys, Grant and Matt, who were sitting with her too.

"Guess Ed wanted her to be here by the time we arrived." I shrugged. "And Nate's not looking at her *like that*," I lied. From where I was standing, he looked like he was all over her like a hot rash.

Alex was always in motion while she spoke: tucking her legs under her, teasing out a strand of hair, managing her hands. While we watched, I saw her lean over the desk and say something to Nate, making him laugh out loud. Then I swear they all looked over to us as Alex said something else, but I guess that could have been a coincidence. Or me being paranoid.

"Who the fuck does she think she is?" Robyn said. Maybe she'd just seen what I'd seen. "Talent show reject," she murmured, her breath creating a circle of mist on the glass, "that's all she is."

"Don't forget the failed record contract as well." I bumped Robyn's arm, but she didn't laugh.

"Seventeen and washed up," Robyn said, "and yet Ed still thinks she can fill Nicole's shoes."

As we continued to lurk behind the door, still glowering at Alex, I saw Grant get up and walk towards us. We stepped back, allowing him to open the door and come out into the corridor. As he passed us, he stopped, threw a look back over his shoulder into the studio, and said, "Met the new girl yet?"

"Figure we're just about to." Robyn looked at the closing door.

"Reckon you've got some competition there," Grant said, starting to walk away again. "Press'll be fighting over who to photograph the most now." His laughter hung around us as he disappeared down the corridor.

Robyn didn't respond. She shouldered the door back open and strode across the studio floor, making straight for Nate, then sidled up next to him, cutting him off midconversation. I watched as she draped her arms round his neck and pulled him in to her, presumably saying something to him because I saw him nod. It was so obvious, it was hilarious. Then I saw Robyn look at Alex and guessed she was speaking to her now, so I entered the room and joined them, then just sort of hung around by the mixing desk, waiting for Alex to look at me so I could speak to her too.

"Hey," I said when her gaze finally came my way.

"Hey."

And that's how it started. As simple as that. No pleasantries, no names. Just one quick greeting each. Alex, it seemed, was a girl of few words. Instead of trying to strike up any kind of conversation with either me or Robyn, she stood in front of us, her thumbs hitched into the back of her jeans, hair tumbling across her eyes, still oozing more confidence than I'd ever seen from any girl before. Especially one on her first day at work. I guessed having just been on one of the most popular TV talent shows gave you that kind of self-assurance.

"So you're Alex?" Robyn said, transferring her arm from Nate's shoulder to mine. "I'm Robyn," she said. "This is Talia. We call her Tally."

"Then I'll call her Tally too." Alex smiled, looked me up and down, then raised an eyebrow, and I could tell straight away from that one tiny thing she totally thought she was the bee's knees. Then she briskly pulled her hand from her pocket and extended it first to me, then to Robyn. "If that's okay?"

I wasn't sure who that was addressed to—me or Robyn—but I nodded anyway.

"And Brooke?" Alex asked. "Ed said I'd get to meet all three of you guys today."

"Late." I rolled my eyes. "She's *always* late. Sometimes I think Be4 should be renamed Be Late, just for her."

No one laughed.

I'm never late. Because Be4 is my life, and singing is my life. It's all I've ever wanted to do, since I first shoved a hairbrush in my hand and stood in front of a mirror singing the words to my favourite song, watching my reflection and loving the way singing made me feel inside. I've never really been one for talking. Conversation isn't my strong point. But singing? Singing's everything to me.

So is Be4. It's been my life for the last four years, ever since me, Nicole, Robyn, and Brooke cobbled together a band for our Year 9 end-of-term concert and discovered we sounded pretty good together. That's when the busking started. Four years ago. Four thirteen-year-olds hanging out outside the shops on Brighton's seafront with our second-hand amp ramped up so loud we'd get moved on after five minutes, but still hoping we'd end up with enough money at the end of the day to be able to buy a takeaway on the way home. We worked hard too. For three years we worked our butts off, busking and gigging weekends and holidays, making a name for ourselves around the town, putting demo tracks that we'd recorded in Robyn's parents' garage out on YouTube, gaining a small group of faithful followers. It was hard work but it was worth it, because even though we didn't know it at the time, we were slowly on our way to living the dream.

"So, are you from round here then?" Robyn was addressing Alex. My head was pounding and I was still miffed that neither of them had laughed at my joke.

"You didn't watch *Sing*, I take it?" Alex's smile was slow. I noticed her hand had been tucked into her back pocket, and her lazy swagger, tightened up slightly when she'd introduced herself to us, was back. "They did a VT of me at home."

"I don't really watch stuff like that," Robyn replied. "So are you from round here?" she repeated.

I saw the flicker of ennui that passed across Alex's face, presumably from Robyn's blatant dismissal of *Sing*.

"Camden," she replied. "Moved there earlier this year."

"Before you did the"—Robyn rolled a hand—"what was it called again?"

"*Sing*." Alex's words dissolved into a sigh. "Yeah. Before that."

"*Sing*," Robyn echoed. "That's right. The reality whatsit."

As an outsider looking in, it was childish but amusing. Think lions on the Serengeti circling a lioness, each one eyeing the other up. Or dogs circling one another for the same tennis ball. You get the picture. I watched the pair of them before I spoke, secretly admiring the fact that Alex quite obviously didn't give a shit about Robyn's provocation, while at the same time wishing Robyn wouldn't keep trying to wind her up.

"Camden's nice." I sounded like a prig.

"I'm sorry?"

"Camden," I repeated. "It's nice."

The blast of air from an opening door took whatever reply Alex was or wasn't going to give and blew it away, and instead signalled the arrival of Brooke, red-faced and mumbling profuse apologies to whoever would listen. Robyn's arm, which was still draped about my shoulder, magically jumped over to Brooke's shoulder, presumably to reinforce to Alex (as if she needed it) that here was the arrival of another member of Team Robyn. Grateful for Brooke's intervention, and tiring quickly of Robyn's puerile motives, I moved away, rooting around in my bag for some painkillers as I did so. I listened to the muffled conversation coming from across the studio as Alex introduced herself to Brooke, while at the same time cursing myself for not having anything with me to dull my throbbing head.

I sank into one of the swivel chairs next to the speakers and rubbed my hands across my face, digging my fingers into my temples, hoping it would help. It didn't. I lifted my head, surprised to see Alex standing in front of me.

"Mind if I…?" She gestured to the chair next to me, flopping down into it before I could answer. "You're right," she said, "it is."

"What is?"

"Camden." Alex smiled. "It's nice."

"Oh. Yes." I returned her smile, then looked away, not knowing what else I could say.

"And you?" she asked. "Where are you from?"

"Brighton originally. We all are." I turned and looked back at her, the movement causing my head to pound. "But now I'm living in Islington." I paused. "Ed likes us all to be *somewhere visible*." I air-quoted. "Islington seemed like the best option."

Well, according to Ed anyway. He'd chosen the Islington bit, I'd chosen the apartment; after all, it was going to be me that had to live there. That was freaky at first. The thought of living in London at seventeen, away from my parents, away from everything I'd known in Brighton. Freaky and scary. Brooke, Robyn, and I had lived together to start with, but even in those first few months I knew it wouldn't stay like that. Sure enough, once Robyn hooked up with Nate she spent more and more time at his place, then Brooke started making noises to me about wanting to be closer to the centre of London—closer to all *the action*. I loved Islington and I loved my apartment. I knew people there; I had neighbours that looked out for me, and friends just a short Tube ride away. I didn't want to move, so I let Brooke do her own thing, and less than a year after moving from Brighton, I was living alone. But by now I wasn't scared or freaked out. I had been London-ized and I'd transformed into the confident, happy seventeen-year-old I am now, relishing my freedom and space. My parents had reassurances from Ed that our record company would keep a close eye on all of us, and so far it was working very well, much to my parents' and Ed's relief.

Ed Manford. Our creator. That made him sound like God, and sometimes he thought he was. In reality, he's our manager, not our creator. *We* were our own creators, but he was the one who saw one of Be4's YouTube demos and decided we had something special, and knew he had the money and the contacts to be able to give us a shot. So he contacted Robyn and it all spiralled from there.

Ed was the one who had the foresight to find himself a producer with enough savvy to remix one of our earliest songs, "Taken," and he was the one who then suggested it could work as part of the soundtrack to a small, independent UK film called *Into the Light*. Thanks to Ed, it worked. Thanks to Ed, *we* worked. Thanks to Ed, Be4 had a couple of top-twenty hits and a relatively successful first album out within a year, and we were now well on our way to even bigger and better things.

"He told me." Alex sat back further in her chair and pulled a hand through her hair. "Whatever's best for the group, hey?"

I smiled but didn't answer. After sixteen months of working with Ed, I didn't always agree with him, but the one thing I did know was everything he did, he did for the band. And for the most part, he did it well, but this time I wondered if he'd got it wrong. Be4 weren't a girl band, as such. We valued our pop-rock edge and took pride from the fact we were different from the other, manufactured bands. I stole a look to Alex. To my mind, she was 100 percent manufactured: created, polished, and then spat out by her talent show when she didn't make the grade. She reeked of girl-band material to me.

I wanted Be4 to be different. I wanted to be the one playing the guitar riffs, I wanted to hear Brooke's grainy voice in our harmonies, I wanted our lyrics to really hit home and make a point rather than float away like fluffy, inconsequential clouds. Be4 were so much more than that, and there were times I wondered if Ed realized that as we hurtled towards making our second album, or if all he thought about was the money he was rapidly making out of us.

Whenever my thoughts drifted that way, Nicole inevitably stole back into them. I slipped another quick look to Alex, her head now bowed over her phone, and couldn't help but wish it was Nicole I was sitting next to rather than her, wishing I didn't feel as though everything had crumbled the day she went.

But it had. Big time.

I didn't like it—this stranger coming in—and I didn't like that me, Robyn, and Brooke had to instantly embrace her and accept her when all we wanted was to have Nicole back. When all I *needed* was to have Nicole back, for the past to have never happened, and for us all to get back to how we'd been.

Before.

Alex shifted in her seat and I looked away, but my thoughts of Nicole had already brought the familiar guilt slithering over me, snaking its way around me, tightening with every fetid memory. Squeezing me, suffocating me.

Except the guilt wasn't the snake. *I* was the snake. And even though Robyn and Brooke had known everything that had happened between me and Nicole, I'd never admitted to either of them that I'd always secretly thought it was thanks to me Be4 had lost her and I'd lost my best friend and my confidante. I glanced again at Alex, still engrossed in her phone. Evidently she'd gotten bored of my company and had given up trying to have another conversation with me. I couldn't say I blamed her, and anyway, it suited me fine. My mood had plummeted and I felt as though I had nothing to say to her, and never would.

Alex wasn't Nicole, Be4 would never be the same again, and as the fresh realization of the situation slowly sank in, my head began to thump even more.

Chapter Two

It was a Sunday when Nicole went away. I remember that because we'd been due to meet up on the South Bank to watch the buskers and she never turned up. I was pissed off, because we hadn't been seeing as much of each other in the months before that and I'd wanted to hang out with her for a bit. I'd waited for her, for over an hour, texting her repeatedly to ask her where she was, getting more and more exasperated when she didn't reply.

Then I received the phone call from Ed that made my stomach feel as though it had filled with rocks.

In the weeks that followed, I often thought that Sunday had been a funny day for her to go to rehab, but then I'd figured rehab didn't work like a doctor's or a dentist. You didn't just ring up and make an appointment that was convenient to you. You just went when you had to go—and Nicole *really* had to go. Ed had made it all go so swiftly too, because Ed was always very good at making things go away.

"It's the best for all concerned." I remember vividly Ed saying that. So he made Nicole go away, and then swiftly—there's that word again—got Alex brought into the band to replace her with such indecent haste that we—me, Robyn, and Brooke—the press, or even the fans couldn't even question why. Just like that. No fuss, no hassle.

Nicole out, Alex in.

Sure, Alex could sing. Her rapid progress through the TV talent show *Sing* had proved that. Until she got booted out in the quarter-finals, that is. That, conveniently for us and Ed, happened around the same time Nicole went into rehab. So Alex transitioned smoothly from being on a TV talent show straight into being in Be4, and I reckoned she had no idea just how lucky she was.

That first day with Alex in the studio was weird on so many different levels. We'd been told by Ed to come in so that we could all put down a new demo track he'd been sent and which he thought would be perfect for the forthcoming album, and also so Alex could record her parts, replacing Nicole's vocals which had previously been recorded on the ten other tracks that were to go on the album. That's why it weirded me out so much; it was almost as if Nicole didn't exist any more. As if any remaining part of her was being erased indefinitely from anything to do with Be4. That's why I was apprehensive that first day too—the thought of no more Nicole, after so many years together, and the thought of having to start over with Alex.

Nicole out, Alex in.

I hated it.

❖

"Man, she sure loves herself." Robyn was the first to speak once Alex eventually left the studio with Ed.

"I reckon she thinks she's it." I couldn't help but agree with her.

"On what basis?" Brooke asked. She's fair like that.

"Hello? Flirting with my boyfriend?" Robyn said. "It's not like she even stopped when I came in, is it?" She threw a look of disdain to the door. "And did you see the way she looked at me when she spoke about that reality show she's just been booted off of as well? Like it was the best thing ever." She made a noise that was halfway between being a laugh and a snort.

"It's a big show." I shrugged. "Saturday night prime time."

"All it does is offer people who are mediocre singers instant fame, because they're in the public eye for five minutes," Robyn countered. "And with it, instant thoughts that you're something." She looked at the door again. "Which, believe me, she thinks she is."

"You think she's mediocre?" I asked. "The bits I saw, she was okay."

Robyn waved my question away with an airy hand.

"And you've got all this from what?" Brooke asked. "That five-minute conversation you had with her just now?"

"I'm talking about the whole package," Robyn said. "She's not a real musician. Just a wannabe."

"Aren't we all?" Brooke asked. "Isn't that why we all do it? For the fame?"

"But we've worked at it," Robyn argued. "Four years. How long did she last on that show? Two months?" She folded her arms. "And then thinks she can just slot in here and become the next Nicole."

"She certainly has…attitude," I said, Robyn's arguments striking a chord with me, "or rather, confidence. It's scary how self-assured one person can be."

"Maybe being on the show gave her that." Robyn frowned. "Maybe being thrown in at the deep end does that to a person. Sink or swim and all that." She sank into a chair. "First week, right, they had to sing big band. First. Week." She shook her head.

"I thought you said you'd never seen the show." I sat next to her.

"Yeah, right." Robyn stretched her legs out in front of her, crossing them at the ankle. "You think I'm going to let *her* know that?" She laid her head back. "Mind you, anyone who can sing a note without sounding like a cat being strangled could have done it. All I'm saying is making them sing big band on a first week is a bit shitty."

"Ed wouldn't get just anyone, you know." Brooke, ever the voice of reason, spoke. "He knew Alex was something special."

"But is she Be4?" I asked. "Will she get it?"

"Not like Nicole did." Robyn shook her head. "She'll never be Nicole."

"I still would have preferred it if Ed had found an unknown." I closed my eyes to my still-pounding head. "Like we were, you know?"

"Ed went through this with us though," Brooke said. "It's not as if he's sprung it on us."

She was right. He had. It was either we agreed to a new fourth member, or he'd have to rethink the whole Be4 bandwagon. None of us wanted that. Not when we'd come this far. Nicole would understand…Wouldn't she?

"Face it, girls," he'd said. "Do you really want this to end now it's just starting?"

Of course we didn't. But I guess none of us thought he'd think to replace our best friend with a reality-TV reject, though. Or so quickly.

"I agree with Tally." Robyn spoke, derailing my train of thought. "What can Alex possibly know? About us, I mean? About the whole Be4 vibe? About our struggle to get where we've got?"

"She can't," I agreed. "So maybe she'll never fit in, and then what?"

"Then once Nicole's better, she can come back," Robyn said, a lazy grin spreading across her face. "Nicole is Be4, not Alex." She threw a glance to the door. "And the sooner both Ed and Alex realize that, the better."

❖

Recording tracks without Nicole sucked. Having to have her vocals replaced on some of our already-recorded songs sucked even more. After Alex finished her tour of the studios with Ed, and after me, Brooke, and Robyn finished tearing her apart in her absence, it was time to start singing together for the first time. I wasn't looking forward to it one little bit.

"So, Alex." Ed was treating her like the new kid in school, being so touchy-feely and saccharine with her, it made me want to hurl. "Just like when you recorded 'Crush' earlier, we're going for this in a single take, okay?"

Alex nodded.

"The instruments have already been recorded separately," Ed said, steering her towards the sound booth, "and the girls' vocals. We'll combine it all later in a mix."

He was talking to her like she'd never been in a studio before, when I knew for a fact—well, Google—that she'd released a single when she was something like fourteen, which had totally bombed.

Still, that was way more than I'd ever done at fourteen, so I wondered why she let him talk to her like she was an idiot, when it was clear she wasn't one. While Ed still blathered on, I watched as Alex slowly pulled her Beats from around her neck, then handed them to Grant, one of the sound guys, saying something to him which I couldn't catch but flashing him a smile that could charm the birds from the trees. Then when Ed finished talking, she sauntered over to the sound booth and again I watched her put some different headphones on with the same casualness, adjust them against her ears, then give Ed the thumbs up.

"Let's hope she fluffs her first lines." As Robyn put her own headphones on, she leant over and drolly whispered in my ear, making me laugh louder than I'd intended. "Then we'll see what she's made of."

As the intro to "After the Rain"—our proposed new single—sounded through my own headphones, I felt bad for Alex then, and even though I agreed with Robyn, there was a bigger part of me that kind of knew Alex would knock those first bars out of the park.

She did.

Even Robyn shut up then.

Alex's singing was insane. As she sang, her hands clamped tightly against her headphones, the high G she hit in the middle of the chorus sent shivers cascading down my spine. Most people I knew in the music business wouldn't have tried to hit it; even Nicole hadn't been able to get up to that G with the same amount of clarity, and Nicole could belt out the high notes like no one else I ever knew. Alex, though, had a different edge to her voice, a husky sweetness and purity I'd never noticed when I'd heard her on TV. Now, singing live right in front of me, her voice drifting into my ears, it was obvious Alex had a voice to die for.

I reckoned she knew it too.

Unlike Robyn, I really hadn't seen any of *Sing*. Not because I was being pompous about it, and not because I thought I was above watching a TV talent show (after all, who can resist skateboarding dogs?) but because, well, I don't really know. Perhaps at the end of a day in the studio, or at the end of a week of exhausting gigging, the last thing I need to do is turn on my TV and see people singing. Perhaps I'm not a fan of TV in general, but all I do know is that the opening credits of *Sing*, with the contestants group-singing on the stage and miming badly, were enough each week to send me scrabbling for the remote.

Sure I'd read some stuff about Alex. While *Sing* was on—as it still was—it was impossible to go onto the Internet without reading another story of another contestant doing something they probably shouldn't be doing, or reading about the latest evictee. I knew Alex had sung an Elton John ballad the night she was eliminated. I knew she'd sung it well. And I knew the country had been in total shock that she'd been voted off.

Alex knew she was good too. I was aware only of her presence in the booth, hands clutching her headphones to her ears, eyes closed as she sang. I guess I couldn't blame her for her confidence earlier that morning, when she knew this was what she would be pulling out of the bag. No one with a voice like Alex's could ever have anything other than a granite assurance in their ability.

Ed, of course, was practically apoplectic, and I figured it was totally unnecessary for him to punch the air quite as many times as he did while she was singing. Moron.

"Sheesh." Robyn turned away and pulled me with her. "'K, that girl can sing."

"He knows it"—I jabbed my finger over my shoulder to Ed—"they know it"—another nod to the sound guys—"the whole studio knows it." I threw a look back over to the sound booth. "But she knows it most of all."

Truth was, Alex destroyed every song she sang that morning. While we all stood out in the studio, watching her sing alone in the sound booth, the looks of appreciation that passed between Ed and the sound guys intensified with each new song and new note that Alex sang. Annoyingly, each of her vocal parts was nailed in one take, but then, I sort of knew it would end up being like that.

Alex, apparently, could do no wrong.

❖

Her vocals were recorded. As we gathered around the mixing desk listening to the recording of us all singing together for the first time, everyone was in rapt attention. Except Alex, that is. Alex had wandered away from the group, which really surprised me, bearing in mind it was her first day with us, and I would have expected her to want to make a good impression. Instead, she was standing, arms folded across her chest, looking at a noticeboard on the wall of the studio as if her life depended on it.

I walked over to her while the music was still playing.

"You're not listening?" I tossed a look back over my shoulder.

"I am." She didn't take her eyes from the noticeboard. "I can hear it from here."

"You sounded good."

"Cheers."

I waited.

How about a *You too*?

Nothing.

"Guess it's a bit different from *Sing*, huh?" I asked, when it was clear she wasn't going to return the compliment.

"Yeah." Finally I saw the hint of a smile. "*Sing* was live. No mistakes. No second chances."

"Like gigging." I frowned. "You know that Be4 were a busking group before all this?" I said, waving a hand to the studio. "That's how we learnt our skills. Live."

"Yeah, I heard."

I watched as Alex continued to study the noticeboard and waited for her to ask me something more. She didn't. I felt disappointed. Let down, even. Knowing how much Be4 meant to me, I wanted her to ask me something about it, about how we came together, about how I came to be in the band. How I felt about it. I knew I wanted her to show an interest in…me. That was strange. I wasn't normally egotistical. I shook the thought away.

"Have you heard much other Be4 stuff?" I asked instead.

"I have." Finally Alex looked at me and smiled. "I heard some stuff from the first album. I liked"—she lifted her eyes and thought—"'Serendipity' quite a lot," she said, "as a ballad." She thought some more. "But I guess my absolute favourite has to be 'Drowning in You.'"

My heart gave a shiver. "Drowning in You" was the only song that I'd ever written alone that I'd thought would be good enough to be recorded. "Serendipity" and all the others had been co-written by me, Nicole, Brooke, and Robyn, but the lyrics and music to "Drowning in You" had come to me late one night and, unable to shake them from my mind, had been played out on my guitar and then hastily scribbled down on a scrap of paper at about three in the morning.

"Why is it your favourite?" I asked.

"I'm not sure." Alex shrugged. "I suppose it's because it's faster and braver than the others. Different." I liked that she knew what she was talking about. "It's got a good guitar solo in the middle too." She laughed. "I can't resist a good guitar solo."

"You play, don't you?"

"I love it." Alex nodded, and I knew I'd piqued her interest just from the look on her face. That pleased me. "It's a shame, you know," she continued, "but they were always reluctant to let me play my guitar on *Sing*, but I feel so much happier when I've got one in my hands. You know the feeling, right?"

"Totally." I smiled.

Little did Alex know, she was voicing my opinions too. Playing guitar ranked a close second to singing, and I never felt happier than when I had mine cradled in my hands.

"I wrote 'Drowning in You,'" I said, hoping Alex didn't think I was bragging.

"For real?"

I nodded, liking the look of approval on her face.

"Well it's very good," she said. "I always thought it should have been released as a single, but…" She shrugged.

"Seriously?" I was stoked. "I wanted it to be released as a single too," I said, "but Ed thought differently." I focused on a spot on the noticeboard, remembering the disappointment when he'd told me, and the feeling of hurt when Brooke and Robyn had agreed with him. "He thought the fans wouldn't get it. Thought it was a bit too much of a shift from our usual stuff." I thought it was good enough, though. Good enough to reach number one too. Perhaps I was biased.

"Well then Ed's an idiot." Alex raised an eyebrow and pulled a face, bringing a smile to my lips. "Trust me, it was good enough."

Before I could answer her or thank her, she walked away. I watched her amble back over to Ed, feeling pleased that she at least was on my side.

For the time being, anyway.

Chapter Three

"Tally. Quick word."

I was summoned to see Ed. Like being summoned to see the Head at school. Or my parents.

Alex was deep in conversation with Ed, who waved me over while she still spoke to him. I was on cloud nine. What should have been a stupidly long day was increasingly turning into a far quicker one than I'd envisaged on my Tube ride over to the studio that morning, mainly thanks to the fact Alex had recorded all her solos without a hitch. Now all we had to do was record a few more vocals and we were free for the day; I could be back in Oxford Street shopping with Robyn and Brooke before the shops closed at this rate.

I quit fiddling with a button on the mixing desk and went over to him. "You're ready to go with Brooke's vocals for 'After the Rain'?" I asked.

"Not yet." Ed put down the iPad he'd been using and nodded briefly to Alex, who moved away. "I think it'd be better for you to record your part first."

"Sure." I unzipped my hoodie and shrugged it off. The sound booth was usually set to a hundred degrees. "You got the lyrics there?" I flung my hoodie onto a chair and held my hand out to Ed.

"We're going for another take on 'Crush.'"

I stopped. "Crush" was going to be the third song on the new album; I'd recorded my solo to it two weeks before and had totally nailed it in one take.

"We already did 'Crush.'"

"Now we're doing it again," Ed said. "Well, you are."

"Because?"

"Because Alex has recorded her part for it," Ed said, "and now I think your part needs a small change." He handed me the lyrics, stapled together and attached to a clipboard. "You'll be singing lines four, six, nine, and twelve."

I slid my glance past Ed towards Alex. She gave me a faint smile, then turned her back, choosing instead to talk to Grant rather than acknowledge me.

"My solos come in"—I ran my finger down the clipboard, seeing for the first time the scribbles across the lyrics—"lines two, five, eight, and ten. Then there's the chorus," I said, "then I continue at lines thirteen and fifteen in harmony with Robyn."

"Can you just try?" Ed asked. I was sure I detected a hint of a sigh.

"Problem?" Robyn appeared at my side.

"No problem." Ed smiled. "Just some minor adjustments."

"*Major* adjustments, he means." I held up the clipboard for Robyn to see. "Like, total change of my solos."

"When Tally wrote 'Crush' with me," Robyn said, taking the clipboard from me, "she wrote her own solos knowing how she wanted to sing them."

"Alex suggested—"

"Alex?" Robyn and I spoke at the same time.

"She suggested a little more light and shade," Ed said. "I agree. Rather than belting it out."

"My parts need to be belted out," I said. "That's how I wrote them."

"Your new lines don't." Ed, infuriatingly, looked away. "We're changing the balance, so you'll now sing more harmony parts. I think it'll work better that way," he said. "Fewer pitching issues."

"Pitching issues?" I looked at him incredulously.

"It's a little…pitchy in places," he said, waving a hand. "We can Auto-Tune it, but if you could—"

"*I'm* pitchy?" I couldn't believe my ears.

Ed sighed. "All I'm saying is I think Alex is right," he said, "and it's just not working the way it is at the moment."

"So now she gets to sing my original parts?" I asked. "Having just recorded some of Nic's too?"

Anger prickled at my scalp. I looked for Alex but couldn't see her. She'd obviously gone. Smart move.

"Is that what you mean?" I pressed.

"It's just testing the waters," Ed said, putting a hand on my shoulder. "Just give it a go. See where it leads."

"Let me get this right," I said, taking the clipboard back from Robyn. "Alex gets to replace both Nic's vocals *and* mine? Would you just prefer it if Alex sang everyone's parts?"

"Just try it, Tally," Ed said. "For me?" He gesticulated to Nate. "We ready to roll?"

That, apparently, was that.

Like the patronizing bastard he can be, Ed put his hands on my shoulder, swivelled me round, and steered me in the direction of the sound booth before I could complain any more. Resigned to it, I wandered up to the door of the booth, kicked it open, and stomped inside, hoping that my stomps would perfectly indicate my anger. Turning round, I could see Ed, the sound guys, Robyn, Brooke...and Alex—who had magically reappeared now I was about to sing—all staring back at me. Great. So Alex had smashed her solos in one go, and now, rather than going home like anyone else would, she'd chosen to hang around and listen to me sing my solos.

I'd show her.

I snatched up my headphones and placed them on my ears, hearing in them voices and sounds coming from the studio floor. At Ed's thumbs up, Nate pressed a button and kicked the drum machine into life, swiftly followed by Brooke's previously recorded vocals, signalling the intro to my first line. With a quick glance to the floor again, I closed my eyes and sang my part, then waited briefly as I heard Robyn's vocals kick in, and sang my next line.

The music in my ears stopped, to be replaced by Ed's voice. I opened my eyes, dismayed to see him with his hand up in the air.

"From *when you went away*, please. Remember the balance."

Of course I remembered the balance. I wrote the fucking song in the first place.

I smiled my best sarcastic smile, raised an eyebrow to Robyn who was staring expressionless at me through the glass, then cleared my throat.

Robyn's vocals sounded in my ears again, fading to allow me to sing my line. This time the music continued, the prerecorded drums and guitars that I always loved so much sustaining the rocky edge that I'd envisaged when I wrote them into it. Brooke's vocals entered my ears, quickly followed by Alex's, much louder than I'd expected, completely throwing me. I missed my cue.

"Sorry, sorry." I waved a hand. "Can we take it from Brooke's vocals first?" I shook my head. "The balance has completely changed. Alex's part is much louder than Nicole's was."

I looked at Alex. She stared back.

"From Brooke." Ed.

I looked away, adjusted my headphones, and waited.

Again, Brooke's vocals sounded, quickly followed by Alex's. This time I sang my line, looking out across the studio floor just in time to see a look shadow across Alex's face. A sort of a pursing of lips. A glance away. And, I was sure, a roll of the eyes.

Bitch.

I stopped singing, wishing I hadn't when I saw Ed raise his hands out to his side.

"What's the problem?" he mouthed to me.

I slid my gaze to Alex, annoyed to see her looking down at the mixing desk, rather than directly at me. I wanted her to see I was pissed off with her. Wanted her to see the annoyance in my eyes.

"Nothing's the problem." I kept my eyes on Alex while I spoke. "Can we go from Brooke's vocals again?" I turned my attention back to Ed, nodding to him when I saw his nod.

The music filtered into my ears again, and this time I was ready. I sang, ignoring Alex, who was looking at me again, focusing instead on Brooke, who was as smiley as ever. When I'd finished, both she and Ed gave me the thumbs up. Alex, I noticed, still held a look of disapproval. The girl was halfway through her first day with us, and she was giving me looks.

I yanked my headphones from my ears and left the booth.

"Hey, Alex," I said as I sauntered over to Alex, "what was with all the looks?"

Alex slowly lifted her eyes to mine. "I'm sorry?"

"You," I said. "Looks. Totally unprofessional."

"What looks?" she asked.

Robyn appeared beside me. Her presence emboldened me.

"Disdain," I said. "Contempt."

"What?" Alex laughed, and I hated the sound of it. "You imagined it."

"I saw the looks." I stood my ground. "When I was singing."

"All imagined." Alex turned away.

"You know," I called out as she walked away, "it's not very professional to be standing there pulling faces at me while I'm singing."

Alex stopped dead.

"And it's not very professional you having three takes to get it right," she said, without even bothering to turn round to look at me.

I felt Robyn's hand on my arm.

"Maybe if you'd not gone sneaking to Ed and messed with everything," I said to her back, "I'd have had more time to rehearse."

"Rehearse a song you wrote?" Finally Alex spoke to me over her shoulder. "You for real?"

That threw me. I swallowed. Damned if I could answer that one.

"Tally knows her lines inside out." Fortunately Robyn was more on the ball. "She focuses on her lines while we focus on ours."

"Well," Alex said, taking her headphones back off Grant, "how about she focuses on something else right now?" She slung her headphones round her neck. "How about she focuses on being an adult for five minutes?" Alex gave a nod to Ed and shouldered past me, scooping her headphones back up onto her ears as she did so, then tipped the hood of her hoodie up over her head. She put her hands in her pockets and sauntered from the studio, shoving the door open with her shoulder and letting it swing back closed with a bang.

I stared at the door she'd just walked through, hardly believing what she'd just said. The silence in the studio was deafening, no one wanting to speak. Awkward glances scuttled between those still there, suddenly people became busy in what they were doing, and all the while my face burned with embarrassment and anger.

Seemed as though Alex Brody wasn't on my side after all.

Chapter Four

My fury refused to abate. I went straight home after our recording session, declining Brooke and Robyn's offer to go into the West End for a little retail therapy and to have a right royal grumble about Alex and her comments while we did it. I wasn't in the mood. In fact, I wasn't in the mood for much more than going home and replaying the evaluation mixes of the songs that Ed had given us all, knowing the only reason I wanted to do it was to satisfy myself that I was right and Alex was wrong.

I wasn't bloody pitchy and "Crush" *hadn't* needed any changes to it.

As I sank down into my sofa and slipped my headphones on, my thoughts strayed to Nicole. I glanced down at my phone next to me and, out of habit, picked it up and found her number.

But I couldn't ring her. The one person who I knew would be able to tell me everything was okay was gone, hidden away in the countryside, probably with no thoughts about Be4, London…or me. I let my hand, phone still clutched in it, flop down next to my leg.

Nicole had been my rock. My shoulder to cry on. My friend.

She would never think to sneak to Ed about my solos, that's for sure.

At that moment, I missed her more than I'd ever missed anyone. I wanted to see her so she could tell me everything was going to be all right. I wanted to feel the familiarity of her presence again, gain the comfort I always used to gain from being around her, but I knew I couldn't, and the frustration of knowing that made tears film against my eyes. Annoyed, I wiped them away with my sleeve. Memories from earlier in the year started to creep back into my mind, memories which I'd done my best to ignore, but which now refused to stay tucked away. Since she'd gone into rehab and all contact with her had been severed, Nicole had never left me.

Could I have done more to stop her sliding into her drug habit? I laid my head back and stared up at the pattern on my ceiling. Could I have been kinder to her after what had happened between us? I blinked as a snapshot from the previous summer quite unexpectedly returned to me, an image that I'd managed to keep buried away in the back of my mind for months.

Nicole and I, alone. Walking through a meadow, a warm breeze on our faces, the grass so high it tickled my bare legs and made my skin itch. Our fingers touched, then parted, then touched again, finally linking as we walked side by side through the grass. A palpable shift in our friendship, one that had excited and terrified me in equal measures. Something new and daring—and away from Brooke and Robyn—the looks that had passed between Nicole and me earlier that day in the studio, looks that had become more frequent in the weeks before, had returned with a new intensity.

Annoyed at the intrusion of this unwanted memory, I closed my eyes, cranked up the music in my ears, and tried to chase the image away, frowning as it repeatedly returned to me.

We were sixteen and experimenting. That's what I'd told myself when we'd kissed that day. The kiss had been threatening for ages, I'd guessed that. Nicole had changed in the months leading up to it; her looks to me had been loaded with meaning, her mood swings unfathomable. One minute all over me, so tactile and friendly, the next acting like she didn't give a damn, and apparently terrified to be anywhere near me.

I'd been so confused. My best friend seeming as though she hated me, and I didn't have a clue what I'd done or said to warrant it, or what I could do to make her like me again. So I asked her. She didn't give me a satisfactory answer, though. She'd just said, "Hang out with me today." That was it. And, "Just me and you. Not the others. It'll be fun."

So we did. That's how we got to be walking in the meadow and how I got to have itchy legs. I hadn't cared though; Nicole wanted to hang out with me, like we'd done before she'd gone all weird on me, and I couldn't have been happier. Just an afternoon, me and her, like it used to be.

Then we'd kissed. Okay, the kiss had come much later in the afternoon, after all the walking and the hand-holding and the finding somewhere to sit where we wouldn't be swamped with long grass.

It had been weird. The kiss. It had taken me by surprise too. One minute me and Nicole had been talking about something we'd been planning to write together, then that conversation had led to another one about feelings, and before I knew it, Nicole was saying things to me that my brain wasn't taking in and looking at me in a way she'd never looked at me before. Then leaning over, brushing the hair from my eyes, and looking straight at me for the longest time, until I started to get a bit embarrassed.

The kiss had taken me by surprise and was over before I'd barely registered what had happened. Nicole's soft lips grazing mine. I remember that I hadn't wanted it to be over so soon, so I'd kissed her again and it had lasted longer that time. I think maybe we would have kissed a third time if Nicole's phone hadn't gone off. That seemed to break the mood. Bring us back to planet Earth.

Shake me into realizing what I'd done.

Nicole had carried on staring at me, biting at her lip, then answered her phone. I'd flopped back onto the grass, wondering what I'd done and how it had all happened, while Nicole spoke to whoever it was that had called her. I remember staring up at a blue sky happily unhampered by any clouds, and tasting my lips.

I know I'd felt a total mess then. I'd liked it, but I knew it had felt wrong, and maybe that was because I knew I'd just kissed my BFF and nothing could ever come of it. How could it? We were best friends and, more importantly, bandmates.

Bad move.

So I told Nicole that I'd really loved kissing her but that the truth was, I didn't want it to mean that it had changed anything between us. I didn't tell her that there and then, of course. Not in the grass. I hadn't wanted to spoil what had been an awesome day, so—being stupid and cowardly—I'd waited a few days, had given myself time to really think about it. Days turned into a week and I still didn't say anything to her. I liked her, I knew that, but I was never sure if I liked her in that way, and I knew whoever I was with, I had to *really* like them. Nicole was…Nicole. Mad, unpredictable Nicole who I'd known practically all my life and knew everything there was to know about. After the kiss, everything felt different, and when I finally made up my mind about what it was I wanted, the conclusion I came to with absolute certainty was that I didn't want everything to feel different any more, and I wanted us to go back to how we'd been.

She cried when I told her that. She actually cried, and that made me feel like the biggest cow ever. Like I'd failed her. Like I'd led her on and then crushed her. But instead of being the supportive friend I should have been, I took the coward's way out and I concentrated on my music instead. Refused to talk to her about it any more than I already had and, instead, poured my guilt over my blurred lines into my writing until the remorse I felt about rejecting her had faded. Nicole would find someone else, I knew. Someone better than me. Someone more worthy of her.

The music I wrote stayed hidden in a secret portfolio marked *Shitty Stuff* and got crammed into the back of a cupboard in my apartment, never to see the light of day again. It's still there now.

Shitty stuff in the cupboard, Nicole in rehab.

Me carrying on as normal.

I pressed *play* on my phone again and the memories of me and Nicole fled. The music from that afternoon flooded my ears, the familiar pounding drums of "Crush" bringing me some comfort, even though the reappearance of Nicole in my mind had unsettled me so much. I rested my head against the back of my sofa and waited for my singing to start.

When it did I closed my eyes and concentrated hard, listening out for my tuning.

I frowned.

I wasn't pitchy.

❖

It was official. “After the Rain” was to be Be4’s fourth single, our first off our new album, and our first with Alex. It seemed Ed was finally satisfied with our recording of it, and now we could leave it to the mixing engineer to clean up the audio and add some effects, and then it would be ready to be burned to disk. When I heard that, I was beyond excited, and all my resentful thoughts about Alex magically disappeared. I think I was so excited because the song was mine, Brooke’s, and Robyn’s first attempt at writing something a little more experimental, and I was desperate for the public to know that Be4 could still exist without Nicole. Despite popular press opinion, constantly speculating about why she’d left—the theories ranged from Nicole wanting to go solo to her being pregnant—and stating that Nicole’s departure inevitably meant the end of Be4, listening to the cut of “After the Rain” for the umpteenth time convinced me that this could be just the beginning for us all rather than the end.

“After the Rain” had some catchy hooks and I knew it was a winner the moment I’d finished writing it. That’s why I was so stoked that Ed thought it good enough to be the new single. I didn’t always agree with him, but I was pleased that, unlike for “Drowning in You,” this time he’d accepted the slight shift away from our normal sound and had seen the potential in it as much as I had, and even though I knew he wanted to change some of the guitar riffs in it, I was happy to comply, just as long as it meant it made the cut. Not all of Ed’s suggestions went as smoothly as this, though. I would say for every twenty songs we wrote, Ed usually wanted to make subtle instrumental or lyrical alterations to at least half of them. Those tended to be the ones that I’d written instrumentals for, and I always knew what he’d want to change about them, because it was the same thing every time, as I liked my music to be more edgy than Brooke and Robyn did. It had always been the same, even when we’d been writing songs together during our breaks at school, but it had always worked out well between us. We compromised back then just the same as we compromised now; an instrumental here and there or a drum intro usually kept me happy. When I wrote music alone, however, the edginess was more apparent. My guitar solos weren't watered down by the others, my words weren't changed, and the angst and grittiness I loved in my writing stayed.

So after various meetings and emails pinging back and forth between us, the version of "After the Rain" that we had recorded a few days before was ready to be released out to the fans. Ed rented out studio space on the twelfth floor of an apartment block in East London so we could rehearse it together, so we'd be ready for all the promo that would soon follow, the first of which was a booking on *The Afternoon Show,* a popular daytime chat show on one of the commercial channels. This was the part of the whole process that I particularly loved: time spent hanging out with my buddies, jamming and singing the music we'd created together, then appearances together on TV, singing our new material to our fans. I never tired of it, and I knew Robyn and Brooke loved it just as much as I did.

I just hoped Alex would, quite literally, enjoy singing from the same sheet as us too.

❖

I'd never been to East London, which was a bit silly considering I'd lived in the capital for over a year now. The rehearsal studio that Ed had rented was in a suburb called Walthamstow, which, to my knowledge, was famous for having a greyhound racing track and not much else. I caught the Tube up from Islington, blending in with the summer tourists as I sat squeezed between them in the insufferably hot carriage, the music playing from my phone drowning out the roar of the train.

No one looked at one another, no one spoke, no one smiled. As the train rocked and scudded through the dark tunnels, I played "After the Rain" on repeat, knowing I wanted to have it completely earwormed into my head before I got to the rehearsal, so that as soon as I opened my mouth to sing, it would feel like I'd been singing it for years. I stared up at the advertising opposite me, listening to Brooke's voice as it sounded in my ears, then Alex's. The harmonies sounded good, and as the train slowed to its next station, I couldn't help the smile that escaped from my lips. My mind tumbled forward to the single's release, to the reception I hoped it would get with the fans. It could be our most popular single yet, I could just feel it.

The train jolted back into life, drawing my eyes away from the advertising. The carriage was quieter now, and now there were fewer people standing in front of me, I could see further down the carriage. That's when I saw her. Alex. She had her hood up, despite the stifling heat of the carriage, and was looking down at the phone in her hands, texting. I studied her for a bit, hoping she wouldn't look up, because I didn't want to have to go and talk to her, even though I figured I ought to.

I turned my head away and looked in the opposite direction. Alex was wearing the same hoodie she'd been wearing at the studio two days before, and just seeing it, and remembering the way she'd so casually dismissed me and sauntered from the room, made my skin warm. Then I wanted to go and sit next to her, so I could ask her just what the hell she'd been playing at, but I also figured having an argument with her in a public place wouldn't be my wisest move.

"After the Rain" finished playing in my ears. I could either play it one more time or switch it off and go speak with Alex. I chose to let it play on again.

I stared at her from across the carriage.

The music played on.

Of course, I *could* just go and talk to her. It didn't have to descend into an argument. The train slowed into the next station, and in the flurry of doors opening and closing, and people coming and going, my attention was distracted from her until the train pulled out again.

I stole another look over to her, half hoping the seat next to her would be occupied now. It was still free. Annoyed with myself, I switched the music off and stood, holding onto a rail next to me for support. I walked down the length of the aisle, swaying in time with the train, and eventually stood in front of her. When Alex didn't look up, I tapped her foot with my foot, then flopped down in the seat next to her.

"Didn't see you here," I lied. "I was sitting over there." I lifted my head. "Just saw you now."

Alex put down her phone and lifted her Beats from her ears. “Sorry?”

She looked annoyed at my intrusion, but that could have been my imagination.

“I was just saying,” I said, pulling my own earbuds out, “I didn’t see you.”

“Oh.” She placed her headphones round her neck. “Right.”

I nodded, just for something to do.

“What are you listening to?” I asked.

“Nothing much.” Alex smiled and plopped her phone into her hoodie pocket. “Bit of Motown.” She lifted her chin to my earbuds, now dangling round my neck. “You?”

“Mixture, really.” I screwed up my nose. Like I was going to tell her what I’d really been listening to?

A yawning silence between us followed, and I wished I was the sort of person that found small talk easy. That’s why I always dreaded anything that involved having someone do my hair and make-up, or visits to the dentist. After all, there’s only so many things you can talk about, and I wasn’t particularly good at any of those things.

I looked around the carriage, wishing my brain would come up with something.

“So, how do you like London?” It was weak, but the best I could come up with.

“London?” Alex asked.

“Yeah,” I said. “How do you like living here?”

“Well I’ve been here nearly a year,” Alex said, “so I guess I’m kind of used to it now.”

I detected amusement in her voice, which pissed me off, and I was equally annoyed that my attempt at conversation with her had bombed, thanks to her sarcasm.

“What about you?” she asked.

“Yeah,” I said, childishly and deliberately not elaborating. “I like it.”

It was all so stilted, it was painful. Fortunately, intervention arrived when at last our train arrived at Walthamstow. I don’t think I’d ever been so grateful to see a station sign.

As I got off the train and headed for the exit, I lost Alex in the melee. I figured I ought to wait for her though, in spite of our awkwardness in each other's company, because despite everything, I thought making her walk alone to the apartment block was a bit mean. I waited for her at the top of the station steps, grabbing her arm as she weaved her way past me in the thickness of the crowds, and I'm certain I didn't imagine the look of relief on her face when she saw me.

Even then, as we made our way from the station, the aching silence between us resumed, and I returned to racking my brains for a conversation starter.

Maybe there would never be one. As we walked stiffly side by side, I seriously wondered if Alex Brody and I would ever have anything to say to each other ever again.

Chapter Five

The rehearsal studio was amazing. I wandered over to the window and stared out at the acres of apartment blocks and roads yawning out below me, watching people scuttling on the streets below me like ants, whilst listening to the sounds of Nate setting up the systems behind me. I couldn't wait to get started. This would be the first time we'd actually be singing together as a foursome, rather than each of us singing our vocals independently and knitting them together as we had done at the studio. Now we had a week of promotion ahead of us, and I was itching to get back onstage and in front of the fans again, so that they too could hear the new line-up for themselves. I couldn't wait. It had been too long, I thought, since I'd stood in front of an audience, my guitar in my hands, and just sang.

I still wished Alex and I could have tried to say something to one another on the short walk from the Tube to the tower block. Instead, we'd both plugged ourselves back into our respective phones, so the silence between us wouldn't become even more embarrassing than it already was, and had just walked side by side, occasionally sidestepping someone walking towards us, before falling into step with one another again.

I would have loved to have been able to pinpoint exactly why it was I found her so hard to talk to, but the conversation just never seemed to flow between us. I'd have thought our shared love of music would at least give us a starting point, but the agonizing silences on the Tube ride over had told me that even talking about what music we had with us wasn't enough to sustain us. But then, I hadn't exactly ever seen either Robyn or Brooke busting a gut to talk to her either. I also didn't sense either of them beating themselves up as much as I was over it.

Now, in the apartment, Alex had done her usual trick of taking herself off to talk to anyone that wasn't me and was busy helping Nate set up the amps. Funny how she could talk to him and Grant quite easily, when she found it so difficult to talk to me. I slid a look to her, chatting so freely with Nate, and I wondered what his secret was. I also knew Robyn, when she got here, would be furious at seeing them together again, and I wondered why Alex continued to hang around Nate when she knew Robyn hated it.

The apartment was awesome and I already knew, just from the voices around me, the acoustics were perfect. I watched Alex moving an amp with Nate and wondered if I ought to go and offer to help; perhaps if I involved myself with my surroundings a bit more—made myself more visible to Alex—then the space that she had created for herself away from me might close a little. I watched them a little longer, thinking that the amps looked way too heavy for me to even try to shift, before intervention arrived in the form of Robyn and Brooke, shoving the apartment door open and bringing with them a blast of chatter and laughter, and some much-needed distraction.

Shifting the amps could wait.

"You're here!" I strode over to them both, grabbed a hand each, and pulled them over to the window. "Tell me if you've ever seen a view as awesome as this."

"So why couldn't Ed rent a place like this when we did the first album?" Robyn peered out of the window. "Rather than that draughty warehouse down by the docks?"

"Because we're making him money now." I laughed. "He's got to keep us onside, right?"

"Damn right." Robyn threw a look over her shoulder, paused, then released my hand and walked over to Nate.

"Is Alex doing it deliberately?" Brooke's gaze followed Robyn.

"If she is," I said, "she's stupid."

"I thought you handled stuff well the other day, by the way." Brooke lowered her voice.

"The other day?" Like I didn't know what she meant. I'd thought of little else since.

"At the recording."

"Right. That."

"I mean, what was she thinking?" Brooke said, turning to face the window again. "Robyn wanted to have a go at her about it, but I told her to leave it."

"You know the crazy thing?" I asked. "I don't even think Alex realized how much she'd pissed me off."

"So maybe you should tell her." Brooke looked at me. "After all, you've got to work with her."

I stole another look to Alex. "You know," I said to Brooke, "I've just sat with her on a train for the last twenty minutes, and I could hardly dredge up two words to say to her." I masked a sigh with a smile. "So telling her she should quit trying to be queen bee and annoying the hell out of everyone around here was always going to be hard."

"But if you don't tell her..."

"It's all right for you." I laughed. "She doesn't think you can't sing. Or Robyn for that matter." I frowned. "Seems it's just me she has a problem with."

"In fairness," Brooke said, wrinkling her nose, "she didn't really say that about you, did she? That you couldn't sing."

"What? Sneaking to Ed and telling him she thought I was pitchy?" I said, tossing a look to Alex, who'd left Nate now that Robyn had turned up and was now fiddling with the wires on her headphones. "And the way Ed just took it from her." I continued to glower over at her.

"Ed's just trying to keep Alex onside right now," Brooke said. "He'll agree to anything she says because he thinks she's the best thing ever."

"You think?"

"I know."

"She's got no idea, has she?" I murmured, more to myself than to Brooke.

As I continued to seethe, Alex looked like she didn't have a care in the world. While Robyn spoke with Nate, I saw Alex, now sitting with her headphones on, oblivious to my eyes boring into the back of her and to my simmering resentment. Our argument at the studio and her words of contempt about me returned, like an annoying mantra that my brain refused to ignore, and I wondered—and not for the first time since she'd said it—just why I couldn't seem to let it go. Maybe because she hadn't brought it up on the train either. Perhaps I was expecting her to say something—apologize, even—but because she hadn't, that made me even more resentful.

My eyes were drawn to her again. Should I tell her everything I'd wanted to say to her on the train? That I thought she'd had no right to rock up at the recording studio—as the new girl—then find fault with my singing? Words like *respect* and *lack of professionalism* swirled about my head, and I sensed adrenaline rising inside me as I imagined striding over to her, yanking off her headphones, and telling her exactly what I thought of both her and her criticism. In front of everyone. Let everyone in the room know in no uncertain terms what I thought of her.

My adrenaline crashed, though, as I saw her get up and walk out through the apartment door, the door banging closed behind her like it had done in the recording studio.

Maybe next time. My breathing slowed again. I shouldn't be nervous about confronting—no, not confronting, *speaking* with her. She was the newbie, not me. She should be nervous about speaking to me; she should understand that she shouldn't make comments about things she didn't understand well enough to possibly have an opinion on.

"What you have to remember," Brooke said, dragging my attention back to her, "is that you are the best bloody singer *ever*. You just remember that next time Alex gets into your head."

I cast another look to the door. Brooke was right, of course. I *was* a good singer. If only the niggling doubt that Alex had planted in me would go away again.

❖

By the time Ed eventually turned up at the studio, my anger had abated slightly. Now, after hanging around for nearly an hour, all I wanted to do was start singing, get the song rehearsed to our satisfaction before going on *The Afternoon Show*, then go home. My parents were heading off for a three-week holiday to Italy later that day, and I wanted to get home so I could speak to them before they left. We spoke a lot, my parents and I. We FaceTimed at least once a day, mostly to reassure my mum that I was okay, that I was eating okay, and that London life was everything I'd told them I'd known it would be when I'd left Brighton to follow my dream. But as much as my parents got reassurance from those daily calls, I got comfort from them too, because I knew my situation was way different to other girls' my age. Most other seventeen-year-olds—certainly my other old school friends—had their parents with them 24/7, looking out for them, being there just when they needed them. Okay, I knew mine would be there in a flash if I ever needed them, but still…it wasn't quite the same.

The rate things were going at the studio now, though, I wasn't sure I'd catch them before they headed off. Alex had disappeared and I was simmering that she was denying me the chance to speak to my mum. Alex had kindly left the room over half an hour before, and the only person who apparently didn't seem to give a damn was Ed. Instead, me, Brooke, and Robyn had been left kicking our heels while he spoke first to Grant, then to Nate, then—infuriatingly—left the room too, without telling any of us what was going on, or when we might even begin to start rehearsing.

Brooke and Robyn didn't seem as bothered as me. While I paced the room, feeling myself getting more and more wound up at the lack of any apparent organization, I heard Brooke talking on her phone to first one person, then another, then another, while Robyn read out as many of the latest #Be4 tweets to me that she could find on her Twitter feed.

I was barely listening. At that moment I didn't care that someone had said, *OMG just seen the blond one from @Be4 getting off the Tube at Blackfriars*, or that *#Robyn totally rocks the LBD look in pics of her coming out of famous nightclub in Kensington @Be4*. Robyn had already told me she'd been papped the night before. She didn't need to read it out to me again right now.

At last, just as Robyn started to read out the next batch of mentions, Ed and Alex returned. No one asked them where they'd been, or why we'd been kept waiting for Alex to come back, so I didn't bother either. As long as we started singing—and soon—Alex could have been to Scotland and back for all I cared; she was back now, and that meant we could finally get started.

Things moved quickly then. People huddled around the sound machine, hands were clapped, orders were shouted out. Our prerecorded instrumental music blared out around the room as Nate adjusted volumes, and Ed moved about everyone, gathering them, shifting them into position, until finally we were ready to start singing.

The opening bars of "After the Rain" rang out and my hunch about the acoustics was right. It was going to sound immense, and as I sang my vocals, I hoped that the studio at *The Afternoon Show* in which we'd be performing it would be as perfect as this. As I waited for my part, Brooke's vocals sounded sweetly around the room. I swallowed, took a deep breath, then sang my vocals, pleased at the quality thanks to the acoustics. A shiver cascaded down my spine as I heard Robyn's vocals kick in, harmonizing perfectly with mine, before Alex came in with her vocals too.

That's when I heard it.

I frowned and shot a look to Robyn, who shrugged and continued to sing her part. Perhaps I'd been mistaken. I sang on, assuming I'd misheard, and stood back from my mic as Brooke sang, then stole a look to Alex as her vocals began again.

I heard it again, and this time there was no mistake. As I watched her sing, my ears picked out a whole different range of notes than I was familiar with: riffs randomly thrown in, lower notes, higher notes. She was all over the place, singing entirely differently to both how the song had been written and how we'd recorded it, and I'd heard enough.

"Wait, wait." I held up my hands. "What are you doing?" I swung round to face Alex. "Where did that lot come from?"

"I threw it in because I think it sounds better with your harmonies when we sing it live," Alex said. She flipped her mic from hand to hand. "Don't you agree?"

"No," I said, "I don't."

Alex didn't answer. Infuriatingly, she just kept throwing her mic between her hands.

"And the riffs?"

"Sounded better."

"You think?"

"I *know*."

"Even though I didn't write it like that," I said when it was clear that was all she was going to say. "As well you know."

"So I ad-libbed." Alex's voice rose.

I threw out my hands. "You can't just start ad-libbing in a rehearsal when you feel like it," I said. "You do remember we're a band, don't you?"

"Of course." Alex looked bored. "And?"

"And a band does things together," I said, jabbing the words out. "If you have one member going off and doing what they feel like in a song, it ruins it for the rest of us."

"Who says it'll ruin it?" Alex asked.

"Tally does." Finally Robyn stepped in. "Sometimes I think you forget you're not a solo artist any more."

"Bullshit." Alex shook her head.

"Or on a talent show," I muttered.

"What did you say?" Finally the mic swapping stopped.

"You have to remember it's not all about you, Alex," I said. "Not any more."

"It never was," she replied, turning away.

"So quit trying to be the big *I am*," I said, shooting a look towards Ed. "Ed? A little backup here, please?"

Ed glanced towards Alex, back to me, then to Alex again.

"Try it back with the original notes," he said to her, "then we'll decide. If your version sounds better, Alex, we'll roll with that."

"Sure." Alex nestled her mic back into its cradle. "We can try it."

"No, no, no." I was stunned. This was *our* song. Mine, Brooke's, and Robyn's. Not Ed's. Not Alex's. She had no right to dictate anything. "We can do more than *try* it. We can *do* it." I looked at Ed again. "We're going to have to perform this on live TV soon enough and you think it's okay for her to start mucking around with it?"

"Who's *her*?" To my ears, Alex practically spat the word out.

"You." I gave as good as I got.

"I was just trying stuff out," Alex said, shrugging, "not *mucking around*, as you so nicely put it."

"Putting in notes that don't exist." Finally Robyn spoke up again. "It's clear Tally doesn't want you to do it." She shrugged. "So quit it."

Alex stared at her.

"You think the same?" she asked Brooke.

"I do." To my relief, Brooke had my back.

"'K." Alex turned away, stared at the floor, then looked back in front of her again. "So…from Tally's vocals?" she asked.

I was done. Even if I'd wanted to, I didn't think I could sing a note right then. My throat was tight. The room was so stuffy, the walls creeping in on me. Everyone was looking at me, waiting for my cue to go again. I felt trapped and light-headed. Frustrated at Alex. It was *my* song, *my* lyrics, *my* tune, and all Alex seemed determined to do was undermine it all. Undermine *me*.

"I need a time out." I crammed my mic back into its cradle and hurried from the room before anyone could stop me. Out on the landing, I looked around for the first door I could see and, seeing one right opposite me, pushed it open a crack and peered in. Seeing it empty, I wandered across the floor and over to the large floor-to-ceiling window, then rattled the handle, relieved to find it was unlocked. I needed some air in my lungs before the heat of the apartment made me pass out. I pulled it open, then stepped out onto the balcony and breathed in the sticky afternoon air. I listened to the sounds of the city below me; somewhere in the distance I heard a train, its wheels screeching against the hot rails; car horns blared at one another on the streets; from somewhere on one of the floors beneath me I could hear the dull thud of music.

I hated her.

I knew I should go back in, be an adult about it. But I couldn't. The festering anger I felt towards Alex, which had been living inside me for days, and which now, thanks to her little show, threatened to spill out of me, prevented me from turning away from the balcony, plastering a false smile on my face, and returning to the others.

I dragged in lungfuls of warm air and stared up at the cobalt sky, narrowing my eyes against the sun to try to see the plane I could hear flying nearby. I looked up to my right, seeing it just as it came into view, bright sunlight sparkling off its fuselage. The plane was low, so was it taking off or landing? I peered up at it some more, trying to make out the livery on its side, and imagined its passengers on board, then wondered where they were going or where they had come from.

While I still stared up at it, leaning over the balcony slightly to watch it until it disappeared from sight, I heard footsteps behind me and, expecting to see Robyn, felt a lurch of dismay. It was Alex. Without saying anything, she came and stood next to me on the balcony, then leant her arms on it and peered over. I slid a look to her as she gazed down, expecting her to speak, but she didn't. The silence between us stretched like elastic, only punctuated by the constant traffic sounds around us. Just when I was starting to feel as though I should either speak or leave, Alex spoke.

"I come from Suffolk," she said, still looking around her, rather than at me. "You know that bit that sticks out on the east coast?"

"I know where Suffolk is," I said, not looking at her either.

"It's very flat and mostly countryside," she said. "Narrow lanes, villages. Stuff like that."

"I know what the countryside is too," I said, more petulantly than I'd intended.

"So when I moved to London," Alex continued, apparently ignoring my childishness, "it was the biggest shock to my system." Finally she looked at me. "I hated it at first. Couldn't get my head around all the change. Wanted everything to be how it used to be."

"Fascinating." I was done with the psychology already.

Alex, apparently, wasn't.

After the longest pause she said, "You know, there's one constant thing that happens in everyone's lives, and that's change." She looked me straight in the eye. "And change is always going to happen, whether we like it or not, because the only thing you can predict in life," she said with a smile, "is the unpredictable."

"I can cope with change." I turned and looked at her too. "If this is what this little chat is all about."

"Yeah, really looks like you can cope with it," Alex said, slowly returning her gaze out to the city, "if that show back there is anything to go by."

"'After the Rain' is my song," I said, "but you seem determined to disrespect it." I paused. "And it wasn't *a little show*, as you so delicately put it."

"What would you call it then?" Alex asked. "I'd call it storming out."

"I needed some time." Even I knew I sounded stupid.

When Alex didn't answer, I carried on.

"You can't just come in and start changing stuff to suit your voice," I said, "when I know how I want the song to sound."

"Have you ever thought that a little tweak here and there might make it sound even more awesome than it already does?" Alex suggested.

"It doesn't need changing." I tried to catch her eye.

"No, you're right."

"So…" I rolled a hand. "Why say it needs to sound better?"

"I didn't."

"You just did."

Alex sighed. "I didn't come out here to argue," she said, "just to explain myself." She stood up straighter. "But if you're too stubborn to even hear me out…"

"Stubborn?"

"You heard me, didn't you?" she snapped.

I bit at my lip. That was me told then.

"We both know the song's perfect," Alex said, "but I also know how my voice works and how I can adapt it to suit your music better." She held my gaze. "So, really, what I'm saying is that the tone in my voice needs to change slightly to work in harmony with your music, so it can be even more awesome than it already is."

"Bullshit." I laughed and looked away. "You just want to be the star of the show because your last two attempts at success in music failed." Gazing out into the distance I added, "So don't tell me you're doing it as a favour to me."

"Is that what you think?" Her voice was soft. "Is that what you all think?"

The quiet edge to her voice made me instantly regret what I'd just said.

"No." I sighed. "I shouldn't have said that." I caught her eye again. "And I'm sorry for what I said about your last two attempts failing."

"Right." Alex leant her arms on the balcony again and studied her hands.

"I'm very protective of my music," I said.

"I get that," Alex said, "I really do." She frowned. "But I also know what can or can't work." She squinted to me through the sun. "Maybe that doesn't come across so well," she said, "maybe *I* don't come across so well."

"You can be a bit full on." I laughed, wanting to add that she irritated the hell out of me most days too.

I heard her draw in a deep breath, then watched as she stepped away.

"I want to try it again," she said, "my way."

"Have you listened to anything I've just said?" I asked.

"Will you just try it?" she asked. "Just once? Please?"

I don't know whether it was the way she said *please*, or the way she looked at me when she said it, but I found myself wavering.

"Please," she repeated. "I really think it can work."

I sighed.

Alex leant her head to one side. "And if it doesn't, you can all call me the biggest jerk in the world."

Not knowing whether I was doing the right thing or not, I nodded, surprised at the smile that my agreement brought to her lips.

Robyn was going to hate me.

CHAPTER SIX

I could tell by the way Robyn was looking at me when Alex and I eventually returned to the room that she knew I'd caved in. I didn't care. I was done. I was tired, both mentally and physically, and now all I wanted to do was get the rehearsal over as quickly as possible so I could go home to ring my parents while I still had the chance. Alex had been convincing in her claim that what she was doing would work, so I figured if she wanted to ad-lib her way through the song and show herself up in front of Ed, then I'd just let her get on with it. Let her have to explain herself to everyone why our rehearsal was going on way longer than it needed to.

As I passed Brooke, she gave me an enquiring lift of her head to ask me if everything was okay. I nodded my reply and slotted myself back behind my microphone. I accepted the bottle of water that was passed to me by Robyn and drank some back, liking the feeling of the ice-cold water coating my hot throat as it trickled down.

"We good?" Robyn asked, taking the bottle back from me and screwing the lid back on.

"All good."

She threw the bottle over to Nate, who caught it one-handed and placed it on the floor next to him. I liked that he smiled at me when he caught my eye, a kind of it'll-all-be-okay smile. At least, that's how I read it. The sound guys were great, and even though I could tell they all liked Alex—after all, they had no reason to dislike her—I also knew they were always, without exception, fair and loyal to us. So I returned his smile, hoping he could read in it my frustration at being put in this situation that I neither felt happy nor comfortable with.

I watched Alex as she sauntered across the floor towards me and Robyn and remembered her words to me out on the balcony. She'd been right; I *was* afraid of change, even though I couldn't admit that to her. But I also knew she'd been right when she'd said there was nothing anyone could do about it; things changed constantly in people's lives, and it was up to us to either suck it up or let it overwhelm us.

I didn't want to be overwhelmed.

Guess it was time to suck it up then.

The intro echoed round the room. The sound of our prerecorded guitars and drums coated the walls, signalling Brooke's cue. As I saw her getting ready to sing, I knew it was time to try it Alex's way now, rather than later. Before I bottled it. And at least that way, we could get it out of the way and move on.

I held up my hand.

"Problem?" Ed snapped the sound machine off.

"I think perhaps," I said, not daring to catch Robyn's eye, "we should try and sing it the way Alex just sang it before, after all." I tucked a piece of hair behind my ear. "Just to see"—I cleared my throat—"how that works with our harmonies."

I didn't need to look at Robyn to see her face. But I did feel her arm on mine as she pulled me away from my mic and over to the side of the room.

"You serious?" she asked. "What was all that stuff before about then?"

"We talked," I said, "out on the balcony."

"No shit."

"I said we'd try it her way."

"And let her win?"

"It's not about winning, Robyn." I sighed and slid a look back over to Alex, who was staring at the floor. "It's about adjusting. Being compliant for the good of the band."

"But you said earlier…?"

"I know what I said," I replied, "but…I don't know. Maybe she's right."

"And if she's not?"

"Then she'll make herself look stupid." I shrugged.

I followed Robyn's gaze over to Alex. Robyn was biting her nails and I knew she was thinking long and hard about stuff.

"Okay, whatever." Eventually the chewing stopped and Robyn spoke. Without waiting for any answer from me she walked back to her mic, leaving me still standing by the wall.

I wasn't sure if that's the response I wanted from her; I also knew whatever I did, I couldn't win. If I gave in to Alex, I made Robyn pissed. If I didn't give in to Alex, I made *her* pissed. It was no-win for me either way.

I wiped my hands down my jeans, sweaty from the heat in the room, and followed Robyn back to the mics. I caught Alex's eye as I slid in between her and Brooke and saw the ghost of a smile pass across her lips. I didn't return it.

"So we're going from the intro again," Ed called out from the mixing desk. Nate slid a button on the desk, allowing music to fill the room, and again I waited for Brooke's vocals before I came in on mine. This time when Alex sang her solo, I listened out for her changes, determined not to let them throw me, and felt pleased at how it sounded when Robyn came in with her vocals, then more pleased when Alex harmonized with her. She belted out her next set of vocals—again, not as I'd written them—and as I came in on my vocals, the softness of my voice in comparison gave the music a different edge to how it had been recorded just a few days before.

My heart hammered in beat with the music as I heard it. This was exactly how I'd imagined it would sound live, in comparison to its recorded version, and it worked. It so worked. As we sang on, I caught Robyn's eye and could tell by the way she was looking at me that she felt the same way. Our harmonies gelled; the clarity of Alex's voice, now she was singing her vocals an octave higher than she had at the studio, would sound immense live. She'd known it all along. She'd probably even known it at the recording, that the recorded version needed to sound different to the live one, because the live version needed to have enough power and rawness to get our audience up on their feet and dancing to it.

As Alex continued to ad-lib through the song, I heard different notes coming from Brooke and Robyn too, as they adjusted their voices to sit perfectly alongside Alex's. Soon, I was doing it too, singing *along* with them to allow our voices to work in conjunction with each other's, rather than singing verbatim, as we'd always done before. It was liberating. More than that, it was huge fun. While we couldn't play around with it too much and allow ourselves to stray too far from what we would be singing live on forthcoming TV shows and in gigs, we did allow ourselves enough slack to have fun with the song and enjoy ourselves, and I knew if we did something similar on *The Afternoon Show*, the audience would absolutely love it.

"Okay, take a break," Ed called out as the music faded. "Ten minutes, then we'll go for another run-through."

I slotted my mic back into its cradle and stepped back. My skin was tingling, my heart still hammering behind my ribs at the sound we'd just made together. Robyn sidled up next to me, grabbed me by my elbow, and hustled me away from Brooke and Alex. She didn't speak. Instead, she looked at me, presumably waiting for me to speak first. So I did.

"So…that went better than expected," I said.

"Better than expected?" Robyn repeated. "It was epic." She lowered her voice at that last bit. "So now we have a problem."

"Do we?" I was confused.

"Alex was right." Her voice lowered even further. "Everything she said was right."

"So?"

"So now what do we do?"

"We go with it?" Just a hunch.

"Then she wins."

I sighed. "Didn't we already have this conversation?" I asked. "It's not about winning, it's about—"

"Compliance. Yeah, yeah." She threw a look back over her shoulder. "It's going to make her insufferable, isn't it?"

I didn't think that was fair.

"I think it's going to make me apologize," I corrected, "because she was right all along. She knows her stuff."

"So you want to do it the same way on this next run-through?" Robyn asked.

"Don't you?" I replied. "It sounded awesome."

"I guess." Robyn sighed. "I just don't want it to turn into the Alex Brody Show, that's all."

"It won't." I squeezed her arm. "She'd be a shit host, anyway."

Robyn laughed and looked over to Alex while she was still laughing. I saw her looking at us and, seeing the look on her face at our laughter, immediately felt bad.

"We'll do it the same way again," I said, giving her arm another squeeze before I walked away.

Alex was still looking at me as I approached her.

"So?" she asked. "Have you and Robyn finished tearing me to pieces?"

"We weren't—"

"Whatever." She turned to walk away. "I'm used to it."

I reached out and grabbed her arm.

"I'm sorry," I said.

"I told you," she replied, moving her arm so my hand fell away, "I'm used to it."

"No, I mean, I'm sorry for doubting you," I continued, slightly hurt that she'd shrugged me off. "Sorry for throwing a fit before." I paused. "The rehearsal just sounded amazing."

Alex stopped.

"The range in your voice," I said, when she didn't say anything, "worked really well with ours. Robyn's in particular."

"Not that she'd ever admit it."

"Maybe she's as stubborn as I am." I smiled and waited for Alex to return my smile. She didn't.

"I knew how our voices would work together." She looked at me. "It's a shame it took me coming after you when you stormed out, and then having to placate you, for you to see that when I knew it would be okay all along."

"I've said I'm sorry," I said, wondering why Alex wouldn't accept it. "What more can I do?"

"You could have had more faith in me to begin with," Alex said, walking away. "You all could."

Chapter Seven

Promoting our music rocks. After our rehearsals in Walthamstow, we had a week of promo ahead of the release of "After the Rain," which meant days of interviews, radio shows, and daytime chat shows. I couldn't wait. I knew it would be a chance for the fans to meet Alex properly for the first time, but more importantly, it would be *our* chance to show everyone that the rumours that had circulated after Nicole's sudden departure hadn't been true: Be4 hadn't fallen apart without her.

Of course, speculation had been rife about why Nicole had left, and the press had already put two and two together and come up with five. The press weren't stupid; emerging pop stars such as Nicole didn't just leave bands for no obvious reason, and I'd heard rumours that reporters had been sniffing around every drug and alcohol rehabilitation centre in the UK, hoping that just one indiscreet member of staff might give them the scoop they were so obviously desperate for.

Even Ed's hastily arranged photo shoot in the Caribbean hadn't fooled them. He'd flown Nicole out to Barbados the day she left Be4 to have a series of photographs taken of her on the beach there. Then she'd been hurried back into the UK the very next day while putting out the message on social media that she was still in the Caribbean enjoying a well-earned break. Nicole was now holed up in Croft House, a drug rehab centre in the middle of the countryside.

Maybe her taking drugs had been her way of punishing me, I don't know. Or perhaps it was her way of severing our long-standing ties, a knee-jerk reaction against me. She'd slackened her ties with me soon after I'd told her I could only be her friend and had fallen in with a bunch of people who were so far removed from me and everything I stood for, it was laughable. Except the drug taking was far from laughable. As Nicole began to spend all her time hanging out with people who wasted their days and nights, I began to wonder if she was doing it so she wouldn't have to think about me and how I'd rejected her. Perhaps that was big-headed of me. I don't know. All I do know is I spent sleepless nights when I knew she was with them, worrying about what she was up to and how it would all turn out.

It turned out to be the worst knee-jerk decision of her life.

I was sitting in the green room of a London TV studio when I had my second proper conversation with Alex, after our chat on the balcony in Walthamstow. We were due to go live on air on *The Afternoon Show,* and after a quick rehearsal of "After the Rain" backstage, Brooke and Robyn had left me so they could go and speak to two guys from another band who were recording a link section for a children's music programme. I wasn't interested enough to give up the comfort of the green room's plush furniture to talk to them, so I amused myself while they were gone by playing a game on my phone, and enjoying five minutes' peace and quiet on my own for a change.

That was, until Alex came in.

We hadn't spoken at all since the rehearsal in the apartment a few days before. After our second and third run-throughs, when it was clear we'd perfected it, we'd gone our separate ways. Alex hadn't travelled back down the Tube the same way she'd come; instead, I'd left her in the foyer of the apartment block with hardly a word and travelled home alone, finally managing to catch my parents on the phone before they disappeared on holiday.

I'd talked to them for over an hour. But with Alex, it was the opposite. I'd thought she'd have wanted to talk some more about the rehearsal, but it seemed almost as if now the rehearsal was over, she wanted nothing more to do with me or any of us, and it was beginning to feel to me as if we'd got to the point where I honestly thought we'd never have anything to talk about ever again. We'd turn up to rehearsals, or recordings, or interviews, do what we had to do, then leave again without a word to one another. That was the way it was going to be, if the last few days were anything to go by.

Now, in the green room, I barely looked up as Alex came in, pretending—however childish it might have been—that the game on my phone was way more interesting to me than her. I saw from the corner of my eye as she switched on the coffee machine to the side of the room, then thumbed through a magazine next to the machine, humming quietly to herself as she did so. Humming didn't normally annoy me, but today it did, because it felt to me as if it was her way of deliberately trying to break up the stifling silence I'd created in the room. As if the silence was my fault. As if everything was my fault.

She grabbed her coffee and snagged the chair opposite mine, casting me a quick look as she sank down into it. I concentrated on my game—which I'd lost interest in long before Alex came into the room—and listened as she first opened a packet of sugar, then stirred it in, then tapped her spoon on the side of her cup, then sipped at it.

The silence returned.

"Brooke and Robyn not around?" Finally Alex spoke.

"Nuh-uh." I shook my head but didn't look up.

I heard another sip. Then a small sniff. A clearing of her throat.

"You not talking today?" Alex asked.

Finally I looked up.

"Just playing, that's all." I lifted my phone.

"You know," Alex said, "if we're to go live on air in"—she looked at her watch—"thirty-five minutes' time and present ourselves to the public as best buddies, we ought to at least pretend like we are in private." She smiled, sat back, and slowly crossed one leg over the other, adding, "Don't you think?"

I put my phone back down.

"I wasn't being funny," I said. "I really was just playing."

Liar.

"You've hardly said two words to me since the rehearsal the other day," Alex said.

"Have you spoken to me?" I asked.

"Have you tried to speak to me?" she answered.

"It's difficult when you just take off like you did the other day."

"I went when it was clear no one was going to bother speaking to me."

We were going round in circles.

The excruciating silence returned.

"You know, if there's any animosity between us, the public will pick up on it straight away," Alex said.

"Learn that on *Sing,* did you?" I asked. "*Lesson One: How to Act Properly in Public.*" I regretted saying it straight away.

"Nope." Alex held my gaze. "That came in lesson four," she deadpanned. "Lesson one was holding a mic, lesson two was the hair flick."

I had to admit, that was funny.

"Lesson three?" she added. "The stage slide."

I couldn't help the smile that broke out across my face at that.

"Don't tell me I just made you smile?" Alex dramatically clutched at her chest. "I must be getting better."

I gave her my best sarcastic look.

"Steady, Tally," Alex continued, "we might have a civilized conversation next."

My sarcastic look stayed on my face.

"Seriously," Alex said, "if you've still got a problem with me, don't you think we ought to sort it out sooner rather than later?"

I took in a breath.

"Do you still have a problem with me?" she pressed. "I thought we sorted stuff at the rehearsal."

"The rehearsal maybe," I said. "But I didn't like…"

Alex crossed one leg over the other. "You didn't like…?"

"At the studio the other day," I said, "you told me I was pitchy."

Alex frowned. "Pitchy?" she asked.

"Well, you told Ed," I said. "I had to lower my key, remember?"

Alex nodded slowly and seemed to want to choose her next words carefully. "I could hear something in the recording that didn't sound like your normal voice." She looked at me. "I've listened to your music, Tally. Don't forget that."

"But…pitchy?" I was like a dog with a bone, I knew.

"Listen, Tally," she said, "when you mixed it up? Wow. Just wow."

That threw me.

"So why didn't you say that to me at the time?"

"What am I?" Alex asked, "Your mother?"

"No, but…"

"Look, I'm sorry if you thought I was harsh that day," Alex said, "and I'm sorry if my lack of diplomacy meant we started off on the wrong foot."

"You showed me up in front of everyone," I said. "And, actually, in the rehearsal the other day," I continued. "Okay, so it eventually worked, but I didn't like how we got to that point."

"But you just said it yourself. It worked," Alex said, sounding exasperated. "Isn't that all that matters?" She shook her head. "Anyway, we talked about it out on the balcony. I thought you were okay with it."

"I've been thinking." I sounded petulant. "And I didn't like the way you handled the whole situation."

"Oh, grow up." Alex sipped at her coffee. "It worked, so why are you still whining about it?"

I had no answer to that.

"Look, I've just apologized to you—twice—for being thoughtless," Alex added, "and you still can't seem to accept it." She leant over, put her coffee cup down, then stood. "I'm trying to hold out the hand of friendship here, but you seem intent on—"

"Stop." She was right. I held up a hand. "I'm sorry."

To my relief, Alex sat back.

"You know," she said, staring at a point on the wall and not to me, "when I was on *Sing*, it was the most cutthroat thing I'd ever done."

"Seriously?"

She nodded. "I hated it," she said. "Everyone talking about me behind my back. Finding fault with everything I did because they were so desperate to win. It was awful."

"I didn't know."

"Why would you?" Alex looked at me. "Look, I know I've come in and taken someone's place who was very important to you all," she said, "and I suppose I'm always expecting you all to find fault with everything I do. I suppose I just need to prove to you all that I *do* know what I'm doing." She picked her coffee cup up again. "But in hindsight I probably went about it all the wrong way as usual."

"So you didn't think I was pitchy at the recording?"

"No. I didn't." Alex rolled her eyes. "Now can we just change the subject?" she asked. "Please?"

Gladly. I chewed on my lip, trying to think of something to say.

Fortunately, Alex got in there first. "Can we try again?" she asked, then leant over to me, extended her hand, and said, "My name's Alex Brody and I'm very glad to meet you."

"Tally." I took her hand, glad that she'd shown initiative when I'd apparently been unable to. "It's actually Talia, but I prefer Tally. Or Tal."

"Talia?" she asked, releasing my hand. "That's a nice name."

"It means gentle dew from heaven, apparently," I said, sitting back again. "My parents are fans of unusual names. My brother's called Jasper."

"Ha." Alex chuckled. "My dog's called Jasper."

"I'll tell my brother that," I said. "Mind you, I suppose it could have been worse. Our parents could have called us Psoriasis and Chlamydia, or something equally bonkers."

Alex laughed out loud and her laugh was so free and genuine that I felt a sudden…what? A sense of achievement and happiness, I suppose, that I'd been the one to make her laugh first out of all of us.

"I know I'm not Nicole," Alex suddenly said, her laughter gone in an instant. "I can't ever be her."

"I know." I nodded.

Alex drew out a long breath. "And I'm sorry I'm not her," she said, "but, hey. There's not much I can do about that either."

"I know," I repeated. I mirrored her sigh. Seemed it was the afternoon for sighs. "I'm sorry if I—"

"All I can be is me," she interrupted. "I don't know how to be anyone other than me."

She was right. I got that. We'd been unfair to her from the off, expecting her to slot straight into Nicole's shoes and to be the same person who'd gone.

And as I looked at Alex and sensed the hint of uncertainty that lay behind her eyes as she spoke, it finally struck me that Nicole really had gone and it was pointless me, Robyn, Brooke, or anyone else trying to pretend Alex was someone she wasn't.

And I figured at that moment that Alex really didn't need to be anyone other than herself, because she was doing just fine being herself.

Chapter Eight

The chat show was awesome. No, better than awesome.

I glanced at Robyn, Brooke, and Alex as we filed off the studio's stage, having totally killed our live performance of "After the Rain," and felt the same chills on the surface of my skin that I'd felt in the apartment, the same hammering-heart sensation. The audience too—just as I'd thought at our first rehearsal—seemed to love it, if the prolonged applause as we came offstage was anything to go by.

"So…Be4." Our interviewer, a guy in his thirties called Hugh Hollis, who used to be a TV chef or something, apparently wanted to ease us into the interview with some bland questions as we all sat down. "You're keeping the name?"

Obviously.

"We are." Robyn smiled her best smile. "We thought we owed that to the fans."

Good answer.

"Even though there was talk of you guys splitting when Nicole left?" Hugh asked.

I shot a look to Robyn. That was news to me.

"There was never any talk we'd ever break Be4 up," I said. "Our fans have stuck with us since the very beginning. We'd never do that to them."

A small cheer went up from a corner of the audience. I lifted my hand and waved, prompting another, more prolonged cheer.

"And Alex." Hugh turned his attention to her. "How's it been, being the new girl?"

"It's been awesome." Alex, sitting between me and Brooke, sat back and looked like she belonged there. "These guys have been lovely. Made everything so easy for me," she said, "it was like joining old friends."

She had the patter, I gave her that.

As she carried on talking, my thoughts drifted. For the first time that day, I really felt as if we'd finally gelled as a group. I know my chat with Alex in the green room had helped, but our live performance of "After the Rain," with all Alex's changes in it, had just gone down a storm with the audience, confirming to me that Alex really had known what she'd been talking about.

Our first TV appearance as the new Be4 had been a hit, and I knew that was thanks to Alex.

I stole a look to her while she was still talking. The first proper look I'd been bothered to give her, and I saw in her eyes an understanding that I was sure I hadn't seen before. She knew her stuff, that was clear. As I watched her from the corner of my eye, the anger and bad feeling I'd directed towards her in the weeks before now seemed to dissolve when I saw how comfortable she was with Hugh and the audience, and when I remembered the shivers I'd felt in my spine at the beautiful music we'd all just created on that stage.

"And I'm so excited for the future…" Alex was still doing great. She was funny, articulate, charming, and I loved how her charisma and apparent natural ease around a live audience had them laughing and hanging on every word she was saying.

Okay, so we knew they weren't entirely our target audience, but we also knew the programme was being aired live at five p.m. when our preferred teenage viewers would hopefully be watching at home, and I guessed Twitter would be our guide later as to how we'd done.

"And have any of you seen Nicole since she left?" Hugh asked, bringing my attention back to him. "Last seen living it up in Barbados, I think." He gave a look to the audience, making them laugh.

"We haven't, no," Brooke started.

"There were rumours she was back in England," Hugh said. "Could you guys clarify that?"

Brooke, Robyn, and I made a big show of looking confused.

"She's still in Barbados, Hugh." Robyn spoke first. "You've seen the pictures, right?"

"You've seen her bikini, surely?" Brooke.

Another ripple of laughter. Good old Brooke.

"Sure," Hugh said, "but those other rumours just won't go away, will they?"

"Other rumours?" Robyn leant her head to one side.

"The rehab rumours," Hugh said. "That she's in Croft House."

"That's crazy." I laughed. "She's in the Caribbean having a break and writing some solo stuff," I said. I wanted Hugh to shut up. "It sounds good too."

"Solo stuff?" Hugh latched on to that. Of course he did, and it was then I wished I'd never said anything. "Are you giving us an exclusive here?" he asked.

"No, no." I laughed, but Robyn fired me a look, so I added, "At the moment, all she's doing is enjoying her time off in Barbados," and knew all I'd done then was just dug a deeper hole for myself.

Fortunately, Alex changed the subject, and in doing so, saved me. She butted in and somehow managed, with an effortless fluidity, to steer the conversation away from Nicole and back round to the impending release of "After the Rain." It was genius. Hugh apparently completely forgot all about Nicole and focused all his attention on Alex, who was doing an awesome job of maintaining eye contact with him the whole time she was speaking, frequently leaning over to touch his leg, and now quite obviously had his entire attention.

I was so grateful to her. I sat and watched her, wishing I'd never said anything about Nicole. It would be all over the Internet like a rash later, I just knew it. Ed was going to have to work some of his magic, and I was going to have to stay out of reporters' ways for a while. I was an idiot. I slipped another look to Alex, who, now Brooke was talking to Hugh, looked back at me and gave me a small wink, as if to tell me everything was going to be all right.

Then our eight-minute slot was up.

Had we talked enough about "After the Rain"? Or Alex's input into the band? I had no idea, but as the programme cut to commercials, the long and genuine applause from the audience told me we'd done okay. I was pleased.

I was less pleased with Robyn's attitude. She'd been giving me evils as we'd left the floor, and her silence was expected, but then it grew longer and more awkward as we walked back down the corridor towards the green room, and I knew the second we got into the room, she'd let rip.

"Why did you say that about Nic back there?" She swung round to face me once she knew we were all alone. "Ed'll be furious."

I followed her in, holding the door open for Alex and Brooke behind me.

"I don't know." I shrugged. "First thing that came into my head."

"Solo stuff?" Robyn said. "Now the press will want to know how, when, why—"

"They won't," I lied, grabbing my bag. "And if they do, then…"

"Then what?" Robyn asked. "You'll make up some more lies to add to the ones you've already told?"

"Look," I said, "Nic forced us into having to tell those lies. I wouldn't lose any sleep over it."

"Yeah, and whose fault was it in the first place," Robyn muttered under her breath.

"What?" I spun round to face her.

"Why are you two arguing?" Alex stepped up next to me. "We've just had an amazing time out there. Totally killed our performance, charmed the pants off the audience *and* Hugh. So why spoil it now?"

I glanced at her, surprised but grateful she had my back.

"Tally shouldn't have said what she said," Robyn said. "There's enough speculation around Nic as it is, without Tally opening her big mouth."

"Okay, that's unfair." Alex spoke before I could. "Tally just said what Nicole's fans probably wanted to hear, that's all." She stared at Robyn. "I think you should apologize to her."

"Oh, you do, do you?" Robyn squared up to Alex.

"Look," I said, keen to avoid any more arguments. I pulled my phone from my bag and tapped up Twitter, then searched the name of the chat show. "You see anyone talking about Nicole on here?" I held up my phone, relieved that her name hadn't appeared.

First Robyn, then Brooke, pulled their own phones out and looked at them. I watched as Robyn narrowed her eyes as she read, the hint of a smile playing on her lips. Thank goodness massaging her ego was more important to her than arguing with me.

I read some of the messages too, searching for Nicole's name, but not seeing it:

.@Be4 are back!

Totally loving the new lineup. Love, love, LOVE #Tally's hair today.

Looking good @TheAfternoonShow there, Robyn.

OMG, Alex is gorgeous! @Be4

After the Rain sounds amazing. #Brooke is the best singer ever.

.@Be4 look and sound awesome.

#Alex from @Be4! Marry meeee.

I laughed at that one. As I scrolled down, Alex's name appeared more and more often.

Okay, so just watched @TheAfternoonShow, and now I'm totally in love with #Alex Brody from @Be4!!

Thought #Alex was amazing on @Sing, but now I love her even more in @Be4.

"They sure like you." I held my phone up to Alex and waggled it.

"Do they?"

Alex wasn't reading her phone. Instead, she had walked away from us and was now sitting with her chin resting in her hands, staring out of the green room window while she waited for our car to come and pick us up. Her casual disregard for the messages about her wasn't forced, I thought. She genuinely didn't seem affected by the praise that was being heaped on her, and while I thought that was a bit weird, I also thought it was totally cool.

❖

Twitter went even madder after that. Our number of followers rocketed, and the phone to Ed's office, according to him, never stopped ringing. He, of course, was stoked.

It seemed as though no one had latched on to my indiscretion about Nicole on *The Afternoon Show.* The rumours that had dogged her since she'd left Be4 still persisted, but my fears that they would escalate just never materialized. Instead, it was Alex and our performance on the show that were all anyone wanted to talk about, and I could sense a palpable shift in our popularity. I could feel it in the vibe that seemed to follow us wherever we went, see it in the photographs that appeared almost daily in the papers, and could read it in the numerous articles that kept cropping up online about us. It all felt different now somehow. More intense. I knew something big was happening. We were finally going places and I knew it was all thanks to Alex, even though I didn't want to admit it to myself. She was the one always being featured in the photo shoots. Her picture was the first one that appeared on the computer when I searched for us. She had more Twitter followers than any of us and I knew that just proved how much the fans had accepted her into Be4.

Nicole, it seemed, was already history.

I know I should have been sad, annoyed, jealous…whatever. But I wasn't. I honestly wasn't. I was just pleased that we'd found the right person, the person that we'd apparently needed all this time, and it was all thanks to Alex that we were heading in that right direction. I knew I had to thank her. There was something about her that the public had seized on, that the fans loved, that the cameras loved. And I could see what it was that everyone loved so much about Alex Brody, because I could see it myself.

She was perfect for us, and even though I'd initially thought she was nothing more than talent-show fodder, it was abundantly clear to me now that she wasn't, and never had been. Instead, Alex was exactly the sort of person I'd always wanted for Be4. I guess I'd always seen Be4 as being a gigging band, the sort of band that plied their trade live as much as they did recorded, and for the first time ever, thanks to Alex, I could totally see that happening.

Nicole had never really wanted that. It had been the source of too many arguments between us all, and those arguments had become more frequent over the years. Robyn and Brooke had always envisioned Be4 the same way as I had: less dance band, more live band. Nicole had always preferred the dancing, but I couldn't somehow see Alex being the dancing kind of girl.

The fact Alex was awesome live hadn't been ignored. Offers of live appearances flooded in, but the second I walked into Ed's office a few days later and saw the look on his face, I knew he had news for us. It was a request to headline the second night of a festival that would be taking place in Hyde Park in two weeks' time, and I don't know who amongst us was more excited about it. Me, probably. His news took my breath away, because I knew it really showed Be4 were on the up. It had always been my dream to headline a summer festival, but I'd never for one second ever thought it would happen so soon into our career. The gigs we'd done since we'd formed the band had been awesome, but a festival in an arena as big as Hyde Park was taking it to a whole new level, and taking it to a size of audience we could only have dreamed about two years before.

It seemed my instinct about us had been right.

Be4 had arrived.

❖

The festival was confirmed. Better than that, Ed had insisted to the festival organizers that we would perform four of our songs—"After the Rain," "Crush," "Drowning in You," plus an extra one, "Take Me There," which had been written with Nicole just before she'd gone into rehab, and which we knew Ed wanted to release once "After the Rain" had dropped back out of the charts.

I knew it was going to be weird performing at the festival without Nicole by my side. I also knew that "Take Me There" had been written by Robyn and Nicole, and that they had put a long guitar solo in the middle of it just for me. I could totally do it, I knew that. But there was a niggling doubt that had gradually wormed its way into me since Ed had confirmed the festival, that somehow I wouldn't nail my solo on the day.

I knew why I felt like that: Alex.

I was concerned about her opinion of my solo, which would be fair enough if I wasn't a good guitar player, but I *was* a good player. But still, the nagging worry that she'd find fault with it, like she'd found fault with my singing at the recording of "After the Rain" a few weeks before, remained.

I knew I was just going to have to prove her wrong.

Chapter Nine

It was so bloody hot. I looked down from the rehearsal stage at the festival, to the parched yellow grass, untouched by rain in weeks, then to the dusty plumes kicked out by passing trucks, wishing that the day would end so I could go home. Or at least go and sunbathe under a tree somewhere.

It was Thursday. Two days before the festival started, two days before Be4 were to play live on stage for the first time as a new-look band.

We had been rehearsing nonstop since Ed had accepted the gig, and now we'd been in Hyde Park since ten that morning, Alex and me working first with Nate and Grant to make sure our guitars didn't blast everyone's eardrums out, then with Brooke and Robyn to perfect our performance. We worked with a choreographer too, the one thing I detested most about performing live. It was always okay when we appeared on television, because the size of the studios didn't allow us to move much, but gigging live always brought with it some sort of choreography, and although I knew it was necessary, and even though I could keep protesting that Be4 were singers, not dancers, I knew we had to get the few moves we did do on the stage absolutely perfect.

But by two p.m. I'd had enough. As the stage lights mingled with the bright sunshine, making my face burn hot, all I wanted to do was grab my guitar and sit in the shade to practise my solo a bit more. Alex and I had managed a twenty-minute practice together after lunch, but I knew it wasn't nearly enough and that my own sanity was crying out for my guitar and some much-needed me-time away from everyone else.

By two thirty I got my wish. I made my excuses to the others and snagged myself a spot behind the stage where I could clutch my best friend to me and let the stresses that had gripped my neck in a stranglehold all day disappear into the late-afternoon sky the second my fingers brushed the strings. It was heaven. As I first picked and then strummed my notes, the smile that had been missing from my face all day returned, and a coolness enveloped my body. I've always loved how my guitar feels in my hands. It felt so solid and trustworthy, and once I started to strum it, it's like I knew everything was going to be okay. It was *my* guitar solo: not Alex's, not anyone else's. It was important to remember that each time the nerves thought to get the better of me.

I'd only been playing for around ten minutes when I heard soft footsteps approaching across the grass towards me. I played on, hoping whoever it was would go away. The footsteps slowed and I heard a nervous cough from somewhere behind the stage, followed by, "Oh, hey."

I looked up. Alex.

"I wondered where you were," she said. "I mean…I wanted to ask you something."

I played on. "Ask away," I said.

"I was thinking." Alex rested a hip against the stage rigging. "About the guitar part in the middle."

"You don't like it?" I immediately stopped playing. What was wrong now?

"No, it's awesome," Alex replied, looking down at her feet. She glanced back up at me. "I just wondered if you wanted to hang out later and practise it some more."

"Sure. If you want." I looked back at her, still unsure. "You think it needs some practice?"

"It didn't feel as though we had much time together today," Alex said. "But it doesn't matter." She pushed away from the rigging and delved her hand into her pocket, pulling out her phone. "I just thought it would be cool to hang out and jam together." She moved out of the shade and back into the sunshine.

"Today?" I asked.

Alex stopped. "We're kinda finished here for the day, aren't we?" She squinted back at me against the sun. "And I'm *totally* done with any more choreography for today." Alex rolled her eyes and shuddered. "I'm at a loose end for the rest of the day, that's all," she said, "but no worries if you're busy."

"No." I jumped to my feet. My tiredness and irritability magically disappeared, and the thought of hanging out with Alex and playing guitar with her for the rest of the afternoon suddenly seemed like the only thing I wanted to do. "I'm not busy."

"Good." Alex's smile seemed genuine. She put her phone back in her pocket. "So," she said, "your place or mine?"

❖

We chose my place. I left Alex at the park, having given her my address, and then arranged for her to come over after five.

It was weird, I thought, as I travelled back across London to Islington, that the thought of Alex coming to my apartment could give me such a sense of anticipation. Weird but exciting. Alex in my sphere, in my personal space. Seeing me out of context, for the first time since she'd joined us. Just me and her.

My apartment, of course, was like a tip. I didn't ever clean, I didn't ever tidy up after myself. Why would I? I'm a seventeen-year-old living on her own in an apartment big enough for six people. The only clean and tidy part about it is the kitchen—that's always spotless, primarily because I never use it. Within a five minute walk of my front door I have a pizza place, an Indian, a Mexican, and a sushi bar that does the best oshizushi this side of the Thames. Why would I ever need to cook?

As I came in through the front door, kicking an errant pair of socks behind a potted plant, my eyes sought out one of my favourite guitars, waiting patiently for me in the corner of my lounge. My salvation. I shrugged my bag and guitar from my shoulders and, knowing I should tidy up, but wanting to play a few chords before Alex arrived more, I grabbed it and sat.

As the music flowed from my fingers, the time passed without me even realizing it. Before I knew it, the sound of the buzzer on my intercom was intruding, cutting through the music like an annoying bee. I stopped playing and stared up at the clock. Four fifteen. I swung round to look at the door, debating whether to ignore it and carry on playing, but as if the person on the other side had read my mind, the buzzer rang again, longer this time.

Irritated, I placed my guitar down and strode to the intercom, kicking yet another piece of clothing out of the way as I did so. I answered.

"Boy, you took your time." Alex's voice took me unawares. I glanced up at the clock again, confirming it was indeed four fifteen and not five p.m., and said, without thinking, "You're early."

There was a pause.

"I can…go away again if it's not convenient."

Alex was early. I shot a look around me, wishing I'd stopped playing earlier and knuckled down to making my place look at least half decent. What on earth would she think?

"No, no. It's good." I pressed the button on my intercom. "Come on up. Fourth floor. Come out of the lift and turn left. It's the second door down there."

I slotted the phone back into its cradle and looked around again. I grabbed six coffee cups from the table—three in each hand—and shoved them into the kitchen, then scooped up an armful of clothes that were apparently on their way to the laundry room and flung them in, slamming the door to it with my foot afterwards. I pulled a face as I saw the remaining mess in the lounge but figured it was too late to do any more, and that Alex would just have to take me as she found me.

She looked good when she finally came in. One thing I'd learned about Alex over the few weeks since she'd arrived was that she was one of these people who look fantastic *all* the time, but you know it's taken absolutely no effort on their behalf at all. She'd changed since the sound check at Hyde Park and was now dressed down more than she had been, in just skinny jeans and a tight black T-shirt, with her hair swept back off her face. It was a really good look, and I so wanted to tell her that. But I didn't. Instead, I held the door open to her, apologized for the state of my apartment, and watched her as she sauntered in, guitar strung round her shoulders, hands deep in her jeans pockets.

"I'm sorry I'm early." Alex turned and looked at me as I closed my front door. "I was hanging out at home, bored." She shrugged. "I figured I'd just come on over." She scooted her guitar off her shoulders and up over her head. "I hope you don't mind?" she asked, leaning her guitar against her leg.

"It's cool," I said, laughing as I remembered the jumble of clothes hastily flung into the laundry room.

"What's funny?" Alex tilted her head to one side and studied me.

"You caught me a bit unawares." I gestured vaguely around the room. "I don't usually live like this."

Liar.

"Just before you arrived, I…uh…tried to tidy up," I said.

"Really?" Alex lifted an eyebrow. "I see." She nodded, but she had a sceptical look on her face.

"Drink?" I started to walk to the kitchen.

"Do you have a Coke?" Alex propped her guitar up against my sofa and followed me. "The Tube was boiling hot."

"I do." I went to my fridge and opened it. "Or beer if you prefer?"

"Ed lets you have beer here?" Alex asked.

"Ed doesn't know." I grinned.

"Coke's good," Alex said, coming into the kitchen with me. "I don't drink alcohol anyway."

"Ed never has to worry about you, does he?" I pulled two cans of Coke out, wishing I didn't have quite so many bottles of beer lined up next to them. "Not very rock 'n' roll," I said, handing Alex her can.

"Not drinking?" Alex asked. "Whatever. Doesn't bother me."

"I didn't mean…" I pulled my glance away. "I was being funny. Sorry."

"It's never been my thing."

I watched Alex open her can with a hiss, then hastily suck up the fizzing foam that bubbled out of it. She wiped her bottom lip with her thumb.

"How did you manage in the contestants' house?" I asked her, signalling for her to follow me back into the lounge. "Group of you all thrown together like that?"

Alex dropped down into one of the chairs. "They did what they wanted to do," she said, "and I did what I wanted to do." She looked at me. "My time on *Sing* was all about the singing, funnily enough. Well, it was for me, anyway."

"The others weren't so serious?" I asked.

"Some were," Alex replied. "Others were just there to live the dream." She took a drink. "The producers banned alcohol, cigarettes… They all got smuggled in somehow. And drugs sometimes." She shuddered. "The producers had no idea."

An image of Nicole's face danced at the edges of my consciousness.

"You weren't tempted?" I asked.

"I might be a seventeen-year-old musician, Tally," Alex said, "but I'm not stupid. What's the point of fucking up my life just for the occasional high?"

"Were you gutted you got booted out before the semis?" I wanted to change the subject. Hustle Nicole's presence out from the room.

"At the time, yeah." Alex sipped at her Coke. "I mean, the fact that a thirty-year-old blues singer who couldn't hit a high note if his life depended on it got through and I didn't really hurt."

I felt for her. Alex had been tipped to win, and rumour was, the bookmakers had stopped taking bets on her during the fifth round, they were so convinced she was going to win. Getting eliminated at the quarter-final stage must have been agony.

I looked over to her and caught her eye.

"That's why this has all been so awesome," she said. "Joining you guys." She held my gaze. "I was beginning to think I was down and out. Career over before it had even started." She laughed, but I could tell her laugh hid her uncertainties. "When you're in that environment, you start to believe the hype. That you could be the next big thing," she said, "and then the next day you're out and you're already history, sick with worry about where your life is heading because all you've ever wanted to do is make music."

I studied her face as she spoke, seeing a vulnerability there that I hadn't seen before. Her mask of confidence that she was so keen to hide behind was showing signs of slipping now that we were alone. Of course, I knew it would be back once we were all back rehearsing together, but for now I was relieved to see another side to Alex. Grateful that she'd shown it to me.

"You know," she said, "I was always happy busking. Scratching a living from gigging. Then one day you're plucked from that and put into the limelight and you're playing your music to a bigger, more appreciative audience, and suddenly you don't want to go back to busking any more. You've had a taste of what it could be like. What fame's like. Then it's taken away from you"—she snapped her fingers—"just like that."

"I guess we've been lucky." I didn't know what else to say.

"I know you didn't want me in Be4," Alex said. She held my gaze. "I know you all thought I wasn't serious enough for you."

"I don't think—"

Alex leant forward in her chair, resting her elbows on her legs. "I'm deadly serious about Be4, Tally. I promise you." She rolled her can in her hands. "I'm grateful for this third chance, and I'll do anything to prove how dedicated I am."

"I'm sure you will," I said, "but—"

Alex held up a hand. "And I know you didn't have any choice but to accept me," she said, "and that must have hurt, knowing how close you all were to Nicole."

"Nicole is a whole different ball game," I said truthfully. And I hated the other honest words that came from my mouth next. "She's gone. She's out of the picture. Nothing to do with Be4 any more." I looked at Alex. "You're the future. *Our* future."

"Even though none of you really like me?"

I sat back in my chair. "What makes you think that?"

"Just a vibe." Alex cut her glance away. "Robyn in particular."

"Robyn thinks she owns Be4," I said, "and if something happens that she's had no hand in, she doesn't want to know."

As Alex stared down at the can in her hands, I studied her, surprised at her openness and wishing her vulnerability didn't get to me quite as much as it did. Perhaps she needed to hear some more truths.

"Anyway," I said, "Nicole could never play a guitar solo quite like you can."

"Nicole never played guitar though, did she?" Alex asked.

"Exactly. So how could she ever play a solo as well as you?" I dipped my head and caught her eye, making her smile. "And we never managed to get ourselves a festival gig until you came along."

Alex's smile stayed. I was pleased.

"I'm sorry if you think we don't like you," I said. "Perhaps we could have been a little more…welcoming."

"Maybe I'm paranoid." Alex shook her head. "I just want you to know I'm loving every second of being with you guys. I just need you to know that."

I looked over to her guitar then back to her.

"Want to jam then?" I indicated her guitar. "You can teach me that awesome riff you manage to nail every time, if you like."

Alex put down her can.

"Deal," she said with a smile.

❖

Alex could play guitar. I mean, she could *really* play guitar.

We sat in my lounge, the last orange hues of the evening sun smudging long shadows across the walls, Alex in one chair, me just across from her, and just jammed. It was magical, it was serene, and for the first time since she'd joined the band, I felt fully comfortable in Alex's company. Strangely, it was as though it was our guitars that finally brought that closeness, almost as if they acted as our common theme. Alex loved her guitar as much as I loved mine, and it really showed in the way she almost caressed it as she played it, the guitar melting into her body, her demeanour relaxed and at one with it.

We didn't speak; no words were needed because our guitars spoke for us. And, unlike the stilted lack of conversation that had plagued us before, it didn't feel awkward or embarrassing. As we played, heads bowed over our strings, I occasionally looked up and caught her eye. That's when I could see the genuine contentment on her face—a contentment that I finally realized had been missing up until now. Once our eyes met, I dropped my head again and concentrated on my chords, only to raise my eyes and see Alex looking back at me this time.

Her dexterity with the strings astonished me too. Her guitar became an extension of her as her fingers became a blur during the uptempo parts of our jam, the coloured bracelets that covered her wrists furiously jangling until Alex slowed the tempo again, and her fingers returned to stroke the strings and produce such sweet notes with an ease which I could only ever hope to have. She controlled her guitar with such grace, but the incredible thing was I genuinely didn't think she knew just how good she really was.

"Wow." I stopped playing at a convenient point and sat back. "You're awesome."

"You're pretty good yourself." Alex's grin was one hundred per cent.

"Weren't we supposed to be practising the middle of 'Take Me There'?" My grin matched hers. "We kinda went off-kilter there."

"I just followed you." Alex unlooped her guitar over her shoulders and placed it up against her knees. "You took it to a whole different level."

"I just love playing." I shrugged. "Why do you think all the guitar parts I write are so awesome?" I grinned at her.

"I'd love to write something some day," Alex said, running her hand over the neck of her guitar. "Something I can really get my teeth into."

"We should totally try writing something together one day," I said. I meant it too.

"I'd love that." Alex's face was open and expectant.

"So which do you prefer?" I asked, mirroring her action of unlooping my guitar. "Playing or singing?"

"Oh, you can't ask me that!" Alex moved her guitar to one side, then shuffled back on her chair and crossed one long leg over the other. "That's like asking—I don't know—do I prefer my mum or my dad?"

"Your cat or your dog?"

"Exactly." Alex grinned.

"So?" I asked. "Cat or dog?"

"Dog." Alex nodded.

"Okay then…tea or coffee?"

"Ooh, coffee I suppose."

"Skateboarding or snowboarding?"

"Hmm." Alex lifted her eyes to the ceiling. "Snowboarding."

"Tom or Jerry?" I asked.

"That's a tough one." Alex laughed. "Tom, but only because he's misunderstood."

"Misunderstood?"

"Totally."

"Okay." I laughed too. "How about doctor or dentist?"

"Ew. Doctor, but only just."

"Donald or Mickey?"

"Donald." Alex nodded.

"Boys or girls?" It was out before I'd even realized it. "Or…" I swallowed, desperately trying to think of something else. "Hotdogs or burgers?" Lame. *So* lame.

"Girls." Alex tipped her head to one side and smiled. "That's an easy one." Still studying me, she added, "And you?"

I felt my face flame. "I can't…" I cleared my throat, annoyed with my inability to answer her. "I guess I can't pigeonhole…I mean, I don't know." I shrugged, defeated. "Girls, I guess." My face burned hotter under Alex's scrutiny.

"You guess?" Alex's arched eyebrow didn't help my awkwardness. "You either know or you don't."

"Well then, I don't know," I said, "and you still haven't answered my question about guitar or singing."

"And you're changing the subject."

"I know."

Alex leant closer in her chair, resting her arms on her knees, and stared at me. "Guitar," she finally said, slowly adding, "I guess."

"Don't laugh at me."

"I'm not." She fell back again. "I'm sorry."

"I've never really been with either a boy or a girl." My voice sounded thin, probably because of the lie I'd just said. "So how can I know?"

"Oh, you'd know," Alex said. "Believe me, you'd know." She looked at me. "You've never kissed a boy?" she asked. "Or a girl?"

Nicole's image appeared in my head. Could I tell Alex about her?

Perhaps not.

"I kissed Josh Mathers when I was in Year Ten." I screwed up my nose. "He tasted of…"

"Boy?" Alex screwed her nose up too.

"Yeah."

We laughed.

"He couldn't kiss for shit." I shook my head. "I thought he was trying to fish something out of my mouth with his tongue."

"Okay, that's revolting." Alex shuddered. "Truly revolting." She settled herself further back into her chair. "I kissed Tom something-or-other"—she flitted a hand—"when I was in Year Ten too." She looked at me. "I only did it as a way of getting over Laura Whitworth, who was two years older than me and who I thought was the best thing since sliced whatnot, and who I used to follow round the school like a lovesick lamb."

"Did she know?" I asked.

"No." Alex shook her head. "Probably just as well. Every time she saw me she'd look at me like I was something she'd trodden in."

"Ouch."

"Indeed." She sighed. "Unrequited love, hey?" She sighed again, deeper this time. "I did a lot of guitar playing back then, I remember," she said. "Proper angsty shit. Probably wrote some of my best stuff back then too, so at least I have her to thank for that."

I looked at the floor, thinking about Nicole's unrequited love for me. Had I treated her like that? Was I just as bad as Laura Whitworth?

My thoughts fought a battle. I wanted to tell Alex about Nicole, but at the same time, I didn't.

"Has there been anyone since then?" I asked. Pushing the subject back to Alex seemed a better option right then.

"Of course." A smile spread across Alex's face. "Laura Bloody Whitworth has been a distant memory for years now, thanks to all the others."

"*All* the others?" The thought pinched at me, and I immediately tried to shake it away.

"Okay, not *all* the others," Alex said, "but there have been others."

"Lots?" Why was I asking?

"Not lots." Alex smiled. "A few." She looked at me. "And you're telling me there's been no one since your disaster with Josh whatshisname?"

"I…kissed a girl."

"And you liked it?" Alex sang back to me.

I laughed.

"It was different to the kiss with Josh, that's for sure."

My pulse quickened at the memory. My kiss with Nicole had been *so* different—softer, more tender. Slower. More meaningful. Not the grubby, stubbly fumbling that Josh had made me endure. Nicole had smelt different too, had tasted different. Nicer. Purer. *Better.*

"Kissing girls is so much nicer than kissing boys." Alex, it seemed, had read my mind. "In my opinion, anyway." She paused. "So what was her name? And why did you say you'd never had much experience with either before?"

"I kissed a boy once," I said, "and I kissed a girl once. Once each. That's not much, is it?"

"I guess." Alex shrugged. "So who was it?"

"Why are you so interested?" I suddenly felt uncomfortable and, for some reason, annoyed with Alex's shrug. "It's in the past. It doesn't matter any more."

"Sorry." I saw Alex's face fall. "I didn't mean to pry." She reached over and picked up her guitar. "Want to jam some more?"

Yeah, I did.

And I *would* tell Alex about Nicole. One day.

Just not today.

Chapter Ten

Prepping for the festival was such hard work. All of it—the sound checks, the stage set-up, the rehearsals. Exhausting. Another long, hot day in the sun, my mouth dry from the endless singing, sweat trickling down the small of my back. Ed on our cases because he wasn't entirely happy with this or satisfied with that. Now *that* really drove me nuts. Okay, I could understand he'd want everything to be perfect—after all, this was our first festival, and our first time singing a set with Alex—but his constant interference made me irritable.

And we were far from finished.

I looked over to Robyn, taking a swig from a bottle of water, and wandered over to her.

"You think we'll be much longer?" I asked her.

She looked at her watch. "It's only two," she said, "so I'm guessing at least another few hours." She passed me her bottle of water, which I took gratefully.

"First set tomorrow," she said. "So it's got to be perfect today."

"You nervous?" I asked.

"A bit. You?"

"Yeah. Very."

Total truth? I was terrified.

"Your 'Take Me There' solo was epic, by the way," Robyn said, looping her arm round my shoulders and pulling me to her. "I felt it today."

"I practised a lot." I shrugged. "Wanted to make sure it was perfect."

"You totally did."

"'Take Me There' is kinda Nicole's song, you know?" I looked at Robyn.

"I know, Tally. I know." Robyn's arm tightened around my shoulders a little. "We all want to do it justice for her."

"I want it to be perfect for her," I said, "even though I know she might not hear it."

That was only partly true. The other, bigger part involved Alex and my wanting her to know how good I was. My eyes travelled over to her, sitting on the edge of the stage, legs dangling over the side, face up to the sun. Hair perfect. Her hair was always so perfect.

"You okay?"

I snapped my attention back to Robyn.

"I practised with her a lot yesterday." I gave a nonchalant lift of my chin in Alex's direction. "Seemed to work."

"With Alex?" Robyn sounded surprised.

"Mm."

"Well you're honoured," Robyn said, letting her arm drop from my shoulders. She took her water bottle back from me and took a long drink. "I still get barely two words out of her," she said when she'd finished, then wiped her mouth.

"She's okay, you know?" My glance drifted back to Alex and I remembered her words to me about her thinking Robyn didn't like her. "Perhaps you should try talking to her. Get to know her better."

"You've changed your tune," Robyn said. I could hear the sarcasm in her voice.

"Maybe we misjudged her, that's all," I said. "Maybe we need to give her a chance."

I suddenly wanted to leave Robyn and go sit with Alex. The feeling had arrived so unexpectedly, it quickened my breath, muddied my senses. Alex was sitting away from me and I desperately wanted to be with her. Wanted to continue the friendliness we'd shared at my apartment the day before. Didn't want to be standing away from her for a second longer.

"I'm going to get another drink." I started to move away from Robyn. "Want one?"

To my relief, Robyn shook her head. I walked away from her, over to the cooler, and grabbed an ice-cold bottle of water from it. I unscrewed it, one eye still on Alex, and drank some back.

I felt weird, but I didn't know why. Slightly nervous. But nervous of what? Alex? I took another drink. I hadn't been nervous with her yesterday, but the thought of being alone in her company right now—and desperately wanting to be in her company—was making my heart beat just that bit faster than it was before.

I was being an idiot. I screwed the lid tight back onto the water bottle and strode over to her.

"Mind if I join you?" I stood next to her and looked down.

Alex looked back up, shielding her eyes from the sun. I saw the smile that spread across her face when she saw me, and I felt a small twinge of something flutter inside me. A flutter that had never happened when anyone else had smiled at me before. A nice flutter. One that I could cope with feeling over and over again.

"Why would I mind?" Alex still smiled up at me.

I flopped down and dangled my legs off the stage, just as Alex was doing.

"Are you as hot and irritable as I am?" I couldn't think of what to say to her. I thought, on reflection, that first sentence was pretty lame. "I mean, it's hot. Isn't it?"

Alex chuckled. "Yeah, it's boiling." She looked at me. "Are you irritable?"

"Not now." That was the truth.

"I'm glad to see you, actually," Alex said.

"You've seen me all day." I laughed.

"Yeah, but not alone." Alex sounded serious. She cut her glance away. "I wanted to say I had a blast at yours yesterday, that's all." She turned back to look at me. "Total blast. We should do it again sometime."

"We should." I nodded. "And, yeah. It was good, wasn't it?"

"I felt…" Annoyingly, Alex looked away again.

I skimmed my sunglasses onto the top of my head and tried to catch her eye.

"You felt?" I prompted.

"Nothing." Alex stretched and her words disappeared into a yawn. "Relaxed." She gave a laugh. "Like I am now apparently."

"You ready for tomorrow?" I asked.

"Our first set together." Alex widened her eyes and pulled a shocked face, making me smile. "Yeah, I'm ready. You?" She reached over and, without asking, took my water from me. I watched as she unscrewed it, one eye still on me, and drank some back, then screwed the lid back on before handing it back to me. It was all so cool and comfortable and genuine and lovely, and just the simple act of her drinking my water had made me feel stupidly happy.

"I'm so ready."

I liked what she'd just done. I liked being with her. Despite initially willing myself not to, I found I liked everything about her.

I liked Alex.

The day of the festival had arrived under clear, blue skies and it was impossible not to feel happy. Everything was clicking into place right now: Alex and Be4 gelled, the fans loved us, we were headlining a festival, the sun was shining, and Alex called me Tal. Weird what makes you happy.

Hyde Park was buzzing when I finally arrived, just after four. I felt like a superstar as my personal driver drove me up Park Lane, past the waiting crowds who immediately swarmed round the car as we approached, past a bunch of scary security guards, and weaved over to the VIP Winnebago where we were to all meet up.

Hyde Park is epic. I'd only ever been there a couple of times since I'd moved to London, and now I felt like a total tourist as I walked up the steps of the Winnebago and turned around, seeing green yawning out in front of me, the Serpentine just visible, London's skyline shimmering through the hot afternoon haze. The air was thick with noise: the buzz of the crowd, screams and shrieks, helicopters hovering overhead, music playing somewhere in the distance. That's when I saw it. The stage. And that's when nerves gripped the pit of my stomach for the first time, because I knew the festival was so much more than any other gig we'd ever done, and that it would produce a whole different feeling to singing in the smaller arena gigs we'd done before. It would be, I knew, like a wild party compared to an intimate dinner. I clung to the handrail of the steps and just gawped at it. To the lights and amps, noise and smoke, its energy practically pumping out over the sea of heads in the pit in front of it and over to me.

A tap on the window pulled my gawping away. Brooke was gesticulating at me, grinning and waving and jumping up and down like a lunatic inside, and as I opened the door and entered, she rushed at me and flung her arms around me.

"Have you seen it?" Her words tumbled out. "Omigod, have you *seen* it out there?"

I returned her hug, and I swear I felt her shaking.

"This is it, Tally," she said over my shoulder. "This is everything we've worked so hard for."

"So why am I so scared?" I laughed into her T-shirt, then pulled away.

"You won't be when you get out there." Brooke went to the window, dipped her head, and peered out. "First chords of 'After the Rain' and you'll forget your nerves."

I was dubious.

Out of nowhere, a guy wired up with headphones and a mic arrived at my side, mumbled my name at me, then looped a bracelet around my wrist. I looked down at it. Shocking pink, with the words *Party in the Park* written on it. I loved it, even though I had never thought of myself as a pink kind of girl.

"Robyn and Alex are out back." Brooke grabbed my hand. "C'mon."

I got pulled through the Winnebago, past people who I'd never met before lounging on chairs, past others who were knee-deep in wires and cables, through a curtain to a separate area where I saw Alex first. She was sitting on her own on an L-shaped sofa, wired up—as usual—to her music, her guitar in its usual place by her feet, her face looking pinched with nerves as she stared down at her phone in her hands. She looked up briefly when we came in, smiled at me, then returned to her music. Strangely, I wanted more from her. A word, or a reassuring look. Something—anything.

Instead, I got that from Robyn, who, just like Brooke before, flung herself at me, nearly knocking me off my feet, told me I looked amazing, and then gabbled ten to the dozen, "Why can't it be ten o'clock already so we can just get out there?"

Before that could happen, though, we had press commitments to do. Then a photo shoot. Then sign some autographs for a local charity to sell at their forthcoming raffle. I knew it was what being a musician was all about, and I'd never felt more ready. Some press guys were gathered in the room with us, looking for our thoughts about the festival, looking for a scoop about what the next single might be after the release of "After the Rain."

While Robyn talked with them, and as if suddenly taking herself out of the zone she'd been in, Alex flipped her headphones from her head, cradled them around her neck, and stood. She came over to me and said something about the size of the crowd outside and it being hot. And she called me Tal for the first time, and I got that weird fizzing thing going on inside. Nothing unusual in that, I suppose, but the feeling it produced inside me came as a surprise. Perhaps it was the fact she felt comfortable enough in my company now to call me it, or perhaps it was the way she said it, or the way she looked at me when she called me it. I don't know. All I do know is that I liked it. Very much. The little ball of fizz in my stomach as I heard her say it told me just how much I liked it. I think the fact she touched my arm when she said it didn't help.

I mumbled something in reply. I put that down to being a bit weirded out by the heat inside the Winnebago and the prospect of going out in a few hours' time and singing live to a crowd of over ten thousand people. It wasn't because of Alex. I told myself that. Definitely wasn't her.

"Do you think she'll be watching?"

Someone was talking to me. Press. London paper, I think.

"Tally? Do you think Nicole will be watching this, wherever she is?"

He was recording me, so I knew I'd have to choose my words carefully.

"If she has the time." I smiled. I figured a smile pretty much covered everything.

"Do you think she'll send her congratulations to you all?" the journalist asked. "Or do you think there might be a small part of her that'll regret leaving you, now things are going so well for you?"

"Nicole always wanted the best for us." Damn, how those lies just flowed so easily. "So I'm sure she'll be pleased for us." I turned my head and looked at another journalist, lifting my chin to her to invite a different question.

The last thing I wanted to be thinking about right then was Nicole. Like a cloud of guilt, she followed me everywhere enough as it was. I didn't want her anywhere near me today because my nerves were bad enough already. I saw the look that passed between Brooke and Robyn, so I steered the conversation back towards Alex.

"Alex is excited to be doing her first set with Be4." I flashed my best smile at Alex. "We all are."

My gratitude when Alex started talking was palpable. Finally the journalists stopped talking about Nicole and turned their attention fully to Alex, who, just like on *The Afternoon Show*, answered their numerous questions with a combination of wit and charm and had the entire press pack hanging on to her every word.

I left the Winnebago and shut the door behind me, then leant back against it. Nicole's cloud floated up to the sky before burning away against the afternoon sun, but I knew it'd be back soon enough. Probably the second I set foot onstage.

It was days like this I wish I smoked.

Chapter Eleven

It didn't come back. Nicole's cloud. Actually, it didn't get the chance to come back because the second my guitar was handed to me and I stepped out onto the stage, into the lights and noise and chaos, the nerves that had been bunched up in my stomach the whole day magically vanished.

Our set was amazing. Purple and black lighting, our name in twenty-foot letters behind us, shards of sparks, and the pulsing drum intro to "After the Rain" introduced us to the baying crowd down in the pit, who had evidently had far too much sun and far too much beer. It was messy, but I loved it. We killed the first song, and any worries I'd had that we might have all sung a bit off thanks to first-song jitters miraculously disappeared, mainly because the crowd just wanted to sing along with each chorus. It was the perfect song to start the set because the electro synth running through it all totally got the crowd rocking and on our side, and I knew each song that followed would work just as well.

We were halfway through our second song, "Drowning in You," when I finally noticed Alex by my side. "After the Rain" had all happened way too fast, and I'd felt like I'd been in a trance through it, determined to nail my guitar parts through shaking hands, eyes fixed on the crowd to gauge their reaction, but now I'd settled down, and I could look around me and quit being so scared.

Alex was singing her part when I looked at her, making eye contact with the crowd while she sang, smiling, loving it. She had her arm high up above her head, her guitar strung loosely around her, her other hand gripped to her mic, and she was belting out her part before Brooke and I joined in. “Drowning in You” was a slower song, and as I sang, I remembered that Alex had told me it was one of her favourites. That seemed to give it more of an edge, for me anyway, and as I kept looking over to her, I wished she’d look back at me, just so I could give her a look that said, *This is your favourite song, and we’re singing it together live for the first time.* I wanted her to feel it as much as I was.

Alex didn’t look at me, though. She seemed to be lost in the moment, and as “Drowning in You” seamlessly drifted into “Take Me There,” my brain took that precise moment to conveniently remind me that this was the last song Nicole had ever written with us, because brains like to do things like that just to be annoying.

The words took on extra meaning as I sang them:

We’ll never be apart,
Best friends forever.
You and me,
Just take me there.

As I continued to glance at Alex while she sang what would have been Nicole’s lines, then past her towards Brooke and Robyn and then back to Alex again, she appeared to me as Nicole. I looked away, back to the crowd, through the sea of swaying mobile phone lights. Refocused. When I looked again, Alex was back and Nicole had gone. I tightly grasped my guitar, even though it wasn’t needed yet, the feel of it moulded into my hands reassuring me. The words that Nicole had written echoed out across the heads of the crowd, almost, it seemed to me, right out of London and across to Croft House. I was convinced she was watching us, wherever she was. Disapproving. Hating.

My guitar part arrived, and I played it gratefully, turning away from my mic and the crowd to face the back of the stage. I saw Nicole lurking in the shadows, questioning me, criticizing me, so I played harder, as if by doing so I’d make her go away and leave me the hell alone. Alex's guitar part rang out, effortlessly linking with mine, and I turned just in time to see her standing next to me. As we played, just like in my apartment that day, we watched each other, smiling, each of us urging the other one to play with even more passion than we already were. It wasn't a competition; we both knew we could encourage the other on just by one look, one nod of the head. One smile. I looked at Alex, her eyes bright and alive, playing the most beautiful notes ever, and sensed Nicole finally slipping away from the shadows behind me.

Alex and I played on, our guitar parts continuing as Robyn's vocals kicked in over them, quickly followed by Brooke's. I turned back to my mic and sang while I still played, now hoping and thinking that Nicole, rather than hating us, ought to be proud of us for how we'd just rocked her song. Before my brain could start to run away with more thoughts of her, though, "Take Me There" ended, and I was relieved I'd managed to get through it without any hitches.

Now mellow, sweet tones were replaced by the thumping synth intro for our last song of the night, "Crush." The crowd, slightly quieter during the two slow songs, responded as expected, and in a heartbeat turned into a heaving mass of arms and jumping and screaming. Suddenly I couldn't hear anything except the pulsing amps behind me which seemed to beat in rhythm with my heart, which I was sure was about to burst out of my chest.

The lights changed from purple and black to blue and white, staccato strobe lights splintered the set behind us, as Alex's guitar screamed into life, immediately followed by mine. Watching Alex spin away from her mic, I focused on my chords and how to bring out the best sound in them to get the crowd even more whipped up than they already were. I moved away from my mic too, to face Alex, our guitars working in sync, then tailing off as Robyn and Brooke sang their opening lines. Stepping back to our mics, Alex and I then sang our harmonies with them, our guitars now hanging loosely under our arms.

Alex grabbed her mic from its stand while she was singing and started walking about the stage, the eyes of the crowd never leaving her. Then she came back over to me, high-fiving Brooke and Robyn as she passed them, and threaded her arm around my shoulder. I looped my arm around her shoulder too, and we sang, arm in arm, leaning against one another, the roar from the crowd now almost drowning out our singing. It was magical, all of it—having Alex and my best buddies on stage with me, hearing the music we were creating together, seeing the reaction our music was creating in the pit in front of us. I sucked up the energy from the crowd, feeling the power coming from them, loving the passion our music was creating.

It was everything I'd imagined it would be, and more, and as the song ended, Alex turned and hugged me, burying her head in my shoulder. Her skin was slick and glowing with sweat, hair damp from the sweat too, a heat radiating off her body as she held me in her arms and gabbled something in a voice so hoarse I couldn't catch it. The crowd had erupted by this point, chanting our names, a pulsating wave of ten thousand cheers surrounding us, swamping us, and as Alex released me from her grip, she spoke again, much louder this time so I heard it.

She just said, *Thank you.*

❖

I wished Nicole would go away. As we came offstage I swear I saw her again. Heard her. *Felt* her. She was asking me questions, wanting to know why Alex was onstage and not her. Bugging me to tell her why I'd found it so easy to connect with Alex, why I'd felt so comfortable onstage with her when I'd only known her for five minutes.

It was stupid. I was acting like Nicole was dead, like it was her spirit following me around and haunting me, when it was my own brain dealing me a whole bunch of guilt cards and scattering them at my feet yet again. Telling me things I didn't want to hear. Constantly testing me.

Nicole wasn't dead. Nicole was, in all probability, shooting some pool with a bunch of other girls at Croft House, or watching a DVD, or talking to her counsellor, or whatever else it was that seventeen-year-olds did in rehab. She probably wasn't even thinking about me, Be4, any of us—so why was I letting my runaway thoughts spoil what had been the most awesome night of my life?

"Did you hear them?" Brooke jumped on my back from behind and slithered off again. "The crowd? I mean, did you *actually* hear them?"

Nicole disappeared back into the darkness.

"I think they loved it." I grabbed Brooke's arm, thankful for her intervention, and pulled it around my shoulder. "Did you see the front row? Mad."

We walked deeper in backstage, and away from the burning stage lights and my thoughts of Nicole, I finally felt myself cooling. If only I could relax now too. Coming down from a gig always took time; coming down from Nicole's presence was apparently taking longer.

"Insane." Alex's voice sounded behind us. "Just insane." Brooke high-fived the palm that Alex offered to her. I did the same.

I could see Alex was totally buzzing. Her hair was still plastered to her forehead, but she'd obviously run her hands through it because it was sticking up slightly. Despite her sticky-up hair, she still looked radiant, ecstatic, and her enthusiasm bounced off her straight over to me. I figured this was what it was all about—the gigs and the fans. The natural high of performing live to thousands of people, seeing their appreciation of the music you've sweated over for months.

Nicole could have had all this too.

"Don't you think?"

Alex was talking to me. I needed to concentrate on her right now, not Nicole.

"Think what?" I asked.

"How much the crowd responded to 'Take Me There.'"

"It's going to be the new single." I released my arm from Brooke's shoulder. "If Ed doesn't make it the next single, I want to know why."

"*And* it'll go straight to number one."

Brooke and Alex both said something similar at the same time, making all three of us break into laughter.

I looked at them as I laughed, feeling a profound sense of partnership for the first time.

"You were awesome." Alex's words slipped in amongst the laughter so quietly I almost missed it.

"Thank you." Our eyes met. "So were you."

"Your riff in 'Crush'? Out of the park."

"Your harmonies in 'Drowning in You'—actually *all* your harmonies," I said, "amazing."

"Just like your high C in 'Drowning in You,' just before I came in," Alex said, shaking her head. "Totally nailed it."

"So I wasn't pitchy?" I raised an eyebrow, then ducked as Alex pretended to hit me.

"Take a compliment when it's given to you," she said, "and quit reminding me of my past mistakes."

"So when you two have finished winding each other up," Brooke said, grabbing my hand, "Ed says there's champagne for us somewhere."

She pulled me away and walked me deeper into the area back of the stage. As I was pulled further from Alex, I turned back to look at her, our eyes meeting one more time before I disappeared into the darkness.

Chapter Twelve

The champagne flowed. When Ed had said he'd treat us, he hadn't been kidding. This was probably about the most generous Ed had ever been to us, an impromptu party laid on just for us, with Ed acting as host. Well, acting like the cat that got the cream. He was stoked at our performance, and while I knew all he was probably thinking about was how much money we were going to make him, there was also a tiny bit of me that hoped he was genuinely pleased at how well we'd all performed together. I guessed he was happy that his hunch about Alex was right too. I couldn't blame him; if I was in his shoes, I'd have been happy too.

As we heard the dull bass of the next band performing onstage pounding through to us backstage, we gathered together, glasses of champagne in our hands, and lapped up the praise that was being heaped onto us. Ed was pacing, muttering to us about the champagne being a treat, and to not drink too much, and afterwards we were all to switch to OJs. His face was flushed red with happiness, and he was using words about the gig that I'd never heard him use before: sensational, worldwide success, stratospheric, historic. I wasn't sure about that last one, but as the champagne bubbles fizzed inside my empty stomach and loosened my muscles, I went with it. Why not? I could still hear the crowd cheering in my ears, could still see the sway of bodies in the pit below me, all singing our music and chanting our names. I could still feel the buzz, the heat from the stage lights; I could still see the blaze of colours from the set, hear my guitar riffs.

Could still feel Alex in my arms.

As I chugged down the last of my champagne and held my empty glass out for a refill, I thought it would be a very long time before the memories of this evening would leave me again.

Ed had rented us two large rooms in a hotel in Chelsea for the night. Now *that* was generous. At the party, as the champagne still flowed, he said something about spoiling us, giving us the chance to let our hair down, and what better place to do that but in a posh hotel in West London? The hotel had a pool, spas, beauty treatments… none of which—apart from the pool—were my thing at all, but then I wasn't about to turn down the chance to spend the night in one of London's best hotels. I wasn't stupid.

It was one of those discreet hotels, totally used to celebrities coming and going. The sort of place where the doorman didn't care if you were a Hollywood A-lister, a washed-up pop star, or an actor on a daytime soap, as long as you tipped him generously on your way in. It was all new to us. The foyer with its enormous sparkling chandelier, the marble flooring that made our shoes squeak, the sweeping staircase. As we trooped in through the revolving front door, it must have been clear to anyone watching that this experience was completely alien to us. We stood in the foyer, all four of us lined up, three slightly drunk, one stone-cold sober, and stared around us.

"I guess we ought to act like we know what we're doing," Robyn said under her breath. "Act like the stars Ed thinks we're becoming."

Alex took the initiative. With a confidence I wasn't feeling, she strode to the front desk, a smile spread across her face, which instantly lit up a mirroring smile on the face of the guy who was serving there. I guessed not many guests normally smiled at him like Alex had just done.

She returned brandishing two key cards in her hand, which she waved in front of our faces once she was back with us.

"Suites thirty-two and thirty-three," she said. "Adjoining rooms." Her smile broadened. "Let the fun begin."

❖

We were like six-year-olds. Jumping on the bed, sweeping the bathrooms for any freebies, channel-hopping on the free satellite TV, opening and closing the minibar so it could illuminate us and we could pull ghostly faces at one another. Embarrassing, really, like children let loose from their parents' grasp for the first time and set free in a sweet shop. I half expected one of us to be sick from all the excitement, but it was all such huge fun I told myself to quit being a killjoy and just enjoy the moment.

The rooms were awesome. Cavernous. And stacked, it seemed, floor to ceiling with stuff we could steal, take home, and deny any knowledge of how it ever got into our respective apartments. A door separated one room from the other, but that was opened immediately so we could have even more space. One of us—Brooke—actually ran between the rooms while another of us—Alex?—timed her on the stopwatch on her phone. My head was spinning with it all: four young, successful pop stars with two whole suites to themselves. A year ago that would have been unthinkable. A year ago, the best we could have hoped for was a five-minute set on a children's Saturday-morning TV programme and a bed and breakfast to bed down in for the night.

"There's more champagne." The game of opening and closing the minibar still hadn't lost its appeal. This time, though, Brooke properly peered inside it and then pulled out a bottle. "It looks expensive."

I took it from her and read the gold label. Moët & Chandon. Classy.

"We're worth it." Robyn crouched down next to us. "Well, Ed must think so anyway."

I looked behind me to Alex, still sprawled on the bed.

"Guess you'll be the only sober one tonight," I said to her, lifting the bottle up. "Shame we don't need a lift anywhere."

Alex raised her head from the bed and flicked me her middle finger.

"I'll make up for it by ordering myself a full English breakfast," she said, resting her head back. "You lot'll be begging for just water to get over your hangovers. I'll be having the works."

While I was still teasing her, I heard our music playing on the TV in the corner of the room. I stood up, grabbed the remote from the side, and turned the volume up higher.

"It's us." I waggled the remote at the TV. "From earlier."

As one, we turned to the TV screen. It was a report, on some music channel, about the festival, the presenter talking excitedly as she spoke about our set and how we'd won the crowd over before our first song had even finished.

I stood, the unopened bottle of champagne still in my hand, engrossed as they showed clips from our set. Damn, we looked good. And seeing it back on screen, I realized I could see what the crowd had seen and loved: four kids playing their stuff and having the time of their lives, loving their lives and their music. It looked insane.

"Guitar solos coming up." I heard Alex speak behind me.

As the camera panned in to me and Alex as we played our "After the Rain" solos, Robyn let out a whoop and pulled me to her, nearly knocking me off my feet.

"Looking good," she said, but I wasn't listening. Instead, my eyes were on Alex and how good she looked. She looked amazing, rocking it out, sucking up the enthusiasm of the crowd, playing better and harder than I'd ever heard her play before. I'd noticed it enough at the festival, but seeing it on playback now, her energy was sizzling, her enthusiasm electric. It sent shivers down my spine.

I suddenly realized I was staring and drew my eyes away. I stared towards the window, hearing the voiceover, hearing snippets of the interviews that followed, but nothing was really going in. All I could see was Alex, guitar in hand, her eyes sparkling, her slender body moving in time to the music.

"So," Robyn said, "analysis of today?"

Robyn's voice finally cut through my thoughts.

"The best day of my life?" I offered, grateful for her interruption.

"The best day of *all* our lives," Brooke corrected.

I sat on the edge of the bed, making the mattress dip and Alex roll a little towards me.

"Is that it?" Robyn joined me. "We just rocked over ten thousand people into the ground, and all you pair of losers can say is that it was the best day of your lives?"

I lurched over to a chair next to the bed, grabbed the cushion from it, and threw it at her. "What would you call it then?" I asked her.

"Monumental?" Alex laughed to Robyn. "Overwhelming?"

"It was the defining moment of my career so far." Robyn made a fist and held a pretend mic to her mouth. "And you, Ms. Brody?" She lifted her fist towards Alex. "How did you feel today?"

"Like"—Alex looked to the ceiling—"I never wanted it to end."

"Lame," Brooke and I chorused together, then fell against each other laughing.

"It was Robyn's defining moment, you know," I said, mimicking Robyn. "Can't you think of anything to say that could better that?"

"Okay," Alex said, threading her hands behind her head. "It was…awesome?" She screwed up her nose. "I'm not so good at this, am I?"

I shook my head. "That was even lamer," I said, slapping her leg. "Try again."

"Okay, how about *you* tell *me* how you felt today instead," Alex asked, sitting up, "if you're so good at it."

"I loved…" I bit my lip. "The intensity of it," I said, smiling. "The passion, the…I don't know, the power of knowing we'd made so many people happy. I soaked up their energy, you know? Used it to feed my own. And when I stepped offstage I wondered if I'd ever get that same feeling ever again, or whether any gig we do from now on could ever match that level of intensity."

There was a silence then. The laughter that had been ebbing and flowing round the bed suddenly stopped.

"I know what you mean," Robyn said, staring down at her fingers. "It was like nothing we'd ever done before. Like no feeling I'd ever had before."

"Me neither," Brooke said softly.

"Like, if I actually stopped and thought about all those people there today, singing our music back to us, dancing to it?" Robyn shook her head. "That'd freak me right out."

"They loved us, didn't they?" I smiled at the faces around me. "Totally loved us."

"Be4 are going places, guys." Alex lifted her hands and fist-bumped first Brooke, then me, then Robyn, immediately bringing the laughter, and with it a lightness, back into the room.

"This *so* needs the champagne." I lifted the bottle that was still in my hands and waited while Robyn scrambled off the bed and grabbed four glasses from the unit above the minibar. The bottle opened with a satisfyingly loud pop and an instant frothing of bubbles out of the neck, down the bottle, and over my hand, prompting loud whoops and yet more laughter.

I looked at everyone's faces around me and loved it all. The solidarity, the joy, the mutual feeling of satisfaction at our successful gig. I poured the foaming champagne and handed a glass to each of them, sharing a look with each as I did so, then taking a large gulp of Alex's drink before I handed it to her.

"Don't want to get you into bad habits," I said, passing her the half-filled glass.

She took it from me, one perfect eyebrow raised.

"To Be4," Robyn said, raising her glass.

We mirrored her action. "Be4." Four voices sounded as one. The champagne disappeared in one mutual gulp.

"So, Brooke," Alex eventually said, "it's your turn now."

"For?" Brooke wiped her mouth with her thumb.

"To spill," Robyn said, reaching for the champagne bottle again. "Tell us what today meant to you."

"Keep it short." I sat on the edge of the bed again. "There's drink to be drunk." I knew what Brooke was like.

"I felt like…wait." Brooke took another drink, making us all laugh. "Like I was in another world," she said, "almost like an out-of-body experience, floating on a cloud."

"Were you high?" Robyn asked. She reached over and playfully punched Brooke's leg. "Did you score before you went on? Nic would have been jealous."

No one laughed at that.

As if realizing what she'd said, Robyn screwed up her face. "Sorry, sorry," she said. "Dumb thing to say."

My stomach balled into a fist, refusing any more champagne. I wanted to tell Robyn how I'd felt coming offstage, when the euphoria had faded. I wanted to tell her how Nicole had taunted me after what should have been the time of my life, and how that had made me feel as if the walls were coming in on me, crushing me. I knew neither Robyn nor Brooke felt the same guilt as I did, and I glared at her, wondering why she'd think to say such a stupid thing. Robyn had totally ruined the moment, and the silence that now scratched through the room was excruciating.

"Didn't I see an Xbox somewhere?" Alex put her glass down and shuffled off the bed. "I'm sure I did."

We watched in silence as she scooted over to the huge wall-mounted plasma-screen TV, fell to her knees, reached under the table that was underneath the TV, then pulled out two controllers.

"I knew it." She turned and lifted them up to show us. "*GTA* anyone? I heard drunk *GTA* is the best game ever," she said, looking back at us, "not that I'd know."

The fist in my stomach loosened its grip a little. I looked over to Alex, crouched by the TV, and as she smiled at me with a face so open and alive, I felt my chest burn with gratitude towards her.

I knew what she was doing, and I loved her for it.

❖

"I'm sorry." Robyn sounded genuine. "What I said earlier about Nic was thoughtless." She'd followed me to the bathroom, leaving Brooke and Alex sitting in front of the Xbox, controllers in hand, shouting at the TV screen.

I sat on the edge of the bath, Brooke and Alex still visible through the doorway. The atmosphere had lifted again slightly, thanks to Alex's intervention, but Robyn's words still hung around the corners of the room like cobwebs, every occasional movement or thought process springing them back to life. But the excitement and exhilaration from before was gone. It was as though Robyn had invited Nicole into the hotel room and she was now in the hotel room with us all, draining the joy from us by telling us we'd had our moment of glory, and that now it was time to stop being so selfish and think about her.

"It's okay." I breathed in, wishing my chest didn't feel quite so tight with anxiety.

"It was a lame joke," Robyn said, coming further into the bathroom and shutting the door behind her. "I got carried away. Should have known when to stop."

"It has kind of put a damper on the whole day." I gave a short laugh. "But then, Nic put a damper on it for me too."

"Want to talk about her?" Robyn asked.

I did. I didn't.

"No." That was the coward's way out, I knew. So I was a coward—nothing new there then.

"If you're sure." Robyn looked away as a shout of laughter came from the room.

The *yeah, I'm sure* died on my lips, to be replaced with, "I can't stop thinking about her."

"Me neither," Robyn said, pulling her eyes back to me.

I stared at her.

"You as well?" I somehow doubted that Robyn had seen Nicole onstage earlier, though.

"Of course." Robyn shrugged. "Because that out there was the first big thing we've done without her, isn't it?" She continued, "And you're feeling bad about it." She smiled. "It's okay. I feel the same way too. It's only natural."

"I guess." I stared down at my hands. "I feel…disloyal."

"To Nic?"

"Mm."

"Because?"

I looked at her. "Because I enjoyed it out there tonight," I said, "and I shouldn't have."

"Of course you should have enjoyed it, Tally," Robyn said. "We've all worked our butts off to get where we were tonight." She frowned. "And, actually, we could have caved after Nic did what she did. But we didn't. If anything, we're stronger than ever."

"That's the other thing that's making me feel guilty though," I said. "Because I think Alex is as good as her."

Robyn thought for a moment.

"Alex is *different* to her," Robyn said, "that's for sure." She looked at me. "She brings something new to the band as well, so I guess it's normal that we'd think she's good for the band too."

The band of tension that had been compressing my chest loosened its grip a little.

"She was fantastic tonight," Robyn said. "Everyone knows it."

"It's weird," I said, "but at first I thought Alex just joined the band for her own personal glory." I glanced back up at Robyn. "You know all that stuff going on at the studio and at the rehearsals?"

Robyn nodded.

"I really didn't like her then." I laughed. "But I was wrong," I said. "I think she genuinely cares for Be4."

"You think Nic didn't?" Robyn asked.

"I don't know." I honestly didn't. "I know she started to resent the fans."

I knew Nicole disliked the fans for one reason: me. I knew she resented every single fan that wrote to me, followed me on Twitter, sent me presents, declared their undying love for me. That she loathed it every time a new bunch of flowers got sent to the studio for me and hated the girls that hung around after recording sessions, hoping for a selfie.

I knew she hated it, but I just didn't know what I could do about it other than hand every bunch of flowers to either Brooke or Robyn, hide the letters from Nicole, and sneak out of back doors to avoid the waiting fans. I couldn't have done any more—could I?

"I know she was jealous of them." Robyn's voice pulled me back to her. "But you know what?" she asked. "As well as thinking every fan out there wanted to sleep with you, I also think she wanted what you had. The adulation. The followers." Robyn sat on the edge of the bath next to me, a smile playing on her lips. "You know what an ego she's got. I mean, come on! It's almost as big as mine."

That made me laugh.

"She saw how many followers you were getting," Robyn continued, "compared to her, and she didn't like it. She didn't like that you were more popular than her, and she didn't like the thought of all these people—girls in particular—wanting you when she couldn't have you."

I stared at her. "I never meant to hurt her." I shook my head, annoyed at the tears that now stood in my eyes.

"I know." Robyn smiled.

A silence settled between us before Robyn suddenly said, "So how many followers do you have now? Compared to me and Brooke?"

"A few." My face warmed.

I never wanted that either. The so-called adulation that Robyn was speaking about. The fame was great, and I loved that fans loved our music—after all, that's why we wanted to do it in the first place, to have our music heard—but the attention that came with it, occasionally unwanted, was sometimes hard to understand. For me, anyway. Robyn loved it, but then Robyn loved everything about being in a band.

Me? I just wanted to write music and sing it to the public. There were times when I longed for the old days, when we'd busk down on Brighton beach, snag a takeaway on our way home with our day's takings, and go home. Just a handful of diehard fans on Twitter. A mention in the local paper if we were lucky. That made me sound ungrateful. I wasn't. But, still…

"More than a few." Robyn said. "Although still way fewer than Alex, am I right?"

I laughed and nodded, and knew Robyn was thinking about her next words before she finally said, "You know what else I think?"

"Hit me."

"I think we all got Alex wrong."

"Seriously?"

"Mm." Robyn nodded. "I think she's more old-school than I thought, and I think what you said just now is spot on." She lowered her voice. "I genuinely think she wants to be in Be4 for the music, not for her five minutes of fame." Robyn scratched her chin. "And that means I'm going to have to apologize to her at some point for being so horrible to her when she first joined us."

I laughed. "You? Apologize? Can we have tickets to see that?"

"Piss off."

"You're right though," I said. "About Alex. You know she wants to start writing some stuff with us?" With me. Alex had said she wanted to write with me. I looked at Robyn. I wasn't about to tell her that, though.

Instead, my mind tumbled back to two nights before. My apartment. A snapshot of Alex and me, heads bowed over our guitars, came back to me with such startling clarity I felt a shiver of pleasure slither down my spine. The memory of how utterly content I'd felt at the time swiftly followed, and I hastily looked away, scared that Robyn would see the expression on my face.

"She told you that?"

"Yeah."

"Could work, that." Robyn nodded slowly.

"We have…similar tastes," I said carefully. "Me and Alex."

"Which means you'll both want more guitar? Yeah, yeah." Robyn laughed. "I might have guessed."

"But even that makes me feel bad about Nic," I said, sighing. "It's like a merry-go-round sometimes."

"You know…maybe you should go and see her," Robyn said. "Nic. Maybe if you spoke to her…?"

I shook my head. "They told us not to see her."

"I know what they told us," Robyn said. "But…"

I saw her shift her position.

"What?" I asked.

"I saw her."

"Nic?" An ache trembled inside me. "When?"

Robyn's expression told me she knew she'd said too much.

When she didn't reply, I asked, "And how is she?"

"Doing okay." Robyn turned her head, as if to make sure the bathroom door was still shut. "But she's got some way to go yet still."

Deep in the centre of my chest I felt the familiar pain, a constant reminder of what had happened to her.

"You think she'll want to see me as well?" I asked.

"Why not?"

Plenty of reasons.

"Was she happy to see you?" I asked. "I still can't believe you didn't say anything. Does Brooke know?" The words tumbled out.

"Yes, she was happy to see me, I know, I'm sorry, and no," Robyn replied, "Brooke doesn't know either."

A thought wormed its way into my brain. Maybe Robyn was right; maybe if I went to see Nicole and could see for myself that she was doing okay, then the guilt might start to fade and I could start to enjoy my successes. Robyn had been right about something else too: we'd worked ourselves into the ground trying to make Be4 a success. Now that we were there, wasn't it time I started to enjoy myself?

A shout from inside the room drew my attention to the door. It sounded like Brooke and Alex's *GTA* marathon was hitching up a gear, and suddenly I'd had enough of talking about Nic. I wanted to go back in and be with Alex, and the thought overwhelmed me. I wanted to be in her presence, to feed off her happiness and positivity after spending the last ten minutes or so wallowing in negativity.

"So will you go and see Nic?" Robyn asked.

Another shout, then laughter, long and loud. The pull of Alex was too much.

"I'll see." I stood and made for the door, knowing that the best thing for my own sanity was for me to try and dredge up enough courage to go and see Nicole, and finally lay some ghosts to rest.

CHAPTER THIRTEEN

Croft House wasn't as I'd expected it to be, although I'm not sure exactly what I *did* expect it to be. A looming, imposing hulk of Victorian granite? Bars on the windows? Pinched white faces pressed to the glass? Guards on duty everywhere? I wasn't sure, and even though there was a certain institutional look about it, Croft House really wasn't as intimidating as I thought it would be when I finally spotted the pleasant, small building that came into view through the passenger window as my cab passed through its wrought-iron gates and made its way down its winding gravel path.

I'd managed to summon the courage to go there. It had been surprisingly quick to arrange too, just two short phone calls, an agreement from Nicole, a day and time set, and a satnav address emailed to me. No one knew other than Robyn. I don't know why I hadn't told Brooke, and I hoped she wouldn't be upset; perhaps I'd tell her after I'd seen Nic. I didn't know.

My driver turned his cab into the car park and pulled up under a tree. Not looking closely at the fare, I handed him some notes and sat quietly while he rooted around in what looked like some sort of money pouch for my change, grateful for those few precious moments that allowed me more time to compose myself. I watched a small, speckled bird through the windscreen as it hopped from branch to branch on a tree in front of the car, suddenly wishing that I could stay there and continue watching it, rather than having to go inside and be confronted by the reality of Nicole's downfall. Finally, with a flurry of wings, the bird left the sanctuary of the branches and flitted away. I craned my neck to watch it for as long as I could, and then, with a grunt of acknowledgement, the driver handed me back some change, and I knew it was finally time for me to suck it up and leave the safety of the cab.

The warmth of the sunshine, after the chill of the cab's AC, was welcome. I stared up at the clear blue sky and wondered if Nicole got to go outside much. I was being ridiculous, I knew. Croft House wasn't a prison. But there was still a small part of me that thought Nicole probably had been locked up in her own prison for quite a while.

I shot a look to the double-fronted main door, with its rusting studs and ornamental handle, and realized I was holding my breath. I looked back to the tree, half hoping the bird might have returned. It hadn't. With a heavy heart, and an impending sense of dread, I walked towards Croft House.

❖

The receptionist was pleasant. Middle-aged, with an open, expressive face that said, *Welcome, but don't mess with me.* I looked at her name badge: Annie. No surname. I guessed the personal touch was deliberate; after all, I kept reminding myself, Croft House was *not* a prison. Nor was it a hospital, but as I approached the reception desk, I couldn't help but smell a slight hospital tang that made me think I might see someone wheeled out on a trolley with wires attached to all their bits and pieces at any moment.

Remember to smile. Try not to look so worried.

I smiled.

"I rang on Monday?" I cleared my throat. "I'm here to see Nicole Kelly."

"If you could fill out this form, please." Annie pushed a clipboard towards me. "And I'm afraid I'll have to ask you to empty your pockets." She smiled slightly. "It's usual practice."

"Sure." I nodded, delving into my trouser pockets.

Once I'd emptied them—a packet of mints which Annie immediately took from me, and a chipped supermarket trolley token which I'd had no idea had been in there—I filled out her form and handed it back to her.

Then I waited. And waited.

Every second stretched by agonizingly and each minute that ticked by made me want to go back out into the sunshine of the car park and look for the small bird again. I turned in my seat and gazed out of the window, feeling suffocated, and nervous, and dreading having to see Nicole all over again. Would she look ill? Or would she look just the same as when I'd last seen her, standing in Regent's Park, yelling at some kid in a baseball cap because he'd nearly hit her with his football?

"Tally."

I snapped my head round and there she was. Nicole. It had been two months, two weeks, and three days since I'd last seen her (yes, I'd counted them all) but seeing her standing in front of me made it seem like we'd just said goodbye that morning. Not that we'd ever got to say goodbye, though. When it all happened. When Ed just took her away, installed her in Croft House, and told me, Robyn, and Brooke that Nicole *needed a break.*

"Nic." I stood.

"Thanks for coming over."

"I would have come before," I said, "only…"

It was all so formal, I wanted to scream.

Nicole shook her head. "I know."

I nodded, afraid to speak. "Yes." I managed. Pathetic.

We hugged, but it was the dry, cold hug you give someone you hardly know, our bodies barely touching. Not the sort you give your once-best friend.

"We'll go to my room." Nicole dropped her arms from me and started to walk away. "We can talk in peace in there."

I followed her, passing by Annie, half expecting her to stop me and strip-search me.

Croft House is not a prison.

The inside was as nice as the outside. As we wandered together down a long corridor, I was struck at how light and friendly the place was, sort of like a hotel but at the same time, *so* not like a hotel. I liked the pictures on the walls: seascapes, even though we were in the Midlands, and paintings of hot-air balloons, for some strange reason. All very bright and optimistic. Positive. There were sayings too, quotations from people whose photos I didn't recognize. Perhaps, I thought as Nicole opened a door to one of the rooms, they were previous patient-guests.

"So what do you think?" Nicole stood in the middle of her room and cast her arms out. "Not quite The Ritz but it's okay."

"It's nice." I nodded and looked around, to the walls plastered with photos and drawings. To her noticeboard with newspaper clippings. To her iPod dock, her TV, DVD. Her Xbox. Everything a teenager should have in their room. I thought about the Xbox in the Chelsea hotel. The fun and laughter we'd had with it. The normality.

Nothing about this was normal.

As Nicole cleared a space for me on her sofa, fussing over the cushions on it, and telling me to ignore the messiness of her room, all I could think was, *You're seventeen. Seventeen-year-olds shouldn't have to go to rehab. Seventeen-year-olds shouldn't have to have their lives monitored for them 24/7 in case they do what you did to yourself. Seventeen-year-olds shouldn't...*

"Coffee?" Nicole asked. "We have all mod cons here." She pointed towards a Nespresso machine on her desk. "Makes the best coffee since Luigi's. Remember Luigi's?"

"Whatchoo laydees want, eh?" I exaggerated Luigi's accent. "Cappoocheeno? Best cappoocheeno thees side of da river, eh?"

Nicole laughed. "I miss Luigi."

"Me too." I laughed with her.

"You don't still go there?"

My laughter stopped. "No."

Luigi's had been our place. The place Nicole and I would go to all the time. Two teenage girls, free in London, money no object. We'd shop, I remembered, until we were exhausted, then head to Luigi's place, just a stone's throw from Harrods, and have anything we wanted from the menu. Including his *cappoocheeno*.

"Why not?" Nicole asked. "You used to love it there."

"Dunno." I shrugged. "Guess it sort of lost its magic after..."

"After I went loopy?"

"You didn't go loopy."

"Whatever, Tally." Nicole turned away, but not before I'd seen her face darken. "So you want one?"

"Want what?"

"A coffee."

"Oh. Yes." I frowned, unsettled by Nicole's sudden change of mood. "Thanks."

I watched her as she busied herself with her coffee machine, unsure whether I should talk some more about Luigi's, or whether it had been that which had changed her mood in the first place. Maybe she didn't want reminding of that time in her life. Before…all this.

"So…how have you been?" I winced. Lame. How did I think she'd have been?

Her answer, though, surprised me.

"I've been good." Nicole turned and rested a hip against the edge of her desk. "Being here has been good for me." She laughed, and to me it sounded empty of any humour. "Even though I didn't think that when they dragged me kicking and screaming in here."

"They dragged you?" I was horrified.

"Figure of speech." Nicole smiled. "I was glad to come here." She paused. "Things had become…too much."

"And…you're clean now?"

"Yeah." She looked away and swallowed. "Thank God."

"I'm glad." I looked across to her, wishing there wasn't so much distance between us, both emotionally and physically. "I never wanted—"

"I know." Nicole shoved away from the desk and returned to her coffee machine, and just like before, I noticed a shift in her mood.

"I mean it." It was important she knew. I loved her as a friend. Just because I never wanted to commit to her as anything more didn't mean I pushed her into all this, did it? "If I'd thought everything would end up like this, then I would have—"

"Told me you felt the same?" Nicole looked back over her shoulder to me. "No you wouldn't. Because you didn't."

"No." I looked away, too ashamed to look at her. "But I would have acted differently if I'd known you'd end up like this."

"An addict?"

"If that's what you want to call it." The tension in my shoulders refused to budge.

"What else would you call it?" Nicole asked. "A bit of fun? 'Cos let me tell you, none of this has been fun."

"I did love you, you know," I said. "I *do* love you."

"Just not in the way I want you to," Nicole said as she handed me my coffee, "right?"

"How long had you been using?"

"Wow." She cut her glance away. "Straight in there with the big one."

"What did you expect me to ask?" I asked. "Did you think I'd come here to drink coffee and reminisce with you?"

"Like I'd want to reminisce about the past?" Nicole gave a shudder. "No, thanks."

"Why didn't you ever tell me you were taking drugs?" I pressed. That had been the worst of all of it, the lies and the deceit. The revelation. The knowledge that I'd never known any of it, despite thinking Nicole and I were close.

"Why would I tell you?" Nicole asked. "When you'd made it clear you weren't interested in me."

"You were still my friend." I heard my voice rise. "Do you know how hurt I was when—"

"Oh, hurt?" Nicole's raised voice matched mine. "You want to talk about hurt? I can give you a whole afternoon on hurt if you've got time."

"Don't."

"Don't what? Remind you?" Nicole's face darkened. "Remind you how everything was okay until I told you I loved you?"

"You said you didn't blame me for what happened to you."

"I lied," Nicole said. "Why do you think I took that first line?" She stood up and walked to her window. "And then the next? And the next?"

"Thanks for that." I put my coffee cup down.

"Truth hurts, does it?" Nicole asked, not looking at me.

"Don't you think I feel guilty enough as it is," I asked, "without you telling me this is all my fault?"

But guilt for what? Putting Nicole into rehab? Or knowing it was Alex I wanted to be in the band rather than her?

"Funnily enough, this isn't about you." Nicole turned and looked at me, looking lost and angry and a whole other range of emotions all jumbled into one. "It's about me."

Oh, it was *so* about me.

"I never wanted any of this," I said. "I just wanted us to go back to how we'd been."

"Except, I couldn't do that," Nicole said. "Everything had changed between us and then everything seemed to happen at once. You and I had kissed and I thought you were The One"—she air quoted that, and it looked weird to me—"but you didn't." She shrugged. "But unlike you, I couldn't stop thinking about you." She looked away again. "Then I had to contend with girls throwing themselves at you." Nicole seemed to focus on something on the wall beside her. "I was hurt. In pain. But then someone came along with something he said would make all the pain and hurt go away. Something he said would make me feel good."

"And did it?" I wanted to know.

"Yeah. It did." Nicole walked back to her sofa and sat. "So I took some more. Then a bit more."

"So why did you never tell us?" I asked again.

My mind scuttled back. To the day Ed told us what had happened. I remembered the shock, the disbelief, the crying. There had been so much crying: Brooke hadn't believed him, I recall. She thought Nicole had left because of something we'd done, a differing of artistic minds that she hadn't been aware of. A desire by Nicole to move away from us and try something different.

If only it had been that simple.

Then, the disbelief. The mutterings of how it *really* wasn't my fault. Honestly, Tally. Nicole chose to do what she'd done. You didn't give her that first line. She *chose* to take it.

I looked back to Nicole. To her gaunt face and shadowed eyes. And if only Brooke knew Nicole really had left because of me. Nicole had been right: I was to blame for her downfall. My rejection of Nicole had changed her overnight, and even though I hadn't seen it at the time, I could now. I could also see that I'd been so immature in thinking we could have ever gone back to how we'd been before. How could we have? How could we have pretended that everything was okay? When the memory of our kiss stood in both our minds, but for completely different reasons?

Drugs had never played a part in any of our lives before; sure, we'd been offered stuff while on the road, but I was confident none of us had ever taken anything, even when our schedules had been so ridiculously hectic and we'd all been so exhausted that it would have been really easy to take something just to see us through to our next gig.

"It was my secret." Nicole's voice sliced through my thoughts. "The only thing you lot knew nothing about, and that made it the one thing I had control over in my life."

"Then you went out of control." I regretted the words as soon as they'd left my mouth.

"Thanks for that."

"I didn't mean…"

"You did." Nicole held my gaze. "And you're right."

"How did you even get in here anyway?" I asked, looking around her room. "At your age?"

"Ed pulled some strings."

"Of course he did." I frowned. "And your parents?"

"They complied." Nicole looked away and I knew me mentioning her parents had hurt her. "They knew it was this or…" She shook her head, as if to shake the thought from it. "Ed told them he thought it was better to keep me out of the public eye for a while." Nicole pulled a face. "You know how it is."

Of course I knew. Remember, everything Ed did, he did for the band.

"So when do you think you'll finish your treatment?" I asked.

Nicole pulled a face. "Another four weeks at least."

"And then?"

"No idea," she replied. "I…" She paused and I waited for her to make some grand revelation. Instead she shook her head and said, "Maybe I'll go home. Back to Brighton." She picked up her coffee. "Ed says he'll work to get me a deal as a solo artist, but I don't know." Nicole looked at me. "It's not like I can come back to Be4. Not now you have this awesome new singer everyone's raving about." A shadow fell across her face.

My thoughts of Alex, until now locked away in the back of my mind, crashed forward again. I didn't want them to. I'd been happy to have her out of my head, even if it had only been for a few hours.

"She's not you," I said. Boy, wasn't *that* the truth?

Nicole smiled but didn't answer.

"She'll never be you."

I tried again, but all Nicole said was, "Congratulations on 'After the Rain,' by the way."

"You heard it?"

Nicole nodded. "So it seems as though Be4 are doing okay without me," she continued.

"It's not the same." Who was I trying to convince—me or her?

Me.

"But we're doing okay," I said. "We did a festival last week which was all types of awesome, and yeah, I'd say things are pretty amazing for us right now." At the look on Nicole's face, I regretted the words as soon as they'd left my mouth.

"Are you for real?" Nicole's mood changed in an instant. "You come in here, telling me how fabulous your life is, how well the band's doing? I'm stuck in here, just trying to get through each day, and all you can tell me is how wonderful your life is right now? I mean, are you for fucking real?"

Her words stung me as if I'd been hit. How could I have been so inconsiderate as to tell her how great my life was when she was here?

I got up and walked towards her. "Nicole, I—"

"Get off me." She slapped me away. "I really am only in here because of you," she spat. "What part of your thick skull still can't get that?"

"Because I couldn't commit to you?" I started to get angry. "Nic, you know you mean everything to me. *Everything.*"

"But it was never enough, was it?" she asked.

"How could we have been together?" I shot back. "The minute we had an argument or disagreed over something, the band would have suffered. Relationships in a band just never work."

"Because it's always been about the band for you, hasn't it?" Nicole said. "Nothing—or no one—is as important to you as the band."

"Wasn't it like that for you too?" I asked. "We had a chance—we *have* a chance—to make something of ourselves after so long trying."

"You might have," Nicole said. "What have I got now? Nothing."

"And whose fault is that?" I asked.

"It's yours," she replied. "All this?" Nicole spread her arms out. "All your doing. So congratulations for totally fucking up my life and my dreams."

My legs felt heavy. I stumbled to a chair and sank down into it.

"Truth too much for you?" Nicole walked over to me. "Look around you. Around my room. See what I'm reduced to." She stood in front of me. "A ten-by-ten room. Daily inspections in case I've managed to smuggle something in. Meetings where I have to spill out my thoughts to other people," she said, "and it doesn't end when I finally leave. Oh no. Then—get this—then I have to attend weekly sessions, *just in case I relapse.*" She air-quoted again. "I'm seventeen, Tally. Seventeen and trapped."

I looked up at her, unable to speak.

"So don't rock up here and tell me how fabulous your drug-free, perfect life is," Nicole said, finally turning away. "Because I don't need to hear it."

She walked to the other side of her room and stared down at her desk.

"Nicole..." I stood up.

"Go," she said, not turning to look at me. "You know the way out."

I hesitated, hoping she might turn and look at me, but she didn't. Finally, when her silence was too much to bear, I left the room and hastened back down the corridor, Nicole's words ringing in my ears and burning on my cheeks.

Chapter Fourteen

The notes wouldn't gel. My guitar wouldn't listen to me. The music I was trying to write sucked.

I'd stumbled from Croft House with Nicole's words raging after me and gone straight home, knowing I needed to do the one thing I'd always done when things were getting too much for me.

So I came home and started writing music, because music was the only thing that ever seemed to make sense in my life.

I don't know how long I sat on the floor of my apartment, papers scattered around me, my guitar by my side. Minutes? Hours? All I did know was I needed to get it out. Get my pain out. Get the smell of Croft House off me. Get Nicole's hate out of me.

My visit to Croft House had been a disaster. But what had I expected? That Nicole would welcome me back with open arms, like I was an old friend visiting her in her swanky new apartment?

I'd come to see her, seeking forgiveness. I'd left with the guilt clawing at my insides so hard that I could physically feel it in my stomach and I hoped no one had seen me hurling into the long grass once I'd reached the sanctuary of the trees in the car park.

Nicole hadn't wanted to listen to me, so the only thing I knew I could do now was put my guilt into music.

If only my brain would switch off long enough to function properly.

I snatched up my guitar again and strummed a few chords, formulating a tune with each change of key. That worked better. I slid my pencil from behind my ear and jotted down the chords I'd written, then strummed another chord. I frowned. That didn't work so well.

Sighing, I placed my guitar down and concentrated on the lyrics instead. Perhaps if I could get those written down, the music would follow naturally. What was I feeling right now?

Haunted.

Guilty.

Empty.

Dead inside.

I wrote a sentence and nodded. It worked.

Friendship.

Caring.

Hate.

It wasn't right. Nicole was in Croft House and I was sitting on the floor of my expensive apartment, writing about her. She never left me. She would never leave me. I wrote those sentences down and felt my throat close. She was my best friend and I'd abandoned her on so many different levels.

I don't know why I did what I did next, but I was glad I did. I lunged over and picked up my phone from the floor, found her number, and called her. Somehow I knew she'd make everything better right now.

She answered and I felt a warmth spread across my chest.

"Alex?" I asked. "Are you busy?"

"Wow." Alex stepped in through the door and took in the scene of chaos that was my apartment. "And I thought this place was a mess the first time I ever came here."

I assumed she was referring to the paperwork. Okay, so there was a lot of paperwork, screwed up pieces of manuscript paper, tossed around the floor, but it was mostly sheets with scribbled notes. Pages and pages of writing. Of thoughts.

"I kind of had a Saturday morning brainstorming session," I said sheepishly.

"No shit." She looked around her as she followed me to the sofa. "And three guitars out. You really mean business, don't you?"

"I was messing around with sounds."

"Did you decide on one?"

"Electro acoustic, maybe." I picked up my guitar and played a chord, just for the hell of it. "I haven't decided yet."

"So…you're writing." Alex sank down onto the sofa with a grin. "I'm astute like that."

"I'm writing." I put my guitar back and flopped down next to her. "You're very astute."

"You always make such a mess when you're writing?" Alex asked.

"Oh, I suppose you sit at an oak desk with a fountain pen, do you?"

"Something like that." Alex let her head fall back against the sofa. "So what are you writing?"

"I'm going to call it…'Perspectives.'" I'd thought of the title a few hours before. "Yeah. 'Perspectives.'"

"Slow or fast?"

"Slow." I nodded. "It has to be slow."

"And you called me over to…what? Help?" Alex asked.

"You weren't busy, were you?" I screwed up my face, suddenly worried I'd dragged her over to my apartment.

"Never too busy to write music." Alex laughed. "Never too busy to write music with you, more importantly."

"You're a star."

"I know."

I caught her eye and smiled. I loved that she was with me. I loved that just by her being here she'd made the anxiety that had followed me from Croft House and back to London, and which had dogged me ever since, magically disappear.

I was right; Alex really did make everything better.

"So I thought at this point," Alex said, as she leant over to grab a piece of paper off the floor, "you should pick the start of the intro rather than strum." She scooted back up closer to me. "Then go into your strumming pattern after that."

We'd somehow managed to end up sitting on the floor together, side by side, backs against the sofa. Just as I'd thought, Alex's input had allowed my music to flow faster than it had all day.

"I like it." I tapped my pencil against my bottom lip. "Leading to the first line which would sound something like"—I sang a line—"then everyone harmonizing into the chorus."

"With me coming in on guitar"—Alex tapped my piece of paper—"right here."

"Perfect."

"See how it sounds." Alex lifted her chin to my guitar across the room.

I tucked my pencil behind my ear, then scrambled to my feet and grabbed up my guitar. I gave it a quick tune while Alex scribbled something down on my piece of paper, then went and sat back down next to her.

"Right, so. The intro will be something like this"—I picked at the strings—"moving to this." I strummed the next chords. Alex nodded. "Then a modulation." I changed key.

"Sounds good." Alex lurched across the sofa and snagged my other guitar. "Then when I come in here later," she said, strumming her guitar, "you move back down a key."

We played together, our guitars working in sync with the other. It sounded awesome.

"Then Brooke sings this line, as our guitars fade," I said as I finished playing. I sang a line, then said, "With Robyn and you coming in here." I sang another bit. "You think that could work?" I asked afterwards.

"Or maybe Robyn could sing her part first," Alex said, "then I come in on the next part, just to add some harmony."

"Whichever." I put my guitar down by my feet. "Both will sound amazing, I think."

I picked up my piece of paper with notes and scribbles across it and drew my knees up to my chest, resting the paper on my thighs. I pulled my pencil out from behind my ear and crossed out a line, adding Alex's name and a question mark next to it.

"Let me see?" she asked, holding her hand out for the paper.

"I added you here." I tapped the end of my pencil on the paper then handed it to her.

We sat on the floor, our backs resting against the sofa, and looked at my notes together.

"I like this line." Alex smiled over to me. "*And when you're lonely, just close your eyes and let me come to you,*" she read. "It's lovely."

"Thank you."

"You write such beautiful lyrics."

My shyness at my own work, never too far away, came to the surface. But like all good shy people, instead of answering her I chose to ignore her comment. Instead, I took the paper from her and said, "I'm not too sure about this bit, though."

"Which bit?" Alex leant closer.

"This. *My thoughts won't leave me alone, even though I try so hard. You said you loved me but it wasn't enough. You said you cared but what did I do? And now the hauntings in my mind follow me around...*"

Alex reached over and tapped her finger on the paper. "This?" she said. "Beautiful. Just beautiful." She looked at me. "Why aren't you sure about it?"

"Would it work with the chords we've written?" I asked.

"Make it work," Alex said. "You can't take a line like that out."

"I guess I could slow it down a little."

Alex tilted her head to one side and studied me. "You should have more faith in your abilities, you know."

"Yeah." I laughed. "Maybe."

"Totally."

"Says the girl who on our first day in the studio together told me I was pitchy." I don't know why I said that. But I was kind of glad I had.

"Tal. Seriously?" Alex shoulder-bumped me. "Haven't I apologized like a *thousand* times for that?"

"You can keep apologizing for it." I laughed and pushed her back, then bowed my head back over my piece of paper. "Line five," I asked. "What do you think?"

Alex leant over again and looked. Her hair tickled the skin on my upper arm, making it goosebump. She didn't answer, and I was suddenly acutely aware of the silence that had filled the room. All I could hear was our breathing. All I could sense was Alex's closeness to me, her hair tickling my arm, her hip and thigh pressed up against mine, her warmth seeping in through the material of my jeans, joining my own increasingly warm skin. My breathing became shallow and I had the sudden crazy notion that I shouldn't breathe on her, so I started to breathe softly through my mouth. That sounded odd though, so I breathed through my nose again, feeling more and more anxious with every breath. Finally, to my relief, Alex leant away again. I shifted my position on the floor, shuffling myself an inch or so away from her.

"Maybe use some extension chords," she said, "rather than basic triads."

I scribbled out some lines, grateful for the distraction.

"Sing it?" Alex asked.

I sang the lines, pleased when Alex nodded and gave a small clap.

"Nice." She looked over to me, our eyes meeting at the same time. "Really nice," she added quietly.

I pulled my eyes away, feeling my face grow hot again. I needed to concentrate, I knew. This was about writing a song for Nicole, to let her know. Alex had no idea about the meaning behind the words, and I wanted it to stay that way.

"This bit here," I said, tapping the end of my pencil on the paper, "should be stripped back in the middle eight so it's just strings, I thought." I stared down at the paper. "I thought violins would give it a more haunting sound."

"That's a shift in direction." Alex nodded, I hoped, in approval. "I think that could work."

"I'd have to run it past Robyn and Brooke, of course," I said, "but I think they'd be okay with it."

I stretched my legs out in front of me, suddenly stiff from sitting on the floor.

"I think violas and cellos," Alex said. "And here too." She shuffled closer to me again, took the pencil from my hand, and put an *X* next to a line of written music. "Lower than violins and more unusual. More mellow too." She scratched her chin with the pencil. "And it'll make the bass more prominent," she added with a grin. "It'll sound immense, bet you."

"Sounds good," I said. "Could we add it again later?"

"It needs a line like"—Alex looked up to the ceiling and puffed out her cheeks—"*love can hurt, but can't you see? The things I did, you'll never understand*. Then back to that awesome line you did before, *And now the hauntings in my mind follow me around*, but this time add the strings."

"Love it." I snagged the pencil back from Alex and wrote it down.

"And a countermelody on the cellos and violas." Alex gave me a small shove. "It'll complement your writing beautifully."

I wrote down *countermelody* on my paper.

"Thank you." I tucked the pencil back behind my ear. "For all of this."

Alex stretched her arms up, locking her hands above her head. "Writing music," she said with a yawn, "is what it's all about, just as much as performing." She let her arms flop back down to her lap and drew her knees up to her chest. "It's a good way of getting thoughts out too," she added, resting her head back against the sofa. "All those innermost thoughts that you can't speak," she murmured.

I didn't reply.

"So who are you writing 'Perspectives' about?" Alex suddenly asked. She rolled her head and gazed at me. "Who's in your innermost thoughts that you have to write about them?"

"No one." Even to my own ears, I sounded sharp. "Why does there have to be someone?"

"You see," Alex said with a laugh, "I was only kidding with you until you said that last bit." She held my gaze. "But the way you answered makes me think perhaps I was right."

"You're not." I scrambled clumsily to my feet, my pencil dropping from behind my ear as I stood. "Drink?" I asked.

I walked to the kitchen, not waiting to hear Alex's reply. Once in the kitchen, I gripped the side of the cupboard, annoyed with myself. I could have laughed it off. I could have just joked with Alex. But no. I had to act all brittle and sensitive. I tossed a look over my shoulder, back to Alex still sitting on the floor. She didn't have to know anything about the song, or about Nicole. My reasons for writing it in the first place. Nothing.

"You didn't answer," I called back to her. "Drink?"

"You got a Dr Pepper there?" she called back.

I pulled two Dr Peppers from the fridge and went back to her, handing her a can as I scooted past her and wiggled down on the sofa behind her.

"Try a sus four here." Alex held the paper up to me. "I think it could work."

"With the guitars?"

"Yup." Alex opened her can. She took a drink then said, "It's important to you, this. Isn't it?"

"'Perspectives'?" I replied. "Of course. All my songs are important to me."

"But there's something about this one," Alex said, "that seems different."

"Nah." I opened my can. "It's no different."

"Mm."

I could tell Alex wasn't convinced.

We drank our Dr Peppers in silence for a while. I watched Alex, her head bent over her lap as she studied the now slightly dog-eared piece of paper with the draft of "Perspectives" written on it, occasionally quietly humming a line to herself.

"Okay, so I wrote it about someone I know," I suddenly said. "'Perspectives,' I mean." I grimaced. Obviously.

"I know." Alex carried on humming again. "See this bit here?" She hoisted the paper up over her head again and shot a look to me. "Should go up at the end, I think."

She sang the line and was absolutely right. It sounded beautiful.

"Change it," I said.

"Yeah?"

"Do it." Instinctively I squeezed Alex's arm. "It sounds lovely like that."

I watched over Alex's shoulder as she rubbed out the music and changed it.

"You think they'll like it?" she asked.

"Who?"

"The person you wrote this for."

"I didn't write it *for* someone," I said. "I wrote it *about* someone."

"Same thing, isn't it?" Alex suggested.

"It's not like that," I said.

I watched as Alex put her can down next to her, then moved slightly as she shuffled herself up onto the sofa beside me. She sat sideways looking at me, one leg tucked under the other.

"So what is it like, then?" she asked. "Are you harbouring feelings for someone?" I saw the mischievousness that danced behind her eyes and immediately felt uncomfortable. "Are you trying to tell someone something?"

My unease escalated.

"Well it's not Josh—what was his name? Year Ten Josh." Alex smiled. "You said it was like kissing a vacuum cleaner, or something like that."

"Stop it, Alex."

"So is it the girl you kissed?" Alex's playful eyes shimmered. "Or another one you're not telling me about?"

"You've got no idea." I shook my head. "So stop teasing."

I saw Nicole in my mind's eye, smirking. I knew what she'd be saying and her voice in my head was crystal clear.

You think you can make everything okay by writing a song about it all? You think that'll ease the guilt? Whatever. If it makes you sleep easier, Tally…

"It is, isn't it?" Alex laughed. Her laugh pushed me over the edge.

"Christ, Alex. You've absolutely *no* idea about any of this." I stood up, kicking over Alex's can of Dr Pepper as I did so and swearing loudly as its contents splashed out across the carpet.

"Shit." Alex sprang to her feet. "I'm sorry. Wait. Let me—"

"It's fine." I brushed her away and strode to the kitchen. I grabbed a cloth and came back into the lounge, then dabbed at the black, sticky mess as it still bubbled and frothed on the carpet, the tears that had been threatening all day filling my eyes.

"I'll go," Alex said. "I'm sorry. I didn't mean to—"

"No," I said, reaching up for her arm. "I'm sorry too. Don't go."

The last thing I wanted was for Alex to leave. Not like that. Not under a cloud after we'd had such an awesome day together.

I looked around for Nicole, but she'd gone.

My hand was still on Alex's arm. While I looked up at her, she put her hand over mine and smiled down at me.

"If you're sure?"

My smile matched hers. "I'm sure," I said.

"It's going to stain, isn't it?" Alex said, looking down at the carpet. "Tal, I'm really sorry."

"I'll ask Ed to get someone in." I followed Alex's gaze down to the carpet. "Place could do with a spring clean anyway."

"It's August."

"You know what I mean."

We were sitting back on the sofa, Dr Pepper cans safely placed away back in the kitchen.

"You think it'll come off?" Alex asked.

The stain. All we could talk about was the stain, like Alex was afraid to speak about "Perspectives" again in case I went off on one like I'd just done.

"Yeah, it'll come off."

The words I wanted to say to Alex about Nicole were just under the surface, just another breath away. Just another long, awkward silence, or another look. But I still couldn't tell her. I knew why, though. I didn't want Alex to feel about me how I felt about myself.

But I also *did* want to tell her. My mind raced.

"Nicole," I finally blurted out. "I wrote 'Perspectives' with her in mind."

"Okay." Alex drew the word out. "Because?"

I chewed at the inside of my cheek. "Remember I told you once before I kissed a girl?"

"Mm-hmm."

“It was Nicole,” I said. “She was my first kiss, and my only kiss with a girl.”

“Was this when you were in the band together?” Alex asked.

I nodded. “About nine months ago.”

“Did you…date?” Alex asked. “Did Robyn and Brooke know?”

“No, we never dated,” I said, “but Robyn and Brooke knew something had happened between us.” I drew in a deep breath. Time to confess. “Nicole wanted to be with me, you know? Like a couple.”

“And you?”

I shook my head. “When we kissed, it took me totally by surprise, and I did really like it at the time,” I said, “but that didn’t mean to say I wanted to be with her.”

“You didn’t fancy her?”

“It was Nicole.” I sighed. “She was my best mate,” I said, frowning. “She was my bandmate. How could I?”

“You didn’t answer my question, though,” Alex said. “Did you fancy her?”

“I don’t know.” I shrugged. “I genuinely don’t know.” I shot Alex a look. “How do you know if you’re into a girl?”

“Oh, you know.” Alex smiled. “She’ll be all you can think about. You’ll go to bed thinking about her, wake up thinking about her. Probably dream about her when you’re asleep too.” She stretched her legs out in front of her. “You’ll do *anything* to please her. Hang on her every word. If you ever make her laugh? You’ll be on cloud nine for hours afterwards.”

I shifted in my seat. I remembered the first time I’d made Alex laugh. I also remembered the feeling of triumph that had accompanied it, and which had stayed with me for a long time afterwards. That had never happened with Nicole. I’d certainly never thought about her all the time either. Never dreamt about her. That had to mean something, surely.

“When did you know?” I asked. “That you liked girls, I mean.”

“Laura Whitworth.” Alex chuckled. “I figured I couldn’t feel that strongly about a girl and not be gay.” She looked at me. “Then, when I met my first girlfriend, it felt so right, you know?”

“But you’re not out?”

"I'm not in either," Alex said. "My parents and brothers know, and that's all that matters to me." She shrugged. "It's nothing to do with anyone else, who I see in my private life."

"I guess not." I looked at her. "So did you tell your parents, or…?"

"My mum had already worked it out," Alex said. "We had the mum chat, and it was the single most embarrassing experience of my life. I was talking to my girlfriend at the time online, you see, and my mum came in on the pretext of asking me if I wanted any laundry doing and then just kind of hung around by my bed while I was having online sex."

"No way!"

"Way." Alex groaned. "She started going on about confusion and the music industry being a hotbed of sexualization and told me to make sure I was comfortable with my sexuality," she said, "and I swear to God I died inside."

"But she was okay with it?" I asked.

"Oh, totally." Alex rested her head back. "My parents are cool like that."

I thought of my own parents. Would they be as cool about it as Alex's? I kind of thought they would be.

"So Nicole liked you, right?" Alex asked, pulling my thoughts away from my parents.

"Yeah."

"Must have been tough for her." Alex paused. "Wait," she said, "is that why she left?"

"We danced around each other for about three months after we'd kissed," I said, "Nicole always hoping I might…" The words caught in my throat. "When I told her I didn't think I wanted to be with her, she, well, she sort of went off the rails a little."

"When Ed approached me to join Be4," Alex said, "he told me Nicole had left to do some solo work."

"She fell in with some people," I said carefully. "Did some stuff."

"Drugs," Alex said.

She made it sound like a declaration rather than a question, but I nodded anyway.

"This is to go no further," I said. "Only a few people know. If the press ever got hold of it…"

"It'll go no further."

I trusted her.

"So where is she now?" Alex asked.

"Croft House," I said, "and two months into her rehab."

"I've heard of it." I saw Alex frown. "A boy from *Sing* talked about it once."

"You know, Ed wouldn't even tell me where she was at first," I said. "I just woke up one day and she was gone. Like she'd never existed." I laid my head back and stared up at a crack on the ceiling. "That was the worst thing. My best mate, just…gone." I rolled my head and looked at Alex. "Whatever had gone on between us, Nicole was still my soul mate."

"You must miss her."

"I do." I looked back up at the ceiling. "The other awful thing is knowing it was me that put her in Croft House in the first place."

"You can't think like that, Tal," Alex said.

"That's not what she told me yesterday."

"You've seen her?" Alex sounded surprised.

"I felt like I needed to," I said. "We were told we couldn't see her at first. When I found out I could, I was straight over there."

"I see." Alex paused. "And?"

"And she hates me." I gave a small laugh. "Still."

"Can't put a Rizla paper between love and hate," Alex murmured.

"Oh, her love for me fizzled out a long time ago, I think," I said. "Now all she feels is resentment that I was the one who put her in rehab."

"Those were her words?"

"Yup," I said. "She said she only started taking drugs because she was so cut up about me."

"That's really unfair."

"Maybe," I said, "but it's probably true."

"Listen, you didn't make her go see those guys in the first place, Tal." Alex looked at me. "There had to be other reasons—something else going on in her life—that made her take that first hit."

"Tell that to the voices in my head."

Alex sat up straighter. "How is she now?" she asked. "I mean, is she clean?"

"She says so." I sighed. "Funnily enough, when I went to see her, she wasn't so keen to talk pleasantries with me."

"And 'Perspectives'?" Alex asked. "You wrote that for her?"

"My lame way of telling her I'm sorry," I said. "Maybe a way of easing my guilt, I don't know."

Alex reached over and took my hand. I looked down at it, nestled in mine, and felt a warmth spread up my arm.

"You have to stop beating yourself up over Nicole," Alex said softly. "People get rejected all the time. It doesn't mean they have to go out and take a shitload of drugs to get over someone." Her brow creased. "That sounded harsh," she said. "What I meant was, Nicole took stuff to ease her unhappiness over…whatever it was that was making her unhappy. You, her life, her music. Who knows?" Alex shrugged. "What you have to remember, when you're down on yourself over it, is that she's in the right place now, getting help." She tilted her head and smiled at me. "Maybe it was all a cry for help. Maybe she just needed a little time out."

"But she told me it was my fault," I said, my voice cracking. "She swore and screamed at me and I hated myself for what I'd done."

"She only said it because she wanted to punish you for hurting her," Alex said. "So she told you something she knew would hurt you back." She indicated to the sheet of paper with "Perspectives" written on it. "Write your song, Tal. Get it out. Show her you're sorry, then try to move on."

I followed Alex's eyes to the paper and sighed.

She was right, I knew. I *did* have to move on. I *did* have to stop beating myself up over Nicole.

Easy, right?

CHAPTER FIFTEEN

It was nearly nine p.m. by the time Alex and I realized we hadn't eaten. Time flies when you're having the time of your life, sitting in the comfort of your own apartment, writing music with someone you liked, I guessed.

"Takeaway?" Alex asked. She extended her arms above her head and gave a sort of yodelling yawn. "I'm starving."

"I've kept you here forever." I dropped the sheet of manuscript paper with all our scribblings on it next to me. "I'm so sorry."

"You're kidding, right?" Alex looked at me. "I've had the best time ever." She pulled her knees up. "And we've got this little beauty all finished." She nodded her head down to the paper on the floor.

I followed her gaze down and felt a rush of satisfaction. "Perspectives" was written and, I thought, was pretty near perfect. I just hoped Brooke and Robyn felt the same way when they eventually heard it. I slipped a look over to Alex. And I hoped they wouldn't be pissed with me that they hadn't been involved in any of the writing.

I tried to push that thought to the back of my head, because I didn't want it to spoil what had been the perfect evening. Now, as the evening light was waning and casting a deep orange glow throughout my apartment, I was happy to let "Perspectives" play over in my head, and for Alex to be with me for as long as she wanted to be. I stole another look to her, her head flopped back on my sofa, and figured she didn't look as though she was ready to go anywhere.

My stomach gave a low grumble, reminding me how late it was.

"You didn't answer my question about a takeaway," Alex said, not lifting her head, "but your stomach just did."

A broad grin spread across her face, making me laugh.

"There's a pizza place downstairs," I said, scrabbling to my feet. "Or Indian. Or Chinese. Take your pick."

"Pizza sounds awesome." Alex got to her feet too.

I grabbed my wallet from the kitchen and thumbed out a note, then turned to see Alex standing in the doorway, watching me. She was resting a shoulder against the door frame, her hands in her pockets, and looked…happy. Content. Like she belonged there. I liked seeing her there. It felt right and, I don't know, comfortable.

As I approached her, she said, "You stay here. I can run down and fetch us something," and held up a scrunched up twenty-pound note in her hand.

I held up mine too and laughed.

"You can't pay for pizza when I've kept you here all day," I said, still laughing.

"Who says?" she asked, not moving from the doorway.

"Me." I stood in front of her. "Seriously, Alex. This is on me. You've no idea how grateful I am you gave up your day to help me."

"I didn't give up anything." Alex shrugged. "I wouldn't have wanted to be anywhere else."

She looked at me for the longest time, until I finally broke the gaze.

"You're still not paying for pizza," I said.

"Okay," she said, reaching over and pulling the note from my hand, "but I'm fetching it."

Before I could protest, she'd pushed herself away from the door and was making for my front door.

"Do you always get your own way?" I called from the kitchen.

"Oh yes." Alex looked back over her shoulder to me, one eyebrow raised. "Always."

❖

“One large pepperoni pizza.”

The smell was amazing. Alex handed me the box, and I lifted it to my nose and sniffed it some more.

“How did you know that was my favourite?” I asked.

“I took a gamble.” She wandered back into the lounge and sank into the sofa. “Guess I was right, huh?”

I followed her in and was just about to ask her about garlic dip when she pointed to a small pot on the table in front of her.

“And before you ask,” she said, “yeah. Garlic dip.”

I sat next to her. Could she be any more perfect right now?

The pizza was awesome, and as I bit into my slice, I made a mental note to tell Anando, the guy that ran the place, that I thought he made the best pizzas this side of the Thames.

“I was thinking about ‘Perspectives’ while I was waiting for the pizza to arrive,” Alex said, putting her half-eaten slice back in the box then wiping her mouth with a tissue. “I think a modulation in verse three could work.”

“You were still thinking about it?” That was cute.

“Of course.” Alex picked her slice of pizza back up again. “It’s an awesome song. It’s officially my new earworm.”

I laughed.

“So are you happy with it?” Alex asked through a mouthful of pizza. She had a string of cheese on her bottom lip which I was just about to point out when she licked it off. “You should play it for me again.”

“Totally.” I crammed the last of my pizza into my mouth and wiped my hands down my trousers, a habit of mine that my mum always loathed, then picked up my guitar. The intro sounded good, and I smiled down at the guitar as I picked at the strings, knowing I had the chords just as I wanted them to sound, and knowing how well they’d melt into the first line.

I sang my vocals, occasionally glancing over to Alex, who was nodding her approval. She reached past my feet and picked up the manuscript paper from the floor, then started singing with me, our voices blending into one another’s. For the first time that day, Nicole didn’t slip into my thoughts as I sang the words I’d written to her.

Instead, I focused my attention on Alex, drawing energy from her singing, feeling a connection with her that was so profound, it was almost overwhelming.

As I played the last chord on my guitar, Alex threw herself back on the sofa, raised her hands above her head, and clapped.

"It sounds amazing." Alex turned to me then, her face flushed from the singing, looking bright and alive.

"I know, right?" I put my guitar back down.

"Our first song that we wrote together." She looked happy.

"Our first number one together, bet you," I said.

"I like your thinking." Alex smiled.

A silence nestled between us, but it wasn't an awkward one. Instead, it seemed to me to be one of a shared satisfaction of a job well done, and of a comfort in one another's company.

As if reading my mind, Alex suddenly said, "This is nice. Pizza, writing music. Hanging out." The look on her face made me smile. "I think I could get used to this."

I loved that she said that.

I figured I could easily get used to it as well.

Chapter Sixteen

I woke up the next morning to a text. From Alex.

Come and play? xxx

She'd left me shortly before midnight the night before, after we'd had another jam of "Perspectives" and then had rounded the evening off watching a crap horror DVD that Robyn had let me have months before, and that was about as scary as *Bambi*. Then Alex had gone, and I figured I must have lain in bed for a good hour thinking about our evening together before I finally fell asleep.

Now, reading her text, I couldn't stop the smile that spread across my face. Couldn't stem the warmth that flooded my body. I read her text for a third time, this time focusing on the three kisses she'd put at the end. Should I have felt this happy? The sense of anticipation of an afternoon hanging out in the sunshine with Alex was profound, and my mind was already racing ahead to what I ought to wear. It was only after I'd scrambled out of bed and had emptied the entire contents of my wardrobe on my bedroom floor that the reality kicked in: it was just an afternoon out with Alex. I should have felt the same as I would have done if Brooke or Robyn had texted me and asked me to hang out too, but I didn't. The prospect of being with Alex was different—*better*—than any afternoon with anyone else, and I knew it was pointless me trying to deny it.

I moved the pile of clothes up into a heap with my foot and, in the process, unearthed a pair of faded jeans I'd not seen in months. I bent down and picked them up. I just needed to throw some clothes on and stop thinking too much about anything. Spend the afternoon with Alex. Eat ice cream. Watch the kids that always hung around the park playing football. Walk. Talk. Like friends do.

Yeah. Just like friends do.

❖

The park was quieter than I'd thought it would be. The heatwave that still hung over the UK showed no signs of going anywhere fast, and it seemed the scattering of people that were there were keen to make the most of it while it lasted. Strolling tourists mingled with cyclists on paths and a handful of children feeding ducks, while somewhere in the distance I was certain I could hear a brass band playing, over, I presumed, in the large bandstand by the café. It was all very…English.

It was midday, and the sun was now at its highest point in the sky. As I walked with Alex, I squinted up into the perfect blue sky, unblemished except for the criss-cross of snowy white vapour trails left by the morning's passing planes.

"Here?" Alex asked, pulling my gaze from the sky back to her. She was pointing to a spot under a tree which was some way from us. "Or would you rather sit out here in the sun?"

I weighed up my options for a moment, then thought about my already deeply suntanned skin, and chose the tree option. I walked with Alex over to the tree, briefly waiting for her as she deviated from her path to kick a stray football back to its owner, then fell back into step with her.

Finally, with the rucksack with our picnic in it dropped at our feet, we both sank down onto the rough grass. A silence followed as we both sat, our backs against the tree, and watched the activities in the park around us. I drew my knees up closer to my chest and circled my arms around them, hugging them closer to me, then blankly watched two dogs chasing each other across the grass.

"This is perfect."

Alex voiced my thoughts, and as I turned to meet her eye, a ghost of a smile touched her lips. She looked so happy. As happy as she had in my apartment the night before, and I did briefly wonder if it was my company that was making her so content, or our surroundings.

My thoughts drifted first to Brooke, then to Robyn, having their shopping marathon just across London. Oxford Street was just a stone's throw from us, but to me, it could have been miles away. My days off in the past had invariably been like that: shopping for clothes I neither liked nor wanted, followed by dinner crammed into a noisy, sweaty London restaurant where we'd have to shout at one another to be heard over the noise.

Back then Nicole had always loved our days off. But it wasn't always the same for me; there were times when I'd have loved nothing more than to just hang out somewhere quiet—a country park, the beach. I'd rarely want to do anything she or Brooke or Robyn wanted to do, but so I wouldn't ever be accused of being boring, or a killjoy, I'd always comply. That's how it had been, more often than not. Appeasement. Submission.

I slipped a look to Alex. This, to me, was perfection. Sitting in the peace and quiet of a park, far away from the hustle and bustle of the city, with someone I really wanted to be with.

I couldn't stop looking at Alex. Her face was raised to the sun, allowing me a few precious moments to properly study her. The sun liked her, I decided, accentuating the smattering of freckles high on her cheeks, while giving her skin a beautiful honeyed tone.

A shout from across the park made Alex open her eyes, immediately pulling my attention away. I gazed out across the park, trying to see if I could see who'd called out, then made some pithy comment to Alex about the moment being ruined, which made her laugh. I liked her laugh, I decided. More than that, I liked that I'd been able to make her laugh.

"Do you suppose it's too early to break open the sandwiches?" Alex asked, looking down at the rucksack next to her. "I thought maybe we could seek out an ice cream van later this afternoon," she said, "if you want?"

Alex wanted a later. She wanted the day to go on.

"Ice cream with chocolate flakes?" I asked, tilting my head to one side.

"Ice cream with whatever you want in it." Alex laughed again, and my sense of satisfaction intensified.

We held each other's gaze, matching smiles on our faces.

Another shout, closer this time, and I turned round just in time to see a dog approaching, its tail a wagging blur. It briefly snuffled around us, then sat next to Alex and leant against her. She pulled on its ears and whispered to it that it was lovely, then scrambled to her feet and pointed to a red-faced middle-aged woman who was jogging towards us, a lead dangling loosely in her hand. I watched as Alex met her halfway, heard the light laugh, the lifting of her hands, the brief touch of the woman's arm that I guessed meant Alex was telling her not to stress about her dog. From where I was sitting, I could see the smile on the woman's face, then saw Alex bend over and ruffle the dog's head, before returning to me.

"She said her dog loved people," Alex said as she flopped back down next to me. "I told her I loved dogs." She blew her fringe from her eyes. "Just as well, hey?"

"How old's yours?" I asked.

"Jasper?" Alex asked. "Four." A smile spread across her face. "I miss him every day."

"We never had dogs at home," I said, opening the rucksack and pulling our tightly wrapped sandwiches out. "Just cats."

"We have a cat too, somewhere," Alex said. She took her sandwich from me and started to unwrap it.

"Somewhere?"

"It lives outside." She shrugged. "Seems happy enough. She comes in occasionally to eat, then disappears into the night again."

"Sounds like Robyn."

Alex grinned as she bit into her sandwich.

"I'm going home this weekend, actually," she said between mouthfuls. "I figured I'd make the most of it being a long weekend."

A small pang of disappointment which had apparently appeared from nowhere, hit my chest. Trying to ignore it, I picked up my sandwich and bit into it.

"Suffolk, right?" I asked.

"You remembered."

"Of course I did." I took another bite.

"Everyone's going to be there." Alex gazed off into the distance. "Parents, brothers."

I'm sure I saw her visibly relax.

"It's been too long, you know?" she said.

"I know." I nodded. "I miss my parents too…" My words disappeared as a wasp decided to choose that moment to land on my sandwich. I flicked it off, annoying it, then spent the next few seconds trying to avoid it. "I try to see them as often as possible, but it's not always that easy, is it?"

Alex shook her head. "Do you want to move away from the wasp?" She batted it away from me.

I shook my head. "It's cool."

She put her sandwich down and sprawled closer over to me, then, leaning on one hand, reached out and flicked the wasp from my shoulder.

"Why do they do that?" I asked, shuddering. "They never leave you alone." I looked around, relieved to see that in fact the wasp *had* finally left me alone.

"Are you sure you're okay here?" Alex tossed a look out to the park. "We could go find a bench somewhere else."

"I'm fine." I touched her arm. "Don't stress."

I carried on eating, thinking about how much I liked how she was with me. I liked the attention, the care. Alex made me feel special, like I was the only one that mattered to her, and while I knew she was probably like this with everyone she knew, I allowed myself to enjoy the sensation while it lasted.

"So what about you?" Alex suddenly asked. "Any plans for the weekend?"

"Staying here." I sighed. "Although London when it's eighty degrees is never any fun."

"My parents live up on the coast," Alex said. "It's lovely when it's like this because the sea breeze keeps things cooler."

"I liked that living down in Brighton," I said. "It's what I miss the most living in London. The sea."

"So go home." Alex picked a blade of grass. "Chill out in Brighton with your parents."

"I wish I could." I screwed up my nose. "But they're on holiday in Italy until the end of the month, so there's no point."

Alex screwed up her sandwich wrapper, then shuffled away slightly from the tree and lay back on the grass.

"Come to Suffolk with me then," she said, rolling her head to look at me. "Meet my bonkers parents."

My heart gave a small jump, and even though I didn't want to think too much about what that meant, my mind was already tearing ahead, thinking about hanging out with Alex in her own home for an entire weekend.

"You're okay." I lay down on the grass too and figured I'd sounded pretty convincing. "Thanks anyway. I wouldn't want to intrude."

"Seriously, Tal." Alex propped herself up on her elbow. "They'd love it." She paused. "*I'd* love it."

I squinted up at her.

"They're planning a barbecue on the beach," she said, smiling down at me. "They'd be disappointed if they knew I'd invited you and you didn't come."

"Your parents don't know me." I laughed.

"They love meeting my friends."

Without warning, Alex reached down and picked a piece of dried grass from my T-shirt and flicked it away, like it was the most normal thing in the world for her to do.

"Please?" she asked.

I looked up at her as she looked down at me and knew at that moment that there was nothing I'd like more than to spend an entire weekend in her company.

"Well if you're sure?" I asked.

"Never been surer." Alex flopped back down next to me. "We're going to have a blast, I just know it."

Chapter Seventeen

Her parents' house was awesome. Way bigger than my parents' place and with a view that stretched so far out to sea I was sure I could see France from it. Of course, when I told Alex that she laughed and said, "We're on the east coast, so you'd have a job from here, Tal," and I felt a bit stupid.

It didn't last, though. Before I even had a chance to go inside and meet her parents, Alex grabbed me by the hand and took me onto her parent's front lawn, where she stood with me, an arm casually flung around my shoulder as she pointed out to sea.

"Down there," she said, flagging a finger to the right, "Belgium if you're lucky." She steered my shoulders to the left. "Denmark is way, way over that way." She straightened me. "Dead ahead is Holland." Then she quickly pulled me to her before releasing me again. "But no France, I'm afraid."

"Geography never was my strong point." I wrapped my arms around myself and gazed out.

"I spent most of my childhood standing on this lawn wondering, if I took a boat out, where it would take me," Alex said. "Then a large chunk of my early teens playing my guitar out here wondering if anyone across the water could hear it." She laughed. "Silly really."

"It sounds lovely."

"It was." Alex smiled. "I was very happy here."

"I can see why." I threw a look over my shoulder as I heard a shout from the house, swiftly followed by excited barking as a small and very hairy ginger-and-white terrier tore out of the house and raced across the lawn to us, its short legs a blur across the grass.

I watched as Alex fell to her knees and embraced the dog, pulling on its ears and rolling it onto its back so she could ruffle the fur on its chest. It lay on the grass, kicking its legs about, making Alex laugh, and I joined her, tickling its chest, albeit less robustly than Alex was.

"Jasper," Alex said, her face shining with happiness. "Your brother's namesake."

"Hello, Jasper." I sat back on my haunches as Jasper righted himself and jumped up to lick my face.

"Okay, enough."

At Alex's command, Jasper stepped back, shook himself, then trotted off to investigate a bumblebee on a flower. I looked up to see a woman, whom I presumed to be Alex's mother, waiting for us in the doorway. I stood up, brushing dried grass from my jeans, then hauled Alex to her feet.

"My mum will probably make some comment to me about introducing you to the dog before her," Alex whispered in my ear as we walked together to the front door, making me laugh.

"We got an earlier train," Alex called over to her mother as we approached. "Hope that was okay."

"It's always okay." Her mother met her on the grass and pulled her into her arms. She said something to her I didn't catch, then smiled at me over her shoulder. "You must be Tally." Her mother released Alex and held out a hand to me. "I've heard a lot about you."

"None of it's true." I smiled, surprised at her announcement, and returned her brief handshake. "Well, not all of it."

"I'm sorry Alex thought to show you off to her dog before me," her mother said, grabbing Alex in her arms again. "I think Jasper comes far higher in her priorities." She squeezed Alex, making her squeal, then released her, ruffling her hair as she did so.

I couldn't look at Alex, because I knew if I did I'd laugh.

We followed her mother into the house, Alex holding the door open for me with a quick wink and a "told you so" quip as I entered the house. As we approached a closed door inside the hallway I heard the low rumble of voices behind it, and for the first time that day, felt a flutter of nerves at the prospect of meeting Alex's family.

A sea of faces hit me as we entered the room.

"So this is the Brody clan," Alex said. She threaded an arm across my shoulder and pointed round the room. "Dad, Joshua my brother, Eva his girlfriend, and some squirt I hardly recognize because he's grown at least another foot since I last saw him." She dropped her arm from my shoulder and went straight over to a smallish boy whose face had lit up the moment he'd seen her, hauling him up as far as she could into her arms before dropping him again. "And you've put on weight."

"So have you, fatty." The boy quickly embraced her, his face flaming bright red, then returned to his seat and the iPad he'd been using when we first came in.

"My younger brother, Sebastian." I nodded and smiled at Sebastian, who flashed me a shy smile in return, then I stood and waited while Alex hugged her father and Joshua, finally accepting the seat that was offered to me, with apologies from her mother for not being a good host.

The next hour was, apparently, catch-up time. I sat and listened, coffee cup cradled in my hands, as Alex spoke excitedly and animatedly, about London and her new life in Be4. About the festival. About the next single. About how much she was loving it all. Occasionally our eyes would meet, and I'd add a thought or an anecdote of my own, but in the main I was happy to sit back and hear directly from Alex just what she was thinking. It was cathartic, I thought, to hear her innermost thoughts about her life with us. With Be4. To hear just how much she liked us, how grateful she was to have had another stab at making it in music, after years of trying. To see her parents' faces so happy to see her, and to hear she was happy too.

That morning in her parents' front room confirmed one vital point to me: Alex really was Be4.

❖

Her room, when we'd finally managed to leave her parents' company, was exactly as I expected it to be. Classily decorated and orderly, but with just a hint of ramshackle threatening around the edges, thanks to the enormous number of vinyls that took up an entire wall.

As I stepped inside, the vinyls were the only thing I could see. Stacked from floor to ceiling, if I'd even tried to count them, it would have been impossible.

"My folks sure like to talk." Alex closed the door and leant against it, puffing out her cheeks. "I'm so sorry."

"Don't be." I went and sat on her bed. "I think they're lovely."

"They worry about me, I think." Alex wrinkled her nose. "The den of iniquity that is the music world and all that."

"When the truth—well for us anyway—is that it's just bloody hard work." I laughed. "My parents are the same. My daily calls home to them to tell them all I do all day is sit in a studio and sing, then go home and sleep, reassure them slightly, I think." I caught Alex's eye. "But only slightly."

Alex smiled. "You said at the park yesterday that you missed them," she said. "Do you find all this as tough as I do?"

"I miss them every day," I replied. "But I'm doing what I've always wanted to do, and as long as I get to see them as often as possible, I'm happy." I looked at her. "And I know my parents well. If I'm happy, they're happy."

Alex shoved herself away from the door and joined me on her bed.

"So tell me how you've managed to get such an epic record collection." I lifted my chin to the wall opposite us. Talking about my parents was making me miss them even more than normal.

Alex followed my gaze. "I'm a compulsive collector of old Motown," she said, and then laughed. "Unfortunately, there's *lots* of stuff I like."

"Motown?" I asked. "How cool is that?"

"Rare Stevie Wonder stuff," Alex said, "other things like that."

I stood up and sauntered to the shelves on the wall, casting my eye over the records. "In alphabetical order," I said. "Impressive."

"Obsessive, more like."

"Maybe a bit." I smiled back over my shoulder. "But still impressive."

"Have you heard this?" Alex joined me. She traced her finger along the line and pulled out a sleeve, then handed it to me. "Recorded live in Paris."

I looked at the sleeve and shook my head.

"And this one is awesome," Alex said, thumbing another one out. "Lounge sessions always sound immense, I think."

I took the record from her.

"They only cut around a hundred copies of this," she said, "but thanks to the Internet, I have one of those hundred copies."

I flipped another one out. "And this one?"

"Only released in the US." Alex took it from me and turned it over. "So I asked around," she said, shrugging, "and I got."

"I love all of these." I held the vinyls carefully in my hand. "You're so lucky to have them."

"The original 1960s version on this is amazing," Alex said, showing me another one. "I think you'd like it." She reached for another. "And this one. The guitar solo in it is beautiful. Almost as good as yours." She shoulder-bumped me. "Almost."

"I'd love to hear it." I put one of the records back. "Well, all of them really."

"I'll burn you some copies," Alex said. "I've got a spare USB here somewhere."

"You don't have to."

"They're all on my PC in London," she said. "It'll be no hassle."

"I'd like that." I was touched she'd even offered.

"You should come over one day," Alex said, nodding, "to my apartment. I've set up a music room. You'd love it."

"I'd like that too." I really meant it.

Alex put one of the records on while I returned to sit on her bed, admiring how carefully she removed it from its sleeve and placed it on the turntable, quite unlike my grab-and-shove technique which always, without exception, left a thumbprint on my CDs.

"The barbecue on the beach is later, by the way," she said as she adjusted the volume. "I hope you're not vegetarian."

"Nah." I shook my head. "I like burgers too much."

"There's still loads I don't know about you." Alex dipped her head to see the volume button better on her stereo, her hair flopping artfully over her eyes, and looked over to me from under her hair. "But I want to."

"Do you?"

"Yeah," she said, returning to the bed. "I really do."

"Okay." I slotted my hands under my legs and sat on them as she joined me. "Well, I like music. You know that."

"I know that."

"I just said." I grinned at her.

"Tell me something I don't know."

"Like what?"

"I don't know." Alex gave a small laugh. "What's your favourite colour?"

"Blue. You?"

"Red."

"Food?"

"Ooh, tricky." I gazed up. "Lasagne, probably." I looked at her. "You?"

"Bacon sandwiches," she said, "with loads of sauce."

"Nice." I nodded.

"Why didn't you want to be with Nicole?" Alex asked.

"Okay, that was random." I pulled my hands out from under my legs and placed them in my lap.

"I just thought of it." Alex shrugged.

I studied my nails, wondering how I could explain about Nicole properly without sounding like I was a horrible person, like I thought I had when I'd told Alex before.

"I already told you before," I said.

"Well, only kind of."

"I wouldn't have wanted to be with someone like her," I said, wishing Alex would change the subject.

"How was she?"

"Chaotic." I laughed through my nose. "Can you say someone is chaotic?"

"I guess."

"She was chaotic then," I said. "Her life was a mess."

"How?"

"She was moody," I said. "Up and down."

"Aren't we all?" Alex suggested.

"But not like she was," I said. "She was my BFF and I loved her like crazy—I *love* her like crazy—but I could never be with someone like her. Not like that." I looked at Alex. "Having Nicole as a girlfriend and having to be in the band with her would have been a total car crash."

"You didn't even want to try?" Alex asked.

"No." I shot Alex a look. Enough with all the questions. "So what do you fancy doing this afternoon?"

"You like to change the subject, don't you," Alex said, "when you don't like the questions."

"And you like to persist with the questions," I replied, "when it's bloody obvious I don't want to answer them."

"Fair point." Alex held up her hands. "Beach?"

"What?"

"We could walk Jasper on the beach."

"Deal."

❖

I'd never seen a dog run so fast. Bearing in mind the temperature outside was still knocking on eighty degrees, Jasper seemed to manage to ignore that fact and run and bark and investigate every inch of the beach near Alex's house as if the sun beating down on us didn't matter at all.

The beach was surprisingly quiet for a Saturday afternoon, just a smattering of kids building sandcastles and a few people venturing into the sea. I walked barefoot along the shoreline, Alex some way ahead of me, my shoes in my hands, my feet squelching into the soft sand as I walked.

We weren't alone, though. When we'd mentioned we were taking Jasper for a walk, there followed a good five minutes of everyone else in the house deciding whether or not to join us, then another five minutes rounding everyone up, until finally, the whole of Alex's family were walking with us.

I kind of minded that, and I knew I shouldn't have. After all, the whole point of Alex coming home was to see her parents, but there was a part of me that wanted to walk with her alone so we could talk about music, the band, anything. I just wanted to talk to her. And that was really selfish of me.

Sebastian too was stoked Alex wanted to take a walk with him. As they walked side by side, I could see in the way he kept looking at her that he idolized her, and it was obvious she loved him just as much. She was fabulous with him too, and the thought that Alex could be so adorable made my heart leap each time I saw another look pass between them or heard a joke made at the other's expense. As I sauntered along, I watched her occasionally chase him in and out of the water's edge, smiling as I heard his squeals escalate as each time she drove him further and further into the water.

While I watched them playing, I saw a girl wave over to them, then approach. I assumed it was Eva, until I looked further up the water's edge and saw her still walking with Joshua. Alex stopped playing with Sebastian, bent down to—I assumed—say something to him, then veered slightly to the left, away from the water, towards the girl, while Sebastian ran on ahead and caught up with Joshua and Eva.

"So Alex tells me you play guitar too."

The low voice beside me made me jump. Her father was talking to me. How long had he been walking next to me? I'd been so absorbed in watching Alex, I had no idea I had company.

"Yeah." I brought my focus back to him. "Classical, acoustic. Any guitar I can get my hands on really."

"We watched a recording of you all on *The Afternoon Show* the other day," her father said. "We try and keep everything Alex does."

"Alex was awesome that day," I said, looking over to her retreating back. "Totally charmed the audience."

"She could charm the birds from the trees, that one." He smiled over to Alex.

She was still walking with the girl; it looked as though they were deep in conversation as they wandered slowly side by side along the water's edge.

An unfamiliar sensation washed over me. I couldn't take my eyes from them as I wondered who she was, and why she was talking to Alex. I shook my head. None of it was any business of mine.

"Alex's been great for us," I said to her father, thinking I ought to talk to him rather than stare at Alex. "Everything's just gone a bit mad since she joined us."

"She's very happy, I know," her father said. "I can tell when my daughter's content."

We were catching them up. I tried to look anywhere but towards them, but my peripheral vision picked out a hug, then the sense that one of them had gone. When I finally looked back over their way, Alex was standing alone, facing us.

As we approached, her eyes were firmly on mine, and I knew I wasn't misreading the look of unease on her face. Her expression was different, guarded, almost as if she was trying to read my face too.

"Was that...?" Her father intervened. "What was her name again?"

"Laurel." Alex's voice sounded different.

"Laurel. That's right." Her father linked his arm in hers. "I haven't seen her around here for ages."

"No."

"She okay?" he asked.

"Seemed to be." Alex's answer was clipped.

As I fell into step beside Alex and her father, I wanted to ask her who Laurel was, and I suppose a part of me thought I shouldn't have to wait to ask because Alex might tell me herself without being prompted. But she didn't say any more about who Laurel is, was, or could be. Instead, she said something to her father about how warm she'd become whilst walking, and I definitely noted a purposeful change in subject from her. Then we resumed our pace, leaving me with a headful of questions and absolutely no answers at all.

The light from the barbecue fire cloaked everything in a warm glow, the occasional spark from the wood sending shards of orange sparks into the night sky, where they danced and twirled for a second before finally disappearing.

I'd eaten far too much, but that still didn't stop me from joining Joshua and Eva toasting marshmallows over the embers. I didn't even like marshmallows, so I had no idea why I was doing it. It just seemed…right. And nice. We stretched out on the sand, still warm from the day's sunshine, and twisted and waved our sticks over the heat of the fire, laughing if one of our marshmallows fell off and into it.

Alex's family were the best, I'd decided. I looked around me, to her mum, dad, brother. To Sebastian trying to encourage a reluctant Jasper into the sea with him. This was Alex's life outside of London and I really liked it. There was an ordinariness about it which was reassuring and a far cry from my life, messy as it could sometimes be. Certainly as it had been with Nicole in it. Having Alex as a friend felt calming, quite unlike the roller coaster of emotions that had accompanied my friendship with Nicole. I missed Nicole, but that evening I realized I missed what we'd had, rather than what we'd become, and I knew with a startling clarity that I could never go back.

So I needed to look to the future. I glanced at Alex, wondering how or if she could feature in that, and my mind started wandering. I felt sleepy from food and conversation, relaxed from feeling comfortable with the company I was in. But even though I was so tired, and my eyes desperately wanted to shut, nothing in me wanted to leave the beach, or Alex. I looked over to her, the slow flickering of the embers illuminating her face, and felt ludicrously happy. She was sitting cross-legged and talking to her dad, but as she did so, she glanced over. Our eyes met across the fire, held, then parted, only to meet again a few seconds later. When it happened a third time, I watched as she said something to her dad, rubbed his arm, then scrambled to her feet and came over to me.

"I've been neglecting you," Alex said, slumping down next to me. "I'm sorry."

"We've been looking after her," Joshua said. "Tally can sure toast marshmallows well."

"I've been busy." I smiled. How could I tell her I wasn't looking at her to summon her over? That I was only staring at her because

I just couldn't help myself? "Want one?" I pulled my stick from the fire and held it up.

She pulled the marshmallow from the stick, then hopped the melting gooiness from hand to hand before blowing on it and taking a hesitant bite.

"It's hot." Alex held it between her teeth, winced, then chewed it back. "Nice, though." She laughed, then took the stick from my hand and slotted another marshmallow onto it.

I watched her as she turned the stick against the heat, tilting her head to one side as she carefully made sure the marshmallow didn't burn. Another wave of contentment washed over me. A sense of peace, and at that moment our life in London seemed a million miles away.

As if sensing my thoughts, Alex pulled her stick from the fire, blew on the smoking marshmallow, and said, "Not quite Camden, is it?" before putting the stick back over the heat.

I drew my knees to my chest and dug my bare feet into the soft sand. I rested my chin on my knees and smiled as I watched her. "Not quite Camden, no," was all I could say.

I lifted my head as Alex pulled the stick from the fire and unthreaded the marshmallow from it. She quickly blew on it and offered it to me, jabbing her stick into the sand and sitting back as I took the marshmallow from her and ate it.

"Dad said he'd like to hear us play together, by the way," Alex said. "Fancy it?"

"A jam on the beach." Joshua pulled his own stick from the fire. "Sounds right up your street."

"Fancy it?" Alex repeated, looking at me.

I nodded. It sounded like the perfect way to round off the evening.

She smiled broadly and got to her feet, then disappeared into the darkness. When she'd gone, Joshua scooted across the sand and sat back down next to me.

"That'll have made her day." He stretched his legs out in front of him and leant back on his hands. "If there's one thing Alex loves in this life, it's having any opportunity to get that darned guitar out and play it to people." He laughed. "I'm joking about the *darned* bit, by the way," he said. "I love that she loves it."

"Oh, I enjoy any chance I get too," I said.

Joshua nodded then looked away. When he looked back to me, he said, "So how long have you two been dating?"

"I'm sorry?"

"You and Alex?"

"Oh, we're not girlfriends." I picked up a handful of sand and let it fall through my fingers. "Just friends." I shot him a smile and hoped that he couldn't see in the darkness what I knew must be my blushing cheeks.

"My bad." Joshua held his hands up. "It's just...well, all I can say is you must be a pretty special friend to her."

"You think?" My stomach gave a small twinge.

"Alex *never* brings anyone here to the house," Joshua said.

My mind tumbled back to the park, when Alex had first invited me over.

My parents love meeting my friends.

That's what she'd said. She'd made it sound as though she invited people to stay all the time. I was on the brink of asking Joshua who Laurel was, and whether *she* had ever come to the house, when he added, "I'm sorry if I got the wrong idea," then glanced over his shoulder as we both heard footsteps approaching. He glanced up as Alex arrived back with us. "Hey," he said. "Got them?"

The music we created was sweet. There was something magical about sitting around the fire, the heat of the day finally lifting from the sand and allowing the night air to spread its cool fingers around us. The water lapping against the shore added to the relaxed atmosphere of the evening, mixing with the sound of mine and Alex's strings as we played.

I loved that everyone sang with us too, as Alex and I played cover versions of well-known songs, occasionally getting the words wrong and making them up as they went along. There was no self-consciousness from any of her family, each person singing as well or as badly as they could, finally falling into a laughing heap when each and every one of us forgot the words to a Beatles song that we should have all known.

"You two should be in a band." Joshua laughed at his own joke when we finished. "You can play, you can sing. What more do you want?"

I caught Alex's eye.

"Shall we?" I asked. "Shall we just forget about Robyn and Brooke and elope somewhere together?"

Alex smiled but didn't answer.

Her silence got swallowed up in the chatter around us as her parents drew the conversation away from Joshua's joke and talked to her about a neighbour that Alex obviously knew very well. I watched her as she listened to them, her eyes occasionally returning to mine. She fiddled with her guitar while she listened, tightening strings and tuning, but I could sense her attention wasn't fully on either her parents or her guitar.

Finally, when others had drifted away from me and I realized I had no one to talk to, I placed the guitar that Alex had given me on the sand, stood, and wandered away from the fire. I sauntered down to the water's edge, the babble of conversations lessening as I walked further away from everyone.

The moon was bright in the clear night sky, casting a wobble of white across the horizon, and illuminating the few boats that were out at sea. There wasn't a breath of wind in the air, with just the sound of the water slapping and sucking against the sand to fill my ears.

I thought of Nicole again. I tried to picture her, wondering what counted for entertainment at Croft House at nearly eleven p.m. on a balmy Saturday night in August. I figured it wouldn't be anything as awesome as everything I'd done that evening. That brought with it the usual claw of guilt, and the return to thinking of her rehab as being a prison, even though now I'd visited it I knew differently. My mind wouldn't have it though, and as I stared out to the sea, I imagined bars on windows and Nicole's face looking out at me.

I cut my glance away, as if doing so would shake the images from my head, and stared out at a boat's mast, gently bobbing like a metronome in the sea.

But they refused to go, and my thoughts about Nicole's life still hung in my mind, the threads of them pulling me back through the doors of Croft House and to her.

Would she ever be the same again? Once she'd finally left Croft House, could she return to normal and stay clean, or would she fall back into her dark days again? Would she ever want to see me again? I just didn't know, and while there was a part of me that couldn't wait for Nicole to come out of rehab, there was another, bigger part of me that was dreading it.

"There you are."

I heard Alex's breathless voice before I saw her.

"I saw you get up and go," she said, finally appearing next to me. "I hope you weren't feeling left out."

"I wanted to look at the sea, that was all." I turned, smiled at her, then returned to looking out to sea. "There's something very relaxing about listening to it, don't you think?"

"Joshua and I used to sometimes camp down here when we were little," Alex said. "I used to love waking up early and listening to it from inside my tent."

"I miss it," I said. "The sea. I ought to go home more often."

I meant it too. I couldn't remember the last time I'd spent more than twenty-four hours at my childhood home.

"It's the downside of fame," Alex said. "No time to do anything but work."

"But the upside is our parents are proud of us," I said. "Your parents in particular."

"You think?"

"The way your parents have talked to me about you today," I said, "I know."

"It must have been awful for them when I told them all I ever wanted to be was a musician." Alex stared out. "I hope I've proved them I was right."

"Your parents adore you," I said. "Anyone can see that."

"They think you're fabulous too, by the way." Alex looked at me. "Dad just said. Back up there." She jerked her thumb over her shoulder.

"I talked to him a lot today." My words slowed. "On the beach earlier," I said, "when you were chatting to that girl."

Alex nodded.

"What was her name again?" I asked, hoping I wasn't being too obvious.

"Laurel."

Without saying any more, she threaded her fingers through mine and rubbed her thumb against my skin. We stood in silence, hand in hand, looking out to sea. It didn't feel weird, holding hands with her. It just felt nice and her hand felt warm in mine. Comfortable. Like it should be there. Like it was always meant to be there.

"Shall we walk?" Finally Alex spoke.

I nodded and allowed her to take me by the hand, following her as she walked along the shoreline. We were still barefoot, and as we walked, the cool sea washed over my feet, tickling them. We walked a couple of hundred feet or so, and then, as if by a silent, mutual agreement, we stopped again. I looked back over my shoulder, the faint glow of the fire the only thing visible to me now.

"I'm glad you came over this weekend," Alex said. "I've really liked hanging out with you."

"I've really liked it too." I gave her hand a small squeeze.

"Laurel's an ex." Alex avoided eye contact when she said it. "She still lives in the village, but that was the first time I'd seen her in ages."

The ex that Alex had told me she'd been on the Internet with when her mum had embarrassed her? Strangely, I didn't want to think about that.

"Cool." The twinge in my chest most definitely wasn't cool. "Did you…date long?" I knew I needed to say something.

"Few months, that's all."

"Bet it was nice to see her again, huh?" I sounded pathetic.

"Not really." Alex laughed. "She dumped me, not the other way around."

I laughed with her, because that's what I thought I should do.

"But it was all a very long time ago." Alex stopped laughing. "A *very* long time ago. You do get that, don't you?"

A look passed between us, and in that one meeting of gazes I sensed a palpable hitching up of something that I knew had already been there, dancing around the edges, but which was becoming more obvious, and more visible.

A silence lingered between us, just the sound of the waves and my own breathing, which I was sure Alex would be able to hear. I let my hand drop from hers, surprised when she took it back again. She pulled me closer to her, turning us both slightly so we were facing one another, and gazed at me for the longest time before reaching over to push a strand of my hair away from my face. She took my other hand in hers but didn't speak, and as I looked up at her, I was unsure what—if anything—I should do or say.

From somewhere in the distance behind me, I heard a shout. A girl's voice. To my ears, it sounded like Nicole. It wasn't, of course, but it was enough to drag me back to reality as I pulled my hands from hers and moved away slightly.

"We should go back." I stepped further away. "They'll be wondering where we've got to."

I gave an embarrassed nod of my head and turned and walked away from her, desperate not to look back at her.

Desperate not to return to her.

Chapter Eighteen

I spent Monday morning thinking about the weekend, going over and over in my head when exactly my feelings for Alex had changed. I tried to focus on the things that had been awesome: how I'd made her laugh, how intently she'd looked at me a few times, looks that had made me feel like I'd been hit by lightning. I hadn't imagined any of it. I thought about how we'd held hands on the beach. How Alex had seemed concerned that I knew Laurel was old news. It was all scary and lovely and messed up at the same time. Alex was my bandmate. Nicole had been my bandmate and I'd sent her spiralling out of control with my selfishness. Alex was too lovely to hurt like that, and I knew I had to stop beating myself up over her like I had with Nicole and keep reassuring myself that it was up to me to make sure nothing was going to happen between us.

We'd arrived back in London at eleven that morning, after deciding on a whim to stay an extra night in Suffolk. That had suited me just fine, because there had been nothing in me that had wanted to end the weekend early and come home, and even though I knew it would be a rush to get to the studio for one for our afternoon of recording "Perspectives," the extra night at her parents had so been worth it.

We'd shared a quick hug before parting at the Tube station, but it had been nothing like the intense hand-holding that we'd had the night before. Had that been deliberate on both our parts? Had Alex figured that the signals we were giving to each other could be misinterpreted? I knew I was riding a roller coaster of emotions right now: the highs of being with her, the lows because being with her inevitably brought Nicole into my head.

All I knew, as I watched her run down the steps of the Tube station without so much as a backward glance back up to me, still standing at street level, was that even though I'd just spent the last three days with her, I missed her the second she disappeared from my sight.

❖

"Liverpool was just the best." Robyn leant against me and I was sure I could smell the remnants of her weekend's drinking still on her breath.

I turned my head away. "Liverpool?" I asked, not understanding.

"The festival?" Robyn made a disapproving sound. "I texted you? Man, I'm thirsty," she said before I could answer her.

I steered an increasingly limp Robyn to a chair in the corner of the studio and sat her down. Then, while she looked at her feet, I fetched her a tumbler of water from the cooler.

"Drink this." I crouched at her feet. "Somehow I reckon you'll need rehydrating."

"Didn't you get my messages?" Robyn took the water from me. "I told you I was in the middle of a field rocking out to some eighties stuff. God, you have to be pissed to listen to too much of that."

"Did you text me?" My brow creased as I pulled my phone from my pocket. Twelve texts, eight of which were from Robyn. I'd not looked at my phone the entire weekend, and the strangeness of it shot through me. Normally I checked it, it seemed, on the hour and every hour. But not this weekend. Not while I'd been with Alex…

"I must have had my phone off." I hastily bundled it back into my pocket. "So I guess you had a good time."

"The best." Robyn leant her head back, then, discovering the back of the seat was lower than she realized, pulled up straight again. "Nate talked about us getting married." She peered at me through heavy eyes. "But he was more drunk than I was, so it doesn't count."

I snuffed out the overwhelming urge to roll my eyes.

"So, Cinderella," Robyn said, shuffling back in her chair, "how was your weekend?"

"Ah, you know," I said, turning my head as I heard the door open. Alex? No, Grant. "Same as ever." I sketched a wave at him as he did the same at me.

"You do anything?" Robyn narrowed her bloodshot eyes. "You didn't reply to my texts, so that either means you were ignoring me or you were having too good a time to bother replying."

I laughed, and had Robyn been a hundred per cent on it, she would have picked up that my laugh was covering my reluctance to elaborate any further. Thank goodness for hangovers.

"There was this band on Saturday night, right?" Robyn said. "Big in the early eighties or something…"

Her voice dissolved around me as my mind wandered back to Alex. How easily she slipped into my thoughts. How happily she sat inside my head.

"You listening to me?"

"What?"

"I was telling you about this band that went on and on," Robyn said.

"Right."

"You didn't tell me how your weekend panned out," she said, and I knew if I lied about spending the weekend with Alex she'd eventually find out, then she'd want to know why I hadn't told her, and then I'd get a whole load of questions that I knew I couldn't handle right now.

"I went to Suffolk," I said, nodding.

"Where the fuck's that?"

"East coast."

"Not London, then."

I laughed. "No, Robyn. Not London."

"So what is there in Suffolk that would keep you there all weekend?" Robyn's words got lost in a loud yawn.

Alex was there.

"Sea, mostly." I paused. "I went with Alex to her parents' house."

"Wicked." Robyn yawned again and I wondered if I was keeping her up. "Her parents nice?"

That was it. No questioning. No surprise from her that I'd spent the weekend with Alex. I felt a strange mixture of relief and disappointment, but I wasn't quite sure why I'd be disappointed. Maybe I wanted to tell Robyn more of what I'd done there. Maybe I wanted to tell her how much I'd loved being with Alex, about how I'd wished the weekend could have gone on even longer than it had.

"I've never been to Suffolk." Robyn sounded disappointed, like it was Suffolk's fault for never inviting her there.

"Well, considering you don't know where it is, that's no surprise."

Didn't Robyn want to know more? Didn't she want to know why Alex had invited me over? Joshua's words to me on the beach returned; he'd said I must be someone special for Alex to take me home. He'd seemed to think it was weird Alex inviting me over, but to Robyn it was nothing. Perhaps I was glad of that; perhaps it really had been nothing to Alex, and I was reading way too much into all the shared looks and hand-holding that had gone on between us.

I glanced down to Robyn, her eyes closed again, and gave an inward laugh. Maybe I'd been thinking too much about Nicole again, and how things had progressed between us from companionship to hand-holding and knowing looks.

"Hey, did I tell you?" Robyn opened one eye and peered at me.

Shared looks didn't have to mean something with *everyone* I met, did it? Wasn't I looking at Robyn right now? I was being an idiot. As always.

"Oi, cloth ears." Robyn sat up straighter. "Did you hear me?"

"Did you say something?"

"I said, did I tell you?"

"Did you tell me what?" I asked. I folded my arms and, unthinking, glanced over towards the door, wondering when Alex might arrive.

"I knew you weren't listening."

"So tell me now." I sighed. I didn't mean to, but it just came out.

"So you don't want to know about the pool party tomorrow?" Robyn asked.

"What pool party?"

"That got you hearing me, didn't it?" Robyn grinned up at me.

"Just"—I rolled a hand—"talk rather than messing about, can't you?" I was tired. And where was Alex? The last thing she'd said to me when we'd parted at the Tube was that she'd see me again at one. I pulled my phone out from my jeans pocket and looked at the time. Twelve forty-five. How could it still only be twelve forty-five?

"Trio Records," Robyn said, kicking her legs out in front of her, "are very pleased with us."

"Because we're probably going to get them their first number one soon?" I offered.

"Because we…yeah, yeah," Robyn said. "So because they're very pleased with us, they're throwing us a party tomorrow. At a pool. Hence, pool party." She held out her hands and looked very pleased with herself too.

"You're hilarious."

"I know."

The noise from across the studio of a door opening immediately took my attention away from Robyn, Trio Records, and pool parties. I saw Brooke first, then Alex, both deep in conversation as they came into the room, and felt a skittering of nerves at seeing Alex again, even though I'd only seen her less than two hours before. As she wandered across the studio floor towards us, Brooke chattering away to her, Alex's eyes sought mine, and the look of pleasure on her face when we finally made eye contact wasn't my imagination.

"We were talking about the party tomorrow." Robyn was the first to speak once Alex and Brooke were close enough to hear. "Tally was wondering what bikini she should wear."

"I wasn't." My face grew warm. "She thinks she's being funny"—I nudged her foot with mine—"but she's not even remotely funny." I didn't want to even look at Alex.

"We were just talking about that," Alex said. Then, hastily, "The party. Not your bikini."

I saw the redness that speckled her cheeks. At least I wasn't the only one dying with embarrassment then.

"Grant just told us out in the corridor," Brooke said. "He's already told us which girl he's inviting."

"Freeloader." I cut my glance away.

"Well, I say it's about time we were rewarded." Robyn stood and pulled down the bottom of her T-shirt that had become scrunched up while she'd been sitting—or rather, slouching—on her chair. "All the hard work we do for this record company," she said, "they should be sending out limos to collect us."

"You reckon they will?" Brooke asked, her eyes wide.

"In your dreams." Robyn.

"Only once we've had five number ones." Alex.

I just laughed a bit.

Movement from across the studio signalled we were needed. Pool party temporarily forgotten, we wandered away from where we'd been standing and headed over towards the source of all the noise.

"Will I…see you there, then?" Alex turned to talk to me while Robyn and Brooke went ahead. "Tomorrow?"

"Of course." I walked with her. Tomorrow couldn't come soon enough, as far as I was concerned now.

"Grant said it should all be getting going by twelve," Alex said. "So I'll come and find you sometime after that if you like?"

"Yeah, right." Robyn interrupted before I could answer. "By the time she's decided which teeny-weeny bikini she can impress everyone with," she said back over her shoulder, "the party will be over."

I swear I could have killed her right there and then.

Chapter Nineteen

I hadn't been to a pool party since the last long heatwave the south of England had sweltered under, when I'd been in Year 11 and we'd all headed down to some girl's house from school (whose name I'd long since forgotten) and created havoc in her parents' pool.

This one would be totally different. This one was being paid for entirely by Trio Records and even though it was being touted by Ed as a thank you to us all, I knew deals would be struck and the paparazzi would conveniently have limited access. That made me spend forever choosing an outfit, something that I hoped would make me look awesome, should any photos get published, while at the same time—remembering Robyn's puerile jokes the day before—making sure I didn't catch anyone's attention too much. Especially Alex's.

The party was in full swing by the time I arrived just before twelve. A swarm of faces, some I recognized, some I didn't, ebbed and flowed around me as I made my way round the side of the pool towards an already bikini-clad Brooke, who had snagged herself a lounger under the shade of a tree.

"Who *are* all these people?" I asked as I sat on the edge of her lounger.

"No idea." Brooke smelled of coconut sun cream and heat. "Ed reckons they're important people but I doubt that very much."

"Anything for an afternoon by a pool, hey?" I looked around me. "Scroungers."

I looked around for Alex, wondering if she was doing the same thing and looking for me.

"Robyn here yet?" I asked. "Or…Alex?"

Just the mention of her name made my voice sound funny, I thought.

"Robyn's talking to Ed over there," Brooke said, lifting her chin. "I saw Alex earlier, talking to some girl, but I haven't seen her since."

"Right." A small jolt passed through me. "I thought she said she'd see me here at twelve but I must have been mistaken." I paused. "Any idea who it is?"

"Who what?"

"Who she was talking to?"

"No idea," Brooke said, settling back down again. "You having a drink?"

"Yeah. Want one?" I stood, moving away at Brooke's nod.

I made my way over to the bar that had been set up under the shade and quickly grabbed us an ice-cold beer each before anyone could see, then picked my way round the loungers and chairs back to Brooke.

"Are we expected to mingle?" I asked as I handed her her beer and put mine down on the table next to her.

"Probably." Brooke took her beer and placed it on the table before settling back and closing her eyes again.

I scraped a lounger over closer to Brooke and sat. I whipped my vest top off over my head and wriggled out of my shorts, kicking them off and dropping them onto the floor next to me, then lay back, feeling slightly self-conscious in my bikini.

I watched the people round the pool, some swimming, some sitting on the edge. All the while my eyes sought out Alex, hoping she wouldn't come over whilst at the same time really wanting to see her, because a part of my brain was surprisingly good just lately at confusing me like that.

"So how was your evening last night?" Brooke murmured, breaking my train of thought.

"Good, yeah." It was a pretty nondescript answer but the alternative was to tell her I'd spent the entire evening thinking about Alex.

"You heard Ed's latest?" Brooke asked. "For some reason he wants to rerelease the first album, but add an acoustic version of 'Drowning in You' on it too."

"You think the fans will buy it?"

"He thinks so," Brooke said. "I just think he's jumping on the bandwagon after the success of 'After the Rain.'"

From the floor I heard my phone buzz. I reached a hand down and rooted in my shorts pocket until I made contact, then lifted my phone above my face, squinting against the sun so that I could read it.

Where are you? xxx

I looked at Alex's name, my stomach feeling mushy but sick at the same time. I let my hand, still clutching my phone, drop to my side.

"I don't know if they'll want to shell out for another album that's essentially the same, but with one extra song on it," I said.

Alex's text bored into my hand.

"I think he just wants to make even more money out of us." Brooke smiled but didn't open her eyes.

I wanted to see Alex. I didn't want to see her.

"But still," I said, just for something to say, "Ed knows his stuff."

I wanted to see her.

I lifted my phone and wrote, *With Brooke by the pool. Talking work.*

Would that put her off?

I stared at my phone until she replied.

Okay, catch you later xxx

Disappointment coalesced with a certain amount of relief, but I knew the disappointment was stronger.

"If it means more days like this," Brooke said, "then I'm all for it."

"All for what?"

"A rerelease, dummy." Brooke looked at me. "Has the sun got to you?"

No, but Alex has.

"A rerelease." I nodded. "Yeah. Sounds good."

I'd drunk all my beer without hardly realizing it. As I drained the last of it, I held the bottle up.

"Another one?" I asked Brooke.

"I'll go." Brooke swung her legs over the side of her lounger. "I've hardly moved since I got here." She stood and stretched. "Gotta pay a visit too, so I'll be a while," she said, then walked away.

Her stretch elicited one from me too. I lifted my arms high above my head, pointed my toes, then relaxed. The sun felt good on my skin, the beer sat happily in my stomach. I closed my eyes and listened to the sounds around me: water slapping against the side of the pool, the squeak of wet bodies on inflatables in it, the chatter of voices vacillating around my ears.

When a shadow fell across my face, I flopped an arm towards the table next to me.

"You were quick," I said. "Just stick my beer on there, will you?"

"Yes, ma'am."

I peered up at the sound of her voice, shielding my eyes from the sun. Alex was looking down at me, some of her hair falling across her face, making my heart give a small jolt. I kept my eyes firmly fixed on her face, trying to ignore the sight of her practically naked body, thanks to the smallest of bikinis I think I'd ever seen.

"I saw Brooke by the bar," Alex said, putting my beer and her bottle of Coke down on the table. "She said to say she'd be back later." She looked at me. "I figured you two had finished talking work, so"—she sank down onto Brooke's lounger—"I thought I'd come over and say hi." The tiniest hint of a smile. It was adorable.

"Hi." I didn't know what else to say.

"Hi." Alex laughed.

She swung her legs onto the lounger and sat back in one fluid movement, raising one knee up. I stared ahead, scared that if I looked over to her she'd be able to see the unease on my face at having a bikini-clad Alex so close to me.

"So what do you think of it?" she asked.

"The party?"

"Mm."

"It's okay, isn't it?" I looked over towards the pool. "No one I recognize, of course."

"Of course. That's how these things work," Alex said. "We do all the hard work and then total strangers get to hang out by a pool with us all day."

"I'm being antisocial." I grinned at her. "Topping up my tan is way more important than mingling with strangers."

"I'd say your tan looks pretty good enough." Alex did that thing of tilting her head to one side and looking at me for so long I was forced to look away. "To me, anyway."

"Thanks." I grabbed my beer and took a long drink. Perhaps I shouldn't have, because the sun and the beer were beginning to make me feel light-headed. I was hot and sticky too, and as I cast a look to the pool, I knew I wanted to go in.

As if reading my mind, Alex sat up and looked towards the pool too.

"Shall we?" she asked, nodding towards it.

She rose and held a hand out to me, pulling me to my feet.

"You know you want to," she said, drawing me by the hand.

We stood at the side of the deep end, each one daring the other to go in first to test the temperature. When it was clear neither of us wanted to go first, Alex reclaimed my hand and, taking a leap, pulled me in with her. The cool water hit me like a brick, sending a spasm of shivers up and down my body as we both plunged under. By the time I resurfaced, my skin had already grown accustomed to the cool, and I swam out to the middle of the pool to grab an inflatable, Alex swimming behind me.

We held on to the inflatable together, one either side, and trod water facing each other across it. The pool had cleared and I was pleased to have it all to ourselves. The water cooled my hot skin, and as I kicked my legs down under me, I stared at Alex, suddenly feeling ridiculously happy.

"What?" Alex smiled at me from across the inflatable.

"Nothing." I wiped some water from my eyes. "It's just nice, isn't it?"

Alex raised her face to the sun and closed her eyes. "It's very nice."

I didn't know if I should say something, so I stayed quiet and just watched her while she still had her eyes closed. The moment was textbook and I didn't want to spoil it; besides, I was enjoying having the chance to look at her while she didn't know.

My eyes roamed her face, bronzed from the sun. I soaked up the sight of her, from her long dark eyelashes to her perfectly straight nose with its smattering of freckles, on to her slightly upturned mouth.

Alex lowered her face and, before I had a chance to look away, opened her eyes and caught me staring. I looked away, embarrassed, and there was a long silence, which I finally broke with, "So Ed apparently wants to rerelease the album." It was lame, but it was all I could think of to say.

"Yeah, Robyn already said." Alex rested her chin on her arm and looked at me.

Before I could say anything else, she released herself from the inflatable and sank under the water, swimming underwater a short while before resurfacing near the edge of the pool towards the shallow end. I released myself too, the inflatable bobbing away from me like a cork, and struck my legs out, swimming over to join her.

I arrived next to her and tentatively placed my feet down, pleased when I knew I could touch the bottom. We stood side by side, facing out towards the deep end, and watched together as some guy dived in, sending a spray of water out over the group of girls he'd just been sitting with, making them all shriek.

"Nice bikini, by the way." Alex reached over and touched the strap on my shoulder. "I meant to say earlier. The colour really suits your brown skin."

I felt every muscle tense as her fingers grazed my skin and I realized I was holding my breath. She held my gaze as she touched me and I knew immediately there was a weird tension between us which hadn't been there before. Sure, there had been a chemistry that night on the beach, but it had been nothing like this. This was… what was it exactly? A new intensity. An amplification in the looks and touching and hand-holding that made me feel both uneasy and ecstatic at the same time.

"Harrods." I swallowed. "I bought it there." I laughed, my laugh sounding strained. "A year ago if you'd told me I'd be buying bikinis in Harrods I wouldn't have believed you."

"A year ago you weren't as famous as you are now," Alex said.

A year ago I was fucking up Nicole's life.

I moved away slightly and sank under the water, hoping I could drown my thoughts. I rose back up and swept my wet hair back off my face.

"Shall we get out?" I asked. "I'm cold."

Without waiting for Alex's reply, I swam away from her to the other side and hauled myself out. I walked back to our loungers, flicking the wet from my fingers, and picked up my towel. As I dried myself, water pooling at my feet, I watched Alex pull herself from the pool and walk towards me, adjusting her bikini top as she did so, without a hint of self-consciousness. My eyes refused to look away this time, apparently eager to look at her long legs, toned stomach, the bikini top that Alex repeatedly pulled at…

Finally I managed to look away. It was agony. I turned my back to her, my mind in turmoil. I felt like I was tumbling away from myself and Alex was the one doing it, taking me further away from what I knew was right, whilst at the same time pulling me towards her with every look and every touch.

"Are you still cold?" Alex asked, pulling my towel tighter round me. She rubbed at my arms, her own skin prickled with goosebumps from the chilly water.

"I'm fine." I took a step back and wiped some water from my brow with the corner of my towel. "Thanks."

Alex nodded but didn't say any more. Instead, she turned and looked back towards the bar, then returned her gaze to me. "Are you hungry?" she asked. "I'm starving. There's food over there."

I remembered I'd skipped breakfast, thanks to oversleeping and worrying I'd be late. At the mention of food, I was suddenly ravenous.

"Actually, I am too." I unfurled my towel from around myself and shook it out. "Shall we get something?"

"You wait here." Alex nudged a lounger closer to me with her foot. "Lie out and dry off. It'll warm you up." She started to walk away. "I think I can figure out what sort of things you'll like," she called back over her shoulder. "After all, I got the pizza right, didn't I?"

I watched her walk back past the pool and weave her way round the myriad chairs and loungers towards the bar. Pulling a dry towel from my bag, I spread it out on my lounger and lay out on it. The sun felt fabulous against my chilled skin, instantly warming it again. As it beat down on my face, my eyes grew heavy and eventually closed, and the sounds around me dipped in and out of my consciousness.

When I opened them again, around ten minutes later, I couldn't see Alex anywhere. I propped myself up on one elbow and scanned around, expecting to see her standing over at the bar. She was nowhere to be seen, and the disappointment that scratched at me was both profound and unnerving. I rolled my legs over the side of the lounger and sat up, scraping my wet hair back off my face, and then shrugging my vest top back over my head.

Finally I spotted her, standing some way from the bar, in the dappled shadows of a tree. She was now dressed back in shorts and T-shirt and was talking to a girl, the girl leaning against the trunk of the tree while Alex spoke with her. I watched them intensely, my eyes never leaving them, a knot forming in the pit of my stomach as I saw how Alex had the girl's entire attention, how her eyes never left hers.

"Oi, Billy No-Mates."

I dragged my gaze from them as I heard Robyn's voice shout across to me from the other side of the pool, then watched her as she sauntered over to me, her footsteps slightly unsteady, thanks, I figured, to the large glass of something presumably alcoholic in her hand.

As if by magic, my eyes slid back to Alex, still talking to the girl. I could hear my own breath in my ears, hear the voices all vying for attention in my head.

"What are you doing, sitting here all alone?" Robyn flopped down on the bottom of my lounger. "Ed said we should network, but

I thought, bugger that when there's free drinks at the bar." She raised her glass and took a long drink from it.

"I just had a swim." Alex. Still there. "I wanted to dry off." Girl. Still there.

I had to concentrate really hard to look at Robyn and not Alex. It was like Laurel at the beach all over again, when her father was trying to talk to me, and all I could think about was Alex talking to her.

"Hey, you know who I just saw?" Robyn asked.

"Who?"

"Tim Westland," Robyn said, "from WestEnd Records."

"Right."

"Well try and sound a bit more excited," Robyn said, slapping my leg. "Tim Westland is, like, *the* biggest thing in record production at the moment." She looked away. "Oh, hey. And guess who else I saw?"

"Who?"

"Guess."

"I can't." I looked back over to Alex. Another girl had joined them.

"Try."

"I've no idea." The knot in my stomach balled tighter.

"Well at least try."

"I said I can't."

"You're so boring sometimes."

Two girls and Alex. One girl was talking and Alex was listening intently, occasionally laughing. The other girl couldn't take her eyes off her.

"Tally?"

I dragged my attention back to Robyn.

"What?"

"I said, you're so boring sometimes."

"Whatever."

"Who's bitten your arse?" Robyn took another drink. "I was just saying, I'd seen CJ Black earlier."

"The DJ?"

"Oh, you are in the land of living then," Robyn said. "I was beginning to wonder."

I hated it. I hated the way it made me feel when I saw how the girls were looking and talking to Alex, and I hated the way she was with them, apparently holding their attention with every word and gesture.

But I had no right to hate it. She was Alex Brody and everyone loved her, and right now I was acting no better than Nicole used to act when she was jealous of the girls I used to talk to.

The thought almost made me gasp and even though Robyn was still talking to me, her words were lost to me. My whole focus was on what was unfolding across the other side of the pool, the wretchedness of my feelings eating away at me, the double realization that I was falling for Alex and now acting no better than Nicole had when she'd fallen for me making my head spin.

The weird tension that had surrounded us when we'd been in Suffolk together hadn't been my imagination, and I knew that while my growing feelings had crept up on me, it was pointless me trying to ignore them any more. The constant looks, the touches. The fact that I was desperate to wring out every last ounce of my time with her because I knew the time I spent with her was never long enough. As I watched her, my heart sitting dully in my chest, I knew without a shadow of a doubt that I wanted her.

And the thought terrified me.

I didn't know what Alex had done to me, but all I knew was that I was aware of myself and of my own actions whenever I was near her. A quickening of the heart, a desire to be noticed. My laughs had become more forced when I was with her, my words more carefully chosen. Had I made her laugh? Had what I'd said been heard and taken on board? Had she liked what I'd said or done? Would she still think about our conversations long after they'd finished, like I did?

Something which I'd once felt around Nicole when we'd been spending a lot of time together. But this was something much stronger and deeper. It felt real. Whenever I closed my eyes, all I could see was Alex; whenever there was silence, all I could hear was her voice. Whenever I saw her, I got a Christmas morning feeling in my stomach; just the sound of my phone pinging, alerting me to a text, sent my heart reeling, hoping it would be from Alex. Then, if it wasn't from her, I'd force a smile through the disappointment, and tell myself it really didn't matter and that not every text could be from her. Then my phone would alert me to another message, and the whole process would be repeated, ending up in absolute bliss when, finally, a text would be from her.

The feeling with Nicole had never felt quite like this, and that's when I became scared because I knew that whatever I'd felt for Nicole, my feelings for Alex were a hundred times stronger.

My life was starting to feel amazing. *I* was starting to feel amazing, and I knew it was all down to Alex. I felt different when I was around her; the sky was bluer, sounds clearer, lines sharper. I wanted to be around her all the time. I hung on every word she said. Felt more alive than I'd ever felt in my life when I was near her. Everything felt different when she was with me. Better.

So why did I feel so scared?

"I've got to go." I snagged up my shorts from the floor and sprang to my feet. "This party's crap."

"What?" Robyn looked up at me from the lounger. "It's only early still."

"I think I've had enough for one day." I knew I'd seen enough for one day, anyway.

I hauled my shorts on, then rolled up my towels, stuffing them both into my bag. From across the pool I was aware of Alex glancing over to me, but I didn't look back. I couldn't.

"Text you later, okay?" I tossed a look back over my shoulder to Robyn as I walked away and made for the house.

I knew I'd have to pass the bar to get through the garden to get to the main gate, and that meant passing Alex. My heart hammering behind my ribs, I strode over towards her, my eyes resolutely looking away from her, even though I knew she'd seen me.

"Tal?" I heard her but didn't respond. Instead, I made for the side of the house, not wanting to see the girls she was talking to, not wanting to know what sort of girls Alex could possibly be attracted to.

I walked round the bar, hearing Alex say something to the girls behind me which I didn't catch in amongst all the other chatter around me, and made my way round the side of the house towards the garden, relieved that Alex hadn't followed me. It was quieter here, the main bulk of people choosing to hang around the pool, and as I walked further away, the hubbub of noise and music left my ears.

I headed for the trees, back towards the main gate I'd come through just a few hours earlier. It was fine, I told myself the further away I took myself from her, that Alex wanted to talk to other girls. It was right. It was normal. It was to be expected.

"Tal." Alex's breathless voice sounded behind me.

I shot a look over my shoulder to see her half walking, half running across the lawn towards me, but I didn't stop. I knew I was being petulant, but I still couldn't make myself stop. Instead, I hitched my bag higher onto my shoulder and ducked in amongst the trees, the main gate now visible.

"Wait." Finally I felt her hand on my arm. "Why didn't you wait?"

"I didn't hear you."

"You saw me." Alex was still breathless. "I saw you look over your shoulder."

I tried to walk away but Alex's grip on my arm tightened. She pulled on me, stopping me from walking any more.

"Were you just going to go" Alex asked, "without seeing me before you went?"

"I figured you'd forgotten about me," I said, "so you wouldn't notice whether I was there or not."

"Of course I would have." Alex looked confused. "Why would you think that?"

"You were busy." I nodded back towards the house. "You kind of went off to get us food and apparently forgot about it."

"I got chatting," Alex said, her hand falling from my arm. "Sorry."

"I saw."

I walked away again. I knew what Alex's face would look like, but I didn't care. Finally she fell into step with me as we walked through the trees.

"Are you okay?" she asked.

"I'm fine."

"You don't seem it."

"I said I'm fine."

I picked up my pace and moved away from her. In two or three quick steps, Alex was in front of me. She swung round to face me and stopped, barring my way.

"You're in my way." I bit at my lip. "I need to go."

"Not until you tell me what's up."

"Nothing's up."

"Why are you being like this with me?" Alex asked, her hand on my arm.

"Like what?" I looked down at her hand.

"Like you don't care."

That cut me. Why couldn't Alex see I was protecting her?

"You're imagining it," I said. I pulled her hand off my arm and walked away, deeper into the trees.

"You do this all the time," Alex called out.

I stopped dead. "Do what?"

"Get close to me one minute, and blank me the next."

"Whatever."

I walked away again, surprised when Alex grabbed me again. She swung me round to face her, then cupped my face in her hands and leant her face closer, so her lips were inches from mine, her warm breath fluttering against my skin, her hair lightly brushing my cheek, like silk.

"You drive me crazy," she breathed, "you know that?"

She pressed her lips to mine, kissing me slowly, a small sigh sounding in the back of her throat as I kissed her back. It didn't feel strange to kiss her. It felt perfect and lovely, as though I'd waited my whole life to do it. As she kissed me deeper, my body melted against hers, and it felt just like…

Just like when Nicole had kissed me.

I pushed Alex off, and the look of hurt and confusion that flashed across her face nearly killed me.

"I can't do this." I lurched away from her, blindly seeking the gate. "Nicole...I can't."

"Nicole?" The confusion in Alex's voice was palpable. "What's Nicole got to do with any of this?"

"I can't. Alex, I'm sorry, I can't."

"Tally, I'm not Nicole!" Alex's cry echoed off the trees.

I stumbled from her, her words lost to me, thanks to the sound of the breeze in the trees and my blood pulsing in my ears as I ran. As I left her standing in the shadows, I knew she was right. Alex *wasn't* Nicole.

But I also knew I'd end up hurting her, just like I'd hurt Nicole.

Chapter Twenty

By the time I arrived back at my apartment, my body was damp with sweat, my bikini uncomfortably sticking to me underneath my clothes.

The Tube ride home had been a total drag, taking far longer than normal. Perhaps that had been my imagination, though, as I'd spent the entire journey expecting to see Alex waiting for me at each station we passed through. Dreading her getting on the train with me and asking me just what the hell I'd been playing at.

I came in through my apartment door, slammed it behind me, and sank down to the floor. I fumbled with my laces with fingers that wouldn't comply, finally managing to wrench my Converses off, then dropped them beside me, enjoying the feel of the cool carpet against my bare feet.

Inside my shorts pocket, the edge of my phone pressed hard against my hip bone. I lifted up from the floor slightly and pulled it out, then stared at the blank screen. No text or phone call from Alex. I didn't know if that made me happy or sad.

I settled on relieved.

I sighed and rested my head against the door. I'd acted like a jerk at the pool. Twice. Now I felt angry, and frustrated, and ashamed, and upset, and a whole other range of emotions that my hot, tired, puddled brain was finding it hard to cope with right now.

I'd allowed myself to think about her way too much. About how she'd looked in her bikini, the way she'd held my gaze as she'd wandered over to me by the pool, the sun honeying her skin. Alex's kiss wouldn't leave me either. No matter how hard I tried, each time I closed my eyes, the feel of her lips on mine, the taste of them, refused to go away, bringing with it a deep ache inside me. I imagined her now, probably still at the party. Talking to those girls again.

My eyes sprang open. I knew they'd love the way Alex walked, the way she talked. The way she made people sit up and take notice of her. How she made them feel inside.

I knew exactly how they felt because I felt it too.

Because, despite trying to ignore it, I was digging myself in deeper and deeper, getting pulled towards Alex more and more. As I sat in the hallway of my apartment, every fibre of me ached to get up and return to her. To tell her I was sorry, and to explain myself to her.

To kiss her again.

My phone buzzed, shaking me from my thoughts, and it felt to me as though I'd been holding my breath the entire time I'd been thinking about Alex.

Robyn: *Where'd you bugger off to?*

I needed a shower, but I couldn't move. I smelled of chlorine and sun cream and the Tube and misery, but I still couldn't move from the hallway. Instead, I sent a reply to Robyn, some lame lie about having to get home for a delivery, and remained slumped on the floor, staring at the wall opposite me.

Tears of frustration pricked my eyelids. I'd always thought of myself as someone who always did the right thing. Didn't hurt people and didn't play games with them. That's why I'd told Nicole the truth all those months before, rather than stringing her along on a lie, and that's why I knew I needed to keep Alex at arm's length now, before we got any closer than we apparently already had done. Before she had a chance to fall for me as hard as I'd fallen for her.

Everything I'd just done had been for a reason. I was a good person, I really was.

I just hoped Alex would understand that.

❖

I saw her again the next day. The timing in my life was lousy sometimes.

As if in sympathy with me, the heatwave finally broke, to be replaced with leaden skies and fat raindrops, and as I scurried through the rain to the studio, I swore it was as if the darker skies had arrived purely to match the darkness in my heart.

It had already been prearranged for us all to meet up at the studio to start recording "Perspectives" for the album. Irony sucks. And of course, just to make matters even worse for me, Alex was already there when I arrived, shortly after ten.

She didn't look at me when I came in, though. Didn't even acknowledge my presence as I stumbled in through the door, dripping wet, then took off my coat and shook the rain from it.

I didn't know what I expected. A text the night before might have been a start, though—an *Okay, we so need to talk about what just happened* text. But there had been nothing, and the minute she saw me, she started acting all weird, refusing to speak to me or even look at me, and now I was sure Robyn and Brooke were acting weird around me too.

They knew. It must have been written all over my face.

Did it matter? Would they freak if they knew Alex and I had kissed?

I slipped another look to Alex. The trouble was, with Alex being all strange like she was, and refusing to speak to me, Robyn and Brook would think me and her had fallen out, and then Alex would leave, and Be4 would split, and…

"So did your delivery come yesterday?" Robyn.

I looked at her blankly. Alex was standing not far away. She was looking tanned and glowing from her afternoon round the pool and was wearing board shorts and a short-sleeved hoodie, despite the rain outside. On anyone else, it would look ordinary. On Alex, like everything else, it looked perfect.

"Yeah. Delivery. Yeah, it came." My words came out more as a sigh than anything else.

Alex moved away, into the shadows of the studio.

"Have you spoken to Alex today?" I asked Robyn.

"Nope." Robyn pulled a pot of something from her bag. Lip balm or something. I neither knew nor cared. I just needed to know if Alex had spilled. "Well, only to say hi." She opened the pot and rubbed something from it on her pouting lips.

"She say anything about yesterday?"

"Why should she?"

"I just wondered if she'd had a good time, that's all." I let my wonderings get lost in a forced yawn, elicited in a sad attempt to cover up my unease.

"I think she left just after you, actually," Robyn said, putting her pot back in her bag. "I saw her a few minutes after you'd gone, packing up her bag."

"Was she okay?" Now *I* was acting weird.

Robyn looked at me strangely. "She was fine. Why?"

"She seemed a bit down when I was talking to her, that's all." The lies flowed easily. "I wondered if she was okay."

"You can ask her yourself." Robyn nodded to the sound booth. Alex was now inside it, staring out at me.

Our eyes met and held, and in those few seconds, it was all I could do to not shove Robyn out of the way and go up to her and explain myself to her. But I knew I couldn't in a room full of people; I needed to be alone with her, tell her I was sorry for what I'd done. Tell her I'd made a mistake.

As I looked at her, a snapshot of the day before came to me with such clarity, I drew in a shaky breath.

Alex, achingly close to me, then her lips, warm and sweet against mine, our bodies finally melting into one another's.

It hadn't been a mistake. I'd wanted it more than I'd ever wanted anything.

And by the way Alex was now looking at me again, it was clear she'd wanted it just as much as I had.

❖

I didn't know how I was supposed to concentrate. The music played, I sang. Ed grumbled. I sang again. My head hurt and my eyes constantly drifted to Alex, willing her to look at me, to acknowledge I was even in the same room as her. But each time our eyes did meet, she'd look away and cut me dead.

I wanted her to keep her eyes on me, though. I wanted her to see that I was hurting just as much as she was, that I was as confused as she was. I wanted her to see in my eyes the reason I'd done what I had, for her to reach into my mind and understand me.

The day just went on and on. Faces came and went in the studio; some I recognized, some I didn't. Awesomely, we wrapped on our first recording of "Perspectives" without any major hitches, or shouting, or re-recordings. The evaluation CD was burned, high-fives were planted all round, and before I realized it, the studio was rapidly emptying of people until suddenly there was only me, Ed, Brooke, Alex, and some sound guy whose name I couldn't remember, left standing in the middle of it. Robyn had gone ten minutes before, talking loudly as she left about her dinner date with Nate. I don't think anyone was listening. I sure wasn't.

Alex was hanging back. I was certain of it. As the others gathered things and collected bags and papers, Alex sat perched on the edge of a stool, making a meal of tightening the laces on her Vans, and searching in her bag for something that caused her to frown and delve deep into it. I knew what she was doing. She was stalling for time because she wanted to talk to me, once everyone else had gone, and the relief I felt that she wanted to hang out with me and talk was tangible.

"You coming?" Brooke asked me. "We can Tube together to Oxford Street if you like."

I looked at Alex, still rooting around in her bag.

"I'll wait," I said. My mind had already wandered in the other direction up the line, towards Kensington. I knew an awesome coffee place there, where the owner constantly called me Tilly but I never minded because he always directed me to one of the more discreet booths where no one could see me. It'd be the perfect place, I figured, for me and Alex to have a heart-to-heart.

I'd ask her. I would. I'd ask her out for coffee, then maybe over a latté and muffin—did Alex even like muffins?—I'd tell her I liked her, because I really did, but that… But that, what? She wasn't as important to me as Be4? The truth was, I had no idea what I was going to say to her. All I knew was I couldn't leave things as they were. I couldn't bear the awkwardness between us, when before we'd been so comfortable around one another.

When finally the room emptied, and there was only me and Alex left, I picked up my guitar, looped it around my shoulder, and, stepping over some cables, wandered over to her. She was standing now, one hand in her pocket, her phone in her other hand, her face a picture of concentration, and I just knew she was choosing songs to listen to for her Tube ride home. And I knew it would be Motown. Because, I figured, I was beginning to know everything about Alex.

"Today went okay, didn't it?" I was the first to fill the silence. "The recording."

Alex looked up from her phone.

"I guess."

Silence then. I looked expectantly at her, hoping she might say some more, but when she didn't say anything further, I said, "We should talk."

"About?" Alex stuffed her phone into her shorts pocket.

"You know what about."

She pulled a face. "Nothing to talk about." Her voice was calm when she spoke.

"But...yesterday," I said. "I...wanted to apologize."

"*Apologize?*" she repeated.

"For...you know."

Alex blew the hair from her forehead and sighed with what sounded to me like exasperation.

"Yeah, okay. Apology accepted," she said with faint sarcasm. She pulled her phone from her pocket again, then brushed past me and headed for the door.

"I thought we could maybe go and have a coffee." Even as I was saying it, I knew what her answer would be.

Her feet slowed, and for one moment I wondered if I'd been wrong. She turned and looked back at me and, after the longest silence, just said, "Sorry. Busy," then yanked the door open and left.

Guess I was having that latté and muffin alone then.

CHAPTER TWENTY-ONE

I wanted to text her. So many times I came close to picking my phone up and sending her a message, but I didn't. Not that Alex texted me either. And the longer the silence between us went on, and the longer neither of us could talk about what had happened at the pool, the worse everything became.

It was only going to be a matter of time before Robyn and Brooke noticed too. We were right in the middle of recording songs for the new album, which meant hours and days cooped up in the studio together, so I had no time whatsoever to get Alex on her own. It had been a week since the pool party, and in that week, I think she and I had barely said two words to one another. Every time I tried to get her on her own, Alex magically had something else to do. Each time I thought I'd mustered up enough confidence to explain myself to her, my confidence slipped away when I knew I couldn't even begin to explain anything.

Alex's coldness towards me was affecting my singing too. How was I supposed to concentrate when all this was hanging over me? Yet I still had to stand next to her in the sound booth and sing with her, gel with her, be comfortable around her.

We were on our fifth take of "Missing You," a fairly short folky sounding ballad which had been written by a freelance composer, which Ed thought would make a good filler song for the album. This was our second album—the dreaded second album—and there had been too much stressing over it, since everyone knew a band's second album had to be way better than the first, if they were to keep their fans happy.

I didn't get "Missing You." It was just a three minute song, which was going to be squeezed in between "After the Rain," and "Perspectives." Whether it was because I hadn't written "Missing You," so I didn't feel it, or whether it was because it seemed like only yesterday we were recording "Perspectives" and now we were recording something completely different, it was difficult to get my head around it, I didn't know. Standing in a tiny booth singing a ballad with Alex, trying not to stand too close to her, trying to make sure our bodies didn't touch, didn't help at all. All I did know was I didn't want to be there. My head was too messed up to be singing words such as *knowing you don't love me* and *this pain is all too much,* and that was making me apparently unable to sing even a single note properly, which was making Ed cranky, and Robyn sigh, and Alex look at me like she'd been looking at me since the pool party.

I wanted to tell them all to fuck off. Alex included.

"What's the problem here?" Ed spoke to me from out on the floor.

I'd taken my headphones off after my third failed attempt to hit a C convincingly.

"Not getting it." Apparently I'd engaged spoilt brat mode.

"What don't you get?"

"Everything." I shook my head. "The song, the vibe."

"Tally," Ed said, approaching the booth, "we've been here three hours already." He screwed up his nose. "It'd be good if we could get this one down by the end of the day."

Like I didn't know that?

"The instrumentals are done," he said, "you're not needed on guitar, so can you just...sing?"

I really loathed him sometimes.

I rattled a look off to Robyn, who replied with a similar expression, then flipped my headphones back on. We started singing again, and Alex, of course, as cool as a cucumber, nailed her vocals. How did she do it? I wanted to look at her, to see if she really was as calm as she was making out. I wished I knew her secret; every movement from her, every soft whisper from her voice sent my focus flying out of the window. I couldn't concentrate; her presence, the fact she was breathing the same air as me, messed with my head. When I did glance at her, memories from the pool came rushing back at me with such stark clarity I repeatedly missed my cues.

What was going through Alex's mind? I wish she'd speak to me, even if it was to tell me that kissing her was messed up and that I was a head-fuck and that she hated me; at least then I'd know that I wasn't the only one that hated me for what I'd done to her. Alex's silence was driving me mad. *She* was driving me mad.

I was done.

I threw my headphones off again and stumbled from the sound booth, nearly tripping over some cables in my haste to get away, and muttering something about idiots leaving cable lying around and me needing a break before I screamed.

Outside in the corridor, I regretted my hasty decision. I braced myself against the wall, looking back to the studio door, expecting it to open any second. It didn't, and I could imagine them all inside talking about me, grumbling about me. About how I'd had another hissy fit, just like I had when we'd been rehearsing in Walthamstow.

When the door still didn't open, I finally pushed away from the wall and stalked down the corridor, away from them.

I was so done.

The buzzing of my intercom wasn't what I wanted to hear. I'd left the studio and come straight back to my apartment, stopping off at the corner shop on the way home to buy the biggest block of chocolate they had. The fact I also bought a six-pack of beer while I was in there was entirely coincidental; I'd be eighteen in five weeks' time, so I was practically legal already. In all the time I'd been going in there, the shop owner had never known who I was, and I figured he wouldn't care if I was Lady Gaga herself, as long as I handed over my money.

My intercom buzzed again. I was halfway through a box set that had been unopened since Christmas, two empty beer bottles at my feet, the screwed up chocolate wrapper still on the floor from where I'd tried to throw it in the bin from the sofa, and missed. When the intercom rang a third time, this time without stopping, I paused the TV and got up.

I yanked it from its cradle.

"All right, already," I said into the phone.

"You always take this long to answer?"

It was Robyn.

"Are you going to buzz me up then?"

Still there.

I sighed down the phone, which Robyn must have heard, because she gave some caustic comment, but buzzed her up anyway. I flopped back down onto the sofa, unpaused the box set, and waited for her.

At the sound of the click of the door, I rolled my head backwards to see Robyn standing in the doorway, and lifted an arm, heavy from the beer, to signal her to come in.

"So this is where you're hiding, is it?" Robyn shut the door and came in.

I paused the box set again. It didn't look like I was going to get to finish it today after all.

"Who's hiding?" I asked.

"You are."

"Whatever. Beer?" I nudged a socked toe to the four remaining bottles on the floor, then waited as Robyn came closer.

She picked up a bottle, slapped my leg to get me to move over, then fell onto the sofa next to me.

Then, just as I knew would happen, silence. Robyn, I guessed, was waiting for me to speak. I didn't feel like speaking.

"So?" Robyn was the first to break. She never did like long silences.

"So?" I repeated.

"Come on." Robyn looked bored. "What's up? Why did you disappear like that?"

"I just didn't get it." I shook my head. "Got frustrated."

"No kidding."

"Did you carry on?" I asked. "After I left?"

"We got our vocals down, yes," Robyn said, "so you'll be recording yours alone, I guess."

"Is Ed angry?"

"He'll be all right."

That was a yes, then.

"It wasn't…" Robyn took a breath, and I knew she was thinking about how to phrase her question. "It wasn't Alex, was it?"

Adrenaline shot through me.

"Alex?" I asked, hoping that Robyn couldn't hear the tremble in my voice. "Why her?"

"Well I thought you'd sorted your shit out with her." Robyn picked up the bottle opener from the floor, then opened her beer. "Now I'm beginning to wonder if you two still don't have a problem with one another."

She had no idea.

"I've not got a problem with Alex," I said. "Why?" I asked, looking at Robyn. "Has she said something?"

"No, but"—Robyn pulled a face—"she did seem upset that you'd gone," she said, "so if it's *you* that still has a problem with *her*, don't you think you ought to sort it out?"

"I already told you," I said, hating the idea of an upset Alex, "everything's fine with me and Alex. It was just the song that I have a problem with."

"It's a good song." Robyn shrugged. "Okay, it's not one of ours, but…"

"I won't have a problem with it next time." If I could sing my vocals alone, without having Alex standing next to me, it wouldn't be an issue.

Robyn looked dubious.

"Well," she said, "I also came over to tell you something which should put a smile back on your miserable face." She leant over and bumped against me.

"Hit me."

"Ed said he wanted to tell us all together," Robyn said, "you know, when we'd finished recording together." She rolled her eyes. "Until you spoiled it."

"Yeah, yeah." Enough with the guilt already.

"It seems," Robyn began, and I could practically hear the excitement in her voice, "that 'After the Rain' is predicted to go to number one tomorrow."

"Seriously?" Now *that* made me smile.

"Yuh-huh. Ed said current CD sales and downloads have outstripped anything else this week."

I wiggled myself up straighter on the sofa and tucked one leg under the other.

"But that's awesome," I said, shaking my head. "Did he say how many sales?"

Robyn shook her head. "Over a million." A grin spread across her face. "We've done it, Tally. Our first number one."

I launched myself at her and threw my arms around her, nearly knocking her from the sofa. We rocked and laughed and whooped in each other's arms, and the craziest thing was, all the time I was doing it, my mind was thinking about Alex, and how pleased she would be.

"Everyone must be stoked." I tore myself away from her and sat back down. "What did...Brooke say?"

"What do you think?" Robyn's face was flushed. "She's over the bloody moon."

"And Alex?"

"Ludicrously happy."

I felt as though my chest might burst with pride. Our first number one. Goal achieved. Even "Taken," our first successful single and the one which put us out there, only managed to achieve number three.

"And Alex is really happy?" The words were out before I'd even thought about it. "What did she say?"

Robyn's laughter slowed as she looked at me.

"Alex is *really* happy, yes," she said. She leant her head to one side. "Is that important to you?"

"It's important that everyone's happy." My voice sounded too unnatural for my liking. "We should celebrate."

"Already sorted." Robyn rested back on the sofa. "Trio Records are presenting us with a platinum disc at some swanky club tomorrow night."

My heart crashed. "Not another party?" I didn't think I could cope so soon after the pool party.

"This, according to Ed, is more of a...presentation," Robyn said. "An announcement of how many copies we sold, and some grand presentation. The press will be there and bigwigs from Trio Records." She shrugged. "It means, of course, that we'll all have to be on our best behaviour." A slow grin escaped from Robyn's lips.

"Yeah, right."

Robyn looked at me. "We did it, Tally." She reached over and fist-bumped me. "We really did it."

Chapter Twenty-two

I didn't like the thought of a presentation. Probably because I hated the fuss of having to get dressed up—even though I can't remember the last time I wore a dress. But when an official party has been arranged by your record company in a swish part of London, and when they want to reward us for all our hard work and ply us with food and drinks, and I don't have to make too much of an effort, or make any speeches or anything else like that, then I'm in there.

Trio Records had hired a club in the West End called Hares. I'd never been before, and I did kind of wonder why there would be a club named after a wild animal in the centre of London, but when I got there, it was clear it was run by some millionaire called Michael Hares. That made more sense then.

The MD of Trio Records must have *really* been pleased with us because, unlike at the pool party, this time she had paid for us all to have two private cars take us into the West End—me and Brooke in one, Robyn and Alex in another. I was glad, because it meant I didn't have to drive through London in a limo with Alex in total silence. As usual, I hadn't left myself enough time to get ready, but at least I hadn't had to stress over what to wear, because I'd already chosen my outfit. After fussing over a pile of clothes, hastily tipped out from the wardrobe that afternoon and spread across my bed, in the end I'd just gone for the easy option and chose black skinny jeans and a black top that clung to me in all the right places. Black was good, I figured. Black covered a whole multitude of things.

Brooke, of course, had turned up in a dress. I thought she looked lovely. Elegant. I knew I was never going to be elegant, but I hoped my black combination still looked good enough to at least not make me look a total mess.

As we exited our car, the paparazzi swarmed around us like bees. Flashlights blinded us, words which I could barely hear were shouted out to us: "Tally! Over here!" "Brooke, give us a smile." We obliged. Standing arm in arm, we allowed the paps their sixty seconds of photographs, then waved, smiled, turned, and disappeared into the blackness of the club. That's when I could finally relax. As the heat and the noise of the club sucked us in, I followed Brooke deeper inside, sidestepping people I'd never seen before, and headed straight for the bar.

"So if the drinks are free," Brooke said, effortlessly getting the eye of the guy serving behind the bar, "I estimate we could be wasted within the hour."

"Stay classy, Brooke." I shoulder-bumped her, making her laugh.

While Brooke ordered our drinks, I leant back against the bar and gazed round. I was looking for Alex. I couldn't help myself.

"Any idea what time Robyn said she and Alex would be here?" I kept my voice as normal as possible.

Brooke looked at her watch. "Their car was collecting her at nine. Then on to Alex's." She looked at her watch again, as if to confirm to herself. "They should be here soon."

Almost the second she'd said it, I spotted Robyn. She was standing across the other side of the dance floor, her arms wrapped around Nate. She looked a little drunk already, in the way that tipsy people do: arms slightly loose, laughing louder than was necessary.

So where was Alex? I took my drink from Brooke, had a sip, then wandered across the floor to Robyn, pulling Brooke with me. When she spotted us, Robyn let out a whoop and walked unsteadily over to meet us. Definitely drunk already.

"You're here!" She embraced us both, spilling some of the drink that was still in her hand onto the floor behind me. I just hoped she hadn't spilled any of it down my back, and that I wouldn't spend the rest of the night stinking of whatever revolting cocktail it was she was drinking.

"I thought you wouldn't be here yet," I said, raising my voice to be heard over the music, which had been cranked up a notch. "I thought your car was at nine."

"Nate and I caught a cab instead." Robyn's voice was already hoarse and I guessed by the state of her she'd been in the club a while.

"What about Alex?" I asked.

Robyn shrugged loosely. "Dunno."

"You were supposed to be getting a car together," I offered helpfully.

"Oh. Yeah." She pulled a face. "Guess she's coming alone then."

I looked around again, wanting to see Alex more than ever now. Other people had arrived, but I still hardly recognized anyone.

The music pumped out, and as the number of people in the room swelled, so did the heat. Robyn had lost interest in my conversation about Alex and had returned to Nate, leaving me and Brooke standing like a pair of wallflowers. The air around us was thick with music and body heat, and just like at the pool, I knew I ought to mingle. Instead, I clung to the wall, drink in hand, and willed Alex to arrive, dreading the thought that she might not bother to turn up.

The alcohol tasted good on my tongue and I took another large gulp, deciding that if tonight was to be the night I would talk to her, I might need some help. I knew I needed to explain myself to her. Make her understand how messed up I'd felt over Nicole, and that I didn't want the same to happen to me and her. Tonight was going to be the night I'd make her understand that we were better off as friends, and then all the worries and angst of the past few weeks would be forgotten.

Suddenly, the music died, and the brief silence was welcome. In those few seconds of silence, I heard a murmuring of voices. I saw heads turn, sensed people nudging one another. My eyes followed the direction that the heads were turned in, and that's when I saw her. Alex. She was stopped just inside the doorway, looking adorably lost, obviously frantically scanning the floor for a face she could recognize. I should have waved at her, beckoned her over, but I was too mesmerized to even lift my hand.

She looked stunning. Like a movie star, a pop star, and a model, all rolled into one. She was dressed even more casually than I was, in faded blue jeans and a tight-fitting long-sleeved tee, but it just worked. Like everything about Alex just worked. Her hair was perfect: shiny and glossy, and teased over her eyes just so. Her make-up, too, was subtle and understated.

Finally, she spotted me and Brooke and, just as the music started again, walked across the floor to us, her head bowed, a shy smile plastered across her face as she passed a multitude of strangers all looking at her. She was obviously uncomfortable at her entrance, desperately uneasy at everyone watching her every step across the floor, and my heart ached for her.

"Bloody Robyn." Alex laughed when she reached us, but I could tell her laugh masked her deep discomfort. "Rang me at eight forty-five and said she was here already, but that my car was on its way."

"Sounds like typical Robyn." Brooke was the first to speak.

My eyes couldn't leave Alex. She caught my gaze, and in those few seconds that we looked at each other, I think we each could see the other's pain. I was the first to look away, my attention drawn from her by Brooke saying something droll to us both about Ed. Alex and I laughed, but it was the sort of laugh that was forced, and sounded unnatural. I don't think Brooke noticed, though.

Someone in a tuxedo carrying a tray of drinks brushed past us, then stopped, did a small reverse, and stood in front of Alex. He said something to her, his words muffled against the loud music, but I took it to be something about a drink, because he handed her a flute of champagne, then carried on his way again. Alex stood in front of me, glass in hand, then took a small sip from it.

"I guess if I ask for an OJ I'll get told I'm boring, right?" she said to me, cradling her glass in her hand.

"You can have what you want," I said. "You want me to…?" I gesticulated towards the bar, but Alex shook her head.

"I'm good," she said.

Brooke had somehow dissolved into the shifting masses, in that way that people eventually do when you're all crammed in together, and now Alex and I were alone. I knew a silence would settle between us, and I wasn't wrong. There were so many things I wanted to say to her, like how I wished we could go back to how we'd been, but the words just wouldn't come. Instead, the music continued to pound around us while we stood next to one another, each of us with glass in hand, while people we neither knew nor wanted to know came and went.

It was Alex who broke the silence first. Completely out of the blue she told me I looked beautiful, and I could tell by the tone of her voice she really meant it.

"Thank you." That sounded so insipid. "You look very nice too." Insipid and *so* lame. I looked down at myself and made some comment about not being very inventive wearing black. Alex replied with a comment I didn't catch.

"I'm sorry?" I cupped my ear against the music and leant closer to her.

"I said black suits you." Alex was so close we were practically touching. "And I love what you've done with your eyes." Her eyes flicked over mine, then away, and the awkwardness that stood between us was excruciating.

I think I muttered something about a new eyeliner I'd bought and just died inside at my inability to string two words together to her. The only thing that would break the awkwardness, I knew, was having a drink, so I drained the last of mine and grabbed myself another full glass from a tray on the bar.

Fortunately, intervention arrived when the music stopped and suddenly I could hear the intro to "After the Rain" belting out around the club. I caught Alex's eye and grinned. We both started nodding our heads in time to our guitar riffs, and then as if from nowhere, my arm was grabbed from behind and I was hauled onto the dance floor. I slammed my drink down on the bar and allowed myself to be dragged along by whoever it was.

It was, unsurprisingly, Robyn. And by the way she was laughing so hard as she pulled me onto the floor, I knew she must have had at least two more drinks since I'd last seen her ten minutes before.

Our music sounded great as it echoed round the club, and even though I didn't much like being the centre of attention in situations like this, the alcohol in my empty stomach had emboldened me sufficiently to actually stay on the dance floor and not flee back to the sanctuary of the darkness where I'd just been.

A huge cheer went up as our vocals kicked in, and the next thing I knew, Alex and Brooke were on the dance floor with us, and I soon forgot that people were watching us. Now I didn't care. Even though I was disorientated by the champagne, I felt bolstered by the throbbing swell of bodies on the dance floor and became increasingly less self-conscious the longer the song went on.

I was squashed in amongst a throng of sweaty bodies, all red faces and limbs flailing, all dancing to our music. Weird. But good weird. Robyn grabbed my hands and kept raising our arms above our heads as we danced, occasionally spinning me round until I had to tell her to stop. Alex and Brooke were doing something similar, laughing and trying to push the other off balance while they did it. I kept catching Alex's eye as we passed one another. She looked happy, reaching out to me and grabbing first my hand, then Robyn's, then releasing them again. I was pleased she was so happy. Relieved, even. I loosened up even more then and allowed myself to get lost in the moment, grateful that the music had allowed me and Alex to be more relaxed around one another than we had been just before.

As the music still pumped out, we joined up and started dancing as a foursome. Brooke with her arms in the air, Robyn with her arms loosely around my neck, her head thrown back, still laughing. Still drunk. We were wedged in amongst other people, some of whom grabbed our arms as we danced, others who linked their arms round our waists and danced with us for a few seconds before moving on to someone else.

Then, suddenly, the bodies on the floor parted and Alex and I were dancing alone, our arms draped around each other's necks. She smelled so good. The heat of her skin set off whatever scent she'd put on, and before I knew what I was doing, I'd pulled her closer and buried my head against her. I pressed myself hard up against her, her body warm and soft against mine, her hair gentle against my skin. It felt just like it had at the pool that day, so comfortable, so right. Like we slotted together perfectly. A matching pair. We danced on, people stumbling against us, not seeing us, occasionally making us loosen our grip on one another, only for us to tighten our hold.

Then, as if by some quirk of fate, "After the Rain" stopped before it was supposed to and was replaced by a slow song which wasn't one of ours. I didn't want to stop dancing with Alex. The slowness of the music and the feel of her melted into my arms were making me dizzy, and I wanted to stay with her like this for the rest of the night. But I knew I couldn't. It was unfair of me to do this to Alex, knowing what we both knew.

"I can't…" I reluctantly wrenched myself from her. "I need to go."

❖

Getting to the toilets was like navigating an assault course. Over the dance floor, past the bar, through a door, and down some steps, then turn left.

I knew I'd left Alex standing in the middle of the dance floor, and I knew what expression she had on her face. I'd stumbled from her, still feeling her body against mine, the memory of it making my skin tingle, like electric currents running through me. I'd barged my way past the others on the floor, knowing if I hadn't left Alex right then, I don't know what I might have done.

I took the steps down to the toilet, the music from upstairs gradually leaving my ears, and pushed my way into the first empty stall I could find, then locked the door and leant back against it. I heard toilets flushing, people coming and going, but all I could think of was Alex and how it had just felt to be with her. All the silences and bad feeling that we'd had since we'd kissed at the pool had been forgotten in those last few minutes when we'd danced together. We'd connected again, and any thoughts I might have had that my feelings for her could possibly go away now counted for nothing. They were never going to go away.

I unlocked the door and walked to the sink. There was only one person in the toilets now, a woman applying lipstick in the mirror. As I washed my hands, I tried not to look as her face twisted in the mirror until she was apparently satisfied with her work. With a quick nod of her head as she passed me, with not a flicker of recognition, she left the toilets. Finally I was alone.

I rested my hands on the sink and studied my reflection. The heat from the club had given my forehead a shine, while my dancing with Alex had made my cheeks flushed. I stared at myself. I didn't look sweaty and terrible, though. Instead, the flush on my cheeks made me look…I don't know. *Alive.*

Nicole had never made me feel like this. Sure, Nicole had made me laugh. But this was something completely new. This should feel wrong, because it felt wrong with Nicole. Except it didn't. This felt…

The door opened. I leant my head closer to the mirror, narrowed my eyes, and swept the hair from my eyes. The door closed. Soft footsteps.

"Tal. We really need to talk."

Chapter Twenty-three

Alex's face was as flushed as mine. I watched her in the mirror as she walked behind me, checking to make sure each stall was empty as she did so, then came to stand at my left side. She leant a hip against the sink, and I waited for her to speak again.

My heart was thumping so hard, I was sure she'd be able to see it beating in my neck.

"We should talk," she said again.

I looked at her reflection in the mirror.

"I tried to talk to you the other day," I said. "In the studio? You weren't interested."

"I was upset," Alex said. "Wouldn't you have been?"

"I'm sorry." I lowered my head and stared down into the sink.

"For what? Everything?"

I nodded, and as I did so, my hair fell across my face so that Alex couldn't see the expression on it.

"I thought we…you know…" Alex said. I lifted my head just in time to see her glance towards the door. "I thought we might have something. You and me."

"I think—" I started, then stopped as the door opened and a girl, about our age, walked in. I was sure she did a double-take when she saw me and Alex, and that was enough for me to want to leave. Next thing I knew, she'd have her phone out and her selfies with us would be plastered all over Instagram. I wasn't in the mood.

I signalled for Alex to follow me and left the toilets, no doubt leaving the girl to text her BFFs to tell them OMG who she'd just seen in the Hares toilets. I navigated my way through the ground floor corridors of the club, testing doors until one finally opened. It was the fire exit, leading out onto a small corrugated iron balcony, with steps down to a small courtyard below. I held the door open for Alex, then joined her on the balcony, pushing the door closed behind us.

"Talk to me, Tal." Alex spoke first. "Tell me everything you're thinking."

I drew in a long breath. "I think we'd be mad to let what happened at the pool ruin our friendship."

"Friendship?" Alex asked. "Is that all you think this is?"

I bit at my lip and nodded. It seemed that lying was the best option.

"Tal, you must know by now how I feel about you," Alex said. "That the feelings I have for you go way deeper than friendship." Her face creased. "I thought you felt the same way."

"I don't know what I feel." I turned and gripped the side of the balcony. "It's like…Nicole all over again."

"I told you before," Alex said, "I'm not Nicole."

"No," I replied, "but I'm still the same Tally." I looked at her. "I can still hurt you, just like I hurt Nicole."

"You'd deny your feelings for me," Alex said, "just because you think I'm going to get hurt?"

"I didn't say I had feelings for you." I didn't want to say that, I honestly didn't.

"So why did you kiss me?" Alex asked.

"I was confused."

"That wasn't a confused kiss," Alex said. "I know the difference. You *wanted* to kiss me." Our eyes held. "Just as much as I wanted to kiss you."

"But it's all impossible," I said, trying to ignore the feeling Alex's continued scrutiny of me was eliciting. "You and I will be impossible."

"Only because you're making it that way."

Alex paused.

"Just tell me what you want," she eventually said.

"I don't want...any of this," I said. "I don't want to have feelings for you. I don't want..." I sighed. "I just want all this to be better again," I said, gazing out across the courtyard. "That's all I want right now."

Alex touched my arm. I turned back and faced her.

"So tell me what I have to do to make all this better," she said.

"You have to not like me." I held her gaze.

"I can't do that."

"You have to, Alex," I said, moving her hand from my arm, "and the sooner you figure that out, the sooner we can move on from all this."

She didn't say another word after that. She looked at me awhile, almost as if she wanted to say more, but instead, left the balcony, slamming the fire exit closed behind her and leaving me standing alone outside.

The fresh air was welcome. I stood for a good five minutes, letting the air cool my skin, knowing I should go back into the party, but not quite feeling ready to do so yet. I held on to the side of the balcony and gazed up into the inky black sky, replaying my conversation with Alex back again to myself in my head. I'd said the right things, I was sure of it. Alex *did* have to not like me, just as much as I had to not like her. It was as simple as that. It would never work. We had to work together every day and to do that professionally, we had to keep our relationship platonic. I had to keep telling myself that over and over again. As I stared up, trying to count the sparse stars in the London sky, I really wished that a big gust of wind would come and take everything out of my hands and send it up into the sky, far away from me.

"What are you doing out here all alone?" Robyn's head appeared round the side of the door. She walked unsteadily onto the balcony, threaded an arm round my shoulder, planted a kiss on my cheek, and muttered, "Loser."

I could smell the alcohol from a good foot away.

"You're having a good night." I reached up and took her hand that was dangling loosely round me. "Had yourself some freebies?"

"We're number one," Robyn said, tightening her grip on my shoulder. "Cut me some slack."

"Slack cut." I laughed. "Sorry."

"Why are you even sober?" Robyn asked. "We're here to celebrate, aren't we?"

With everything that had happened with Alex, I wondered if I'd forgotten that.

"You should take a leaf out of Brody's book," Robyn said, leaning against me for support, "and let your hair down."

"Alex?"

"Yup."

"Why?" I asked, "What's she got to do with anything?"

"Who?"

"Alex."

Robyn frowned and I could see she was trying her hardest to focus on my face.

"What?"

She was driving me mad.

"Alex," I said. "You said I should take a leaf out of her book."

"Oh. Yeah," Robyn said, then puffed out her cheeks. "She came in from God knows where just now." Her gaze drifted away.

"And?"

"And what?"

"Robyn!"

"Hey, I thought you said she didn't drink?" Robyn jerked her head back to me.

"She doesn't."

"She does." A slow grin escaped Robyn's lips. "Downing shots in there." She jerked her thumb over her shoulder. "Atta girl."

"Alex doesn't drink," I said. "Never has done."

"Yeah, right."

I carefully removed Robyn's arm from my shoulder and made for the door, holding it open so she could follow me back in. After helping her past the toilets and back up the stairs, and once I knew she was safely away from the stairwell, I left her and walked back towards the main part of the club.

It was still bursting. The music had been hitched up a notch, and as I made my way back towards the bar, past the heaving crowds, the bass of the song that was being played pummelled my chest. Lights flickered around me, making it difficult to make anyone out, and the DJ kept shouting out, eliciting cheers, which was making my head pound with confusion as I desperately looked around the floor, trying to find Alex.

I needed to apologize. I couldn't leave things the way they were. If she was drinking, it was because of me. Because I rejected her, just like I'd rejected Nicole. I wasn't about to let it happen again.

For someone drunk, she was really quiet. I eventually saw her, tucked away in the corner, leaning against the bar, with only Brooke standing next to her with her arm round her shoulder. When I approached her, Alex stood up straighter, turned, and looked right at me. She lifted the glass she was holding, shrugged, then knocked it back in one. All the time she did it, she kept her eyes on mine. When her glass was empty, it was filled again by the barman, without Alex even having to ask.

It was grotesque. Wrong. Alex wasn't like this.

I stood next to Brooke and stared at Alex.

"You okay?" I lifted my chin to her.

"Fine." Alex picked up her next drink. "You?"

I shot a look to Brooke, who pulled a face at me as if to say she had no idea either. Except I *did* have an idea. I knew full well why Alex was behaving like this.

The next drink went down. Another one arrived soon after. The barman was a jerk. If a story appeared in the next day's papers, I'd know who to come looking for.

"Alex…" I put out my hand. "You want me to take you home?"

"I don't want anything from you."

I looked around me, hoping that no one other than Brooke could see.

"Alex, you don't drink." I reached over and took the glass from her hand. "You need to stop this."

She snatched the drink back from me, spilling some of it on the floor. "What are you," she said, "my keeper?"

While Brooke looked on, Alex drank her shot back in one go.

"I said, didn't I?" Robyn. I'd no idea she'd turned up. "You said"—she prodded me hard in the ribs—"that I was talking bollocks."

I rubbed my side.

"Alex." I held my hand out again. "Let me get you home."

"What do you care?" Alex suddenly sounded sober. "What do you care about me?"

I cared.

"Alex, please." I wished she'd take my hand.

"Don't act like you give a shit about me," Alex said, crossing her arms and tucking her hands underneath, "when we both know the truth."

Robyn and Brooke were watching, so I took the coward's way out. I pulled a confused face at them and acted like I didn't know what Alex was talking about, and felt worse than I'd ever felt in my life.

I locked my eyes onto Alex, hoping she'd see my desperation. All it took was for one idiot to photograph her on their phone, and she'd be plastered all over the Internet within the hour, and with it her reputation would get a right kicking. I knew if I let her be demeaned like that, I'd never forgive myself.

I kept my hand held out until finally—thankfully—she took it. Once she did, I pulled her to me. She felt soft and loose, thanks mainly to the alcohol she'd consumed. I didn't care. She was safe, she was quiet, and no one had seen apart from us three and the barman. Ed could deal with him later, I figured.

"I'll see her home," I said, still holding Alex. "Go and enjoy yourselves."

"Let me." Brooke approached me. "It's cool."

I didn't know if I wanted to let Alex go, but before I could think about it too much, she'd been transferred from me to Brooke and was now leaning heavily against her, staring at me but not speaking.

Then she was gone.

CHAPTER TWENTY-FOUR

I didn't stay on at the party after that. What was the point? Despite Robyn's grumbling that we'd all abandoned her and that we'd miss the presentations, I said my goodbyes and caught a cab straight back to my apartment. As I sat in the back of the cab while it drove through London at one a.m., my mind tumbled over, replaying everything that had happened that night.

There were so many things I could have done differently. So many chances missed.

I leant my head against the cool of the cab's window and watched the city lights as they coalesced; whites and oranges and reds became a blur as my driver made the most of the quieter night roads. I pulled my phone from my pocket and checked it, although I had no idea why I thought Alex would have texted me. She'd seemed incapable of anything, and I suddenly became worried that something bad might happen to her, so I rattled off a text to Brooke asking her to make sure Alex was okay.

By the time I'd put the key in my apartment door, Brooke had replied.

She's fine. Don't stress. Anyway, I'm going to stay at her apartment with her tonight x

The tears started flowing before I'd even gone in through the door.

❖

I woke up the next day with a pounding head, which was ironic considering I'd only had a handful of champagnes the night before. Before any other thoughts had a chance to filter their way through my foggy mind—what the time was, what to eat for breakfast—Alex was already in there. Because she was always in there. I turned over and stretched under the duvet, pointing my toes until my muscles stung, then buried my head into my pillow, and lay like that for two or three minutes, listening to a light rain rap against my window.

I lifted myself up onto my elbow, reached out a woollen arm, and grabbed my phone from the cabinet to the side of my bed then switched it on, narrowing my eyes against its harsh light in the rainy gloom of my room.

Nine a.m.

There was a text too. From Brooke.

I flopped back down against the pillow and read it.

Sleeping beauty. LOL.

She'd sent a picture of Alex, asleep. I knew Alex would be furious if she found out, because I was sure I'd be just as annoyed if anyone did that to me.

It didn't stop me from looking at her photo, though. Even asleep she was beautiful. Asleep and hung-over. She was lying on her side, her head sunk deeply into a pillow. Her thick eyelashes rested against her cheeks, and I stared at her closed eyes for the longest time, imagining how it would feel to be lying next to her right now, gazing at her. Alex's hair was flopped over her eyes so that her fringe landed just above her eyelashes, and she looked so peaceful it was hard to connect the girl in the photo with the same girl that was rapidly heading out of control the night before.

I scrolled away from the photo, then sent a message to Brooke: *You shouldn't have photographed her.*

I lay back and stared up at the spotlight on my ceiling, then felt my phone vibrate in my hand.

She's already seen it, you numpty! And she's totally cool with it x

Alex was awake. I imagined the pair of them, sitting in Alex's apartment, talking about anything and everything. I held my phone up above my head and wrote, *She okay this morning?*

Brooke wouldn't read that as, *Did Alex talk while she was drunk last night?* Would she?

Evidently not. A message came back saying, *She's fine. Bit quiet but she says she has the headache from hell, so not surprising. You up to much today? x*

I let my hand flop back onto my stomach, phone still clutched in it, and let out a long breath. Was I up to much today?

Yes, stressing mostly.

❖

"Lightweight."

Robyn had invited herself round. Great. I'd planned my day off down to the last minute, and it hadn't involved anything more arduous than a cheesy afternoon TV movie, a long soak in the bath, and my daily exercise to the pizza place downstairs. Now Robyn was here, looking as fresh as a daisy and taking the piss out of me because I'd had the audacity to leave the party before five a.m., which was when, as Robyn was now telling me in the minutest detail, she eventually fell out of Hares.

"So I'm a lightweight because…?" I asked.

She was stretched out on my sofa, legs dangling over the arm.

"Because people our age can usually make it a bit further past midnight than you did," she said.

"It was past one."

"Big shot." Robyn pulled a face. "And then I come round here and find you still in your PJs watching some trashy film on Channel Five."

"She's been betrayed by her new husband," I said, rolling a hand in the direction of the TV, "framed for a murder he did."

The look of disdain on Robyn's face was evident.

"Six months ago," she said, "you would have been coming out of the club with me at six." She threaded her hands behind her head. "Six months ago, you'd have been celebrating hitting our first number one single like there was no tomorrow."

"I *did* celebrate," I said. "I had champagne."

"Woo-hoo." Robyn lifted her hands up and shook them.

"Don't."

"Don't what?"

"Take the piss."

Robyn lifted her legs from the arm of my sofa and sat up straight.

"I'm here with you," she said, gazing round my apartment, "Brooke is with Alex, and according to her, she's as flat as you are."

"What are you both?" I asked. "The mood mafia?"

"See, it's comments like that," Robyn said, looking at me, "that make me know everything isn't okay at Tally Towers."

I should have answered, but I didn't.

"So what's up with you and Alex?" she asked. "Still?"

I felt adrenaline prickle my chest.

"Nothing." If I knew I didn't sound convincing, then Robyn certainly wouldn't be convinced.

"Try again," she said.

I shook my head.

"Listen," she said, "when I said to you the other day that you two need to sort your shit out, you said there was nothing to sort. Didn't look like it from where I was last night."

"It's not like that."

"So tell me what it *is* like."

"I can't."

"You told me you and her were cool," Robyn said. "You gave me a whole lot of bull about it being 'Missing You' that you weren't cool with, but you recorded your vocals for it the other day, and we all agreed everything had worked out okay in the end."

"It had. It *did*."

"So?" Robyn pressed. "What's your problem with her now?"

"I told you," I said, objecting being backed into a corner, "there is no problem."

"Okay," Robyn said. Now it was her that sounded annoyed. "You know that if the papers find out that this perfect image we've created is all bullshit, then the fans will feel duped, and…"

"It'll be like Nicole all over again."

"Exactly."

"It *is* like Nicole all over again," I said.

Robyn propped her elbows on her knees. "Alex is on something?" She looked confused. "Sure, she got wasted last night, but…drugs?" When I didn't reply, she pulled her hands through her hair. "Great. Just great."

"No. I didn't mean like that."

"So?" Robyn flitted her hands at me. "Explain."

I bit at my lip.

"I got confused," I said. "Thought I liked Alex too much."

"Like Nicole?" A look of understanding shadowed Robyn's face.

"Just like Nicole," I repeated. "I kissed her too. Just like Nicole."

"You're making a habit of this, aren't you?" Robyn laughed.

"See? This is exactly why I didn't want to say anything to you." My voice rose angrily. "It's not like I deliberately go out of my way to make out with all my bandmates."

"You've never tried with me." Robyn bumped my leg with hers.

"That's because I don't fancy you."

"You fancy Alex?"

"Yes. No. I don't know." I put my head in my hands. "Yes." I peered up at Robyn through my fingers. "I think I do." I buried my head again. "I'm so confused."

Robyn scooted closer and put her arm around me.

"I'm guessing," she said softly, "that the way Alex has been acting just lately, she feels just as confused as you."

"No, I think she'd go for it in an instant," I said. "It's me that's making her act the way she is."

"Because you're messing her around?"

I nodded.

"But you kissed her," Robyn said. "Why would you do that if you're not sure how you feel about her?"

"Like you've never done that with someone?" I asked her.

"Fair point." Robyn pursed her lips. "But did you like it?"

"Kissing her?"

"Of course kissing her, you idiot."

My stomach twinged at the memory. The way Alex's eyes had darkened. Her breath fluttering against my skin, her soft lips on mine.

"I loved it," I said, "which makes all this even more messed up."

"And it's messed up because…?" Robyn asked.

"Isn't it obvious?" I lifted my head. "I can't date her, can I?"

"Of course you can." Robyn looked at me like I was mad. "You're free to date whoever you want."

"And when it all ends?" I asked. "What then? That'll mean the end of all of this. Everything we've worked so hard for all these years."

"Who says it'll end?"

"Being on the road twenty-four-seven?" I suggested. "Living in each other's pockets?"

"Nate and I manage." Robyn shrugged. "I love having him with me all the time." She looked at me. "Are you saying me and Nate will end?"

I let out a long breath. "No."

"Well then."

"I don't want to ruin her life like I did Nicole's either," I said. "I don't want her to end up how she has."

"What? When it all *ends*?" Robyn air-quoted.

"I saw it happen with Nic."

"None of that was your fault," Robyn said. "Nicole was a ticking time bomb, as well you know." She thought for a moment. "Alex is different from her in so many ways."

"And that's why I know I like Alex way more than I ever liked Nic."

"That's cute."

"It's not cute, it's agony," I said.

Robyn was saying all the right things, I knew. But she could keep telling me over and over again that Nicole was okay, that I hadn't wrecked her life. I knew different. I knew that, even as Robyn and I were talking, sitting comfortably on my plush sofa in my plush apartment, Nicole was still holed up in rehab, still blaming me for putting her there.

I'd already wrecked one girl's life. I knew I'd do everything I could to make sure I never had the chance to wreck another one's.

Chapter Twenty-five

For someone who'd probably spent most of her Sunday recovering from her hangover, Alex looked perfect when I saw her again at the studio on Monday morning. I know if it had been me that had downed as many shots as she had on Saturday night, I'd have been in bed for at least three days, but then maybe Robyn had been right. Maybe I was a lightweight.

Recording albums can take forever. All the fans see is the finished, polished version. What they didn't see were the days spent in the studio recording and mixing. The hours spent hanging around waiting for technicians to do their thing, so we could just get on with our singing. That's all I wanted to do just lately: sing, record, go home. Think about Alex. Not think about Alex. Think about her anyway. My life, it seemed, was a total train wreck right now.

❖

"Have you spoken to her yet?"

Robyn arrived at the studio cranked right up into agony aunt mode. It was irritating, whilst at the same time strangely comforting.

"I know I should," I said, pulling Robyn away slightly from the mixing desk, "but I don't know what to say to her."

"How about, good morning, how are you?"

"She's not talking to me." I shot a look over to Alex, sitting in her now-usual spot, on her own. "I can't say I blame her."

"Did you think about what I said to you yesterday?"

I nodded. I'd thought about nothing else.

"There's just always something that stops me," I said, "but I wish there wasn't."

"If it's Nic that's stopping you, and we both know it is," Robyn said, "maybe you should go and see her again."

"It won't change what's going on up here," I said, tapping the side of my head.

"Or here." Robyn tapped her finger on my chest, just about where my heart was.

The studio was filling up. I glanced over to Alex again and knew Robyn was right. I needed to speak to her; ignoring her was just childish. Wouldn't resolve anything. Would make the awkwardness that now sat between us even worse.

I nodded to Robyn and made my way over to Alex, sidestepping the amps and cables as I did so. I stood in front of her and, when she didn't make any move to look up or speak to me, sat next to her.

"Hey."

"Hey."

It was just like how our first ever conversation had started, yet so different.

"You feeling okay?" I asked.

Alex looked slowly up at me, and the look on her face sent a large sliver of doubt slicing right through any tiny bit of confidence I might have previously had before I'd spoken to her.

"No," she finally said, "I'm not okay."

The conversation was going about as well as I thought it would do, and I didn't know whether I should stay and weather it out, or get up and leave.

I chose the former.

"I'm sorry if what I said to you on Saturday night made you… do what you did," I said. "I hate myself for making you do it."

"Not as much as I hate myself."

"Or me?"

Alex looked at me again for so long, I wondered if she was ever going to answer me. "I don't hate you," she said. "I could never hate you."

“Everything I’ve done,” I said, “I’ve done for a reason.” I touched her arm. “You do get that, don’t you?”

Alex looked at my hand on her arm, then slowly removed it. Instead of answering my question, she stood, put one hand in her jeans pocket, and stared out at a point behind me.

“I want you to have this,” she said, looking down at her pocket. She fished around and pulled something out, then handed it to me.

It was an iPod shuffle.

“Remember at my parents’ house?” she said. “I said I’d put some stuff together for you?”

I looked at it in my hand.

“I did it last night,” she said quietly. “Somehow it felt right to do it last night.”

I didn’t say anything.

“You’ll listen to it, won’t you?” Alex asked. “It’s important you do.”

“I will.” I crammed the shuffle into my jeans pocket and raised my hand as I saw Brooke coming over to us. I don’t know why I’d acted quite so much like I couldn’t have cared less about her music, but when I turned back to Alex and looked up and saw the look on her face, I knew what I’d known for a long time now.

It was official. I was a Class A bitch.

Chapter Twenty-six

In the dead of night, the mind wanders. Tortures. Every time I closed my eyes, the expression of hurt on Alex's face kept appearing, burned, it seemed, into the backs of my eyelids.

I'd been odious to her, and she'd so not deserved that. I don't know why I'd felt the need to be so horrible to her when I knew now what I'd been denying for weeks. I loved her. She was everything to me, and I'd acted like I couldn't have cared less that she'd gone to the effort of putting together some music for me.

I missed her too. I missed just hanging out with her, hearing her laugh. I wanted us to get back what we'd had before; I could love her as a friend, I was sure of it. The only thing I wasn't sure about was how I could even begin to make that happen right now.

Giving up on sleep, I fumbled for the light switch. I squeezed my eyes tight shut against the pain of the light's glare and, opening them again just enough to see, snagged up my phone from next to my bed. I sank my head back and found myself trawling back through mine and Alex's text messages. There seemed to be hundreds of them: some serious, some silly, some with deliberate misspellings to make the other one laugh. Because that's what we did. We made each other laugh.

My eyes left my phone and fell to my jeans, crumpled in a heap on the chair where I'd flung them the night before. Pulling back my duvet, I scrambled over the bed and reached for them, fishing in the pockets until my fingers made contact with the shuffle. I always had a spare pair of earphones never very far away, and once I found a fluorescent yellow pair stuffed into the back of my bedside cabinet, I scurried back under the duvet and pulled it back over me again.

The music that sounded in my ears was rich and warm. I switched the light back off and nestled back down into my pillow, staring up into the pitch-black of my room. As my eyes grew heavy I allowed the music to wash over me. Everything we'd looked at in Alex's room was on there: the Stevie Wonder music that Alex had managed to find in America; a Marvin Gaye song which I'd never heard before, but which had the most beautiful lyrics. Alex had added other stuff too, mostly older mellow stuff, but some new music too, from bands which she'd told me in her room that she liked. There were bands I'd never heard of, musicians the whole world knew. It was certainly an eclectic mix and I absolutely loved it.

I closed my eyes and allowed the music to take me away from my thoughts. I felt my muscles relaxing, easing the tension that had been gripping my neck, and I knew sleep wouldn't be far away now.

One song faded, and after a brief pause, the next one started with an acoustic guitar playing. It sounded warm and soft, like a blanket being wrapped around me, and I immediately loved the soothing sound it made. When the vocals started, my eyes opened. I blinked up into the darkness, hearing the familiarity of the voice.

The simplicity around the sound of the guitar playing told me it wasn't a studio recording, and I instinctively knew that Alex had written it and was now singing it. Her a cappella singing was raw and echoing, and I immediately recognized the nuances in the voice I was now so familiar with, the slight huskiness that always sent shivers down my spine.

The music was achingly beautiful, the lyrics haunting. I stared upward into the dark and imagined Alex singing, seeing in my mind's eye the way she always closed her eyes when she sang, how she gripped her headphones, the way she breathed, how she sometimes tapped her leg as she sang.

I absorbed every word she sang. I let them form in my mind, let them speak to me:

One day you'll wake up and you'll know. You'll just know. If you keep me close, right next to your heart, you'll know.

The chorus made my breathing slow, as I heard the words come from Alex's mouth: *Am I so insignificant? Can't you see? Without you I can't live, I can't breathe.*

I blinked.

Just take my hand, let me lead you there. I promise you, I promise you. I can wait, I can live. You'll tell me when. You'll tell me when, I know.

The song faded. Before it had even finished, I'd pressed play again.

It was six a.m. by the time I decided I didn't need to listen to it again. By then, though, I knew the song word for word. Nothing else on the playlist mattered other than Alex's song, and as I finally drifted back off into a deep sleep, I knew that nothing else would ever matter to me quite as much as Alex did.

My phone was shrill. Shriller than it ever sounded when I was awake. I flung my arm out of the bed to pick it up, and in doing so, knocked it to the floor.

"Shit."

I lurched over the side of the bed, knocking Alex's iPod and my headphones off the bedside cabinet as I did so, and scooped my phone up from the floor.

"What?" I answered it, not caring how I sounded.

"You always take this long to answer your phone?" Robyn.

"It's…" I pulled the phone from my ear, trying to see the time, but couldn't. The bright light around the edge of the curtains, though, told me it was late. "What time is it?"

"It's past eleven." She sounded grumpy. Like I cared.

"It's a day off," I said, rubbing my face awake.

"Have you been on the net yet?" she asked. "Or seen the papers?"

"I'm still in bed." I rolled onto my back. "Give me a chance."

"Call me back when you've seen it," Robyn said. "I've got to dash."

"What?" I ran a hand through my hair. "When I've seen what?"

"Just get your arse onto the net," Robyn said. "Google Nicole's name and then call me back."

She hung up. I pulled my phone away and stared at it, trying to focus on the screen so I could hang up too. I wiggled myself more upright and, yawning, opened the browser on my phone, then tapped in Nicole's name. What so-called scoop had the papers come up with this time? Releasing another yawn, I screwed up my eyes and opened them again just in time to see Nicole's name appear on my screen. Along with it were a whole pile of headlines:

Nicole Kelly talks Be4, rehab, and the future.
Nicole Kelly from Be4 spills the beans on what REALLY happened after she left.
Tempers, tantrums, and a whole heap of backstabbing. Read the real reason Nicole Kelly quit Be4.

My eyes darted over the screen, hardly believing what I was seeing. I scrolled down further, the nausea in my stomach increasing with each new salacious and loathsome headline.

"Yes I've been away," says Be4's Nicole Kelly, "but now I'm ready to rock again."

Nicole was out of rehab. I did a quick calculation in my head and figured she had to be out at least two weeks early. And spilling her heart out to the tabloids, by the looks of it. Anything for a fast buck, it seemed.

I rang Robyn.

"What do we do?" I asked her.

"You've seen them then."

"Of course I have."

"I don't know what we do." Robyn sounded scared. "Apart from let Ed sort it out."

"Has she mentioned me in any of them?" I asked. "I've mostly read the headlines and that was enough."

I heard Robyn let a long breath out.

"No," she eventually said, "she's not mentioned anything that happened with you."

Relief flooded me.

"But she's talked about rehab?" I asked.

"Rehab," Robyn said, "how we didn't support her. Blah, blah, blah."

The anxiety I'd been feeling instantly shot through into disbelief and eventually arrived at a boiling rage at Robyn's words.

"But we *did* support her," I said. "Well, as much as we could. It wasn't our fault Ed never told us."

"Tell that to the papers."

"I will, if necessary." I cut the call, too disgusted to speak another word.

A text arrived from Brooke: *Have you seen it? I'm in bits* :(

I snapped a reply back to her: *Are you? I'm fucking furious.*

Ignoring Brooke's reply, I pulled open the first story to appear on my screen. My eyes scanned the article, getting drawn to words that made my anger intensify:

I couldn't understand what was happening to me. Worse than that, I couldn't understand why none of my bandmates ever came to see me. Tally and I had been so close once, and yet here I was, alone in rehab, and she couldn't be bothered to even write to me, let alone come and see me. I was heartbroken. I thought better of her.

The irony made me gasp. Nicole had thrown out her cold, hard-nosed judgement on me to the papers without a second thought—me, who'd defended her time and again and had nearly driven myself mad with guilt over what I thought I'd done to her.

Well, enough.

I threw my phone down on the bed then just as quickly picked it up again. I dialled Ed's number, unsurprised when it went straight to voicemail.

"Ed," I said, "I don't know where Nicole has scuttled off to now she's out, but you find her. You find her and you tell me where she is the minute you do."

Chapter Twenty-seven

Everything was a mess. I'd ruined my friendship with Alex and now Nicole had done a hatchet job on me to the press. I sat cross-legged on the floor of my lounge and laid out the copy of the lucky newspaper that had grabbed its scoop on Nicole's story, seeing her photo looking back at me in the two-page spread. The headline was the same one I'd seen on the Internet earlier that morning, but underneath this one, in bold, black letters was the word EXCLUSIVE, which I took to mean the paper had paid Nicole a whole mountain of money for her story.

I looked down at Nicole's face. The main photo showed her leaning against a wall, her arms crossed, looking straight at the camera. She looked perfect: immaculate hair, skin. Slight tan. Expensive clothes. She looked for all the world to see as though she really *had* been in the Caribbean for the past few months. Another smaller photo showed her sitting with her guitar. Another one sitting at a desk, for some strange reason.

As I stared into her eyes, a fresh wave of loathing washed over me. How could she have done this to us? Words from the article swam in front of my eyes: how we'd rejected her, how I'd failed her. How Be4 had been everything to her, and then she'd had it all taken away. The slow realization that Nicole was playing the game of her life gathered pace the more I read. She claimed she was the one who was weak, and it had been us who had taken advantage of that weakness. We, according to her, were the ones who could have stopped her taking drugs; we were the strong ones and we should have known better.

It was detestable.

As my eyes darted from sentence to sentence, my bewilderment and hurt increased. Nicole had done her best to rubbish us all; as far as she was concerned, she was the strong one now, and we had all been weakened by Alex. Alex didn't belong, according to Nicole; Alex would cause the downfall of Be4 because Alex wasn't a founding member, and sooner or later me, Brooke, and Robyn would tire of her and strike out as a trio. I looked away, too furious to read any more. She'd had no right to bring Alex into any of this, sweet Alex who loved being with us, and who'd helped us get more success than Nicole ever had.

My eyes fell back to the paper. The talk of disloyalty was laughable, when it was clear, the more I read, it was Nicole who was now betraying us by trying to tell the fans that everything we'd ever stood for had been a sham. Disgusted, I shoved the paper away, but as I did so a sentence with a name in it, one I didn't recognize, caught my eye.

Freya.

I reached over and pulled the paper back to me, my eyes scanning the article until I found the sentence again.

> "If it hadn't have been for Freya, I think my life could have worked out very differently."

The words ebbed and flowed.

> "I'm in love for the first time…"
> "Now I finally know who I really am."

I sat back and stared at the wall in front of me, and kept staring at it, as if it held the answers to all the questions tailspinning through my mind. Only the buzz of my phone on the table behind me brought me back to reality, the sound worming its way into my ears and breaking my trance. I stumbled to my feet and, seeing Robyn's name flashing on and off the screen, snatched my phone up and answered it.

"I know I'm not the sharpest tool in the box," Robyn said, sounding breathless, "but am I right in thinking Nicole just came out to the entire country?"

❖

Alex had written me a song. Nicole had dumped a whole pile of nastiness right on me. I kept telling myself these two things as I sat on the Tube over to the studio.

Ed had called. He'd been quiet, which was more worrying than if he'd yelled at me. In fact, I think I'd have preferred it if he *had* yelled, even though none of this was any of my fault, because then at least I'd know what he was thinking. Silence didn't give me anything to go on. Just being asked to *Head over to the studio as soon as you can* gave me even less.

Everyone was there when I arrived. Alex too.

Alex had written me a song.

I smiled over to her as I threaded my way around the equipment, disappointment knifing me when she turned away and started to do something on her phone. I didn't get a chance to go over to her; my arrival apparently signalled the start of the impromptu meeting and, while Alex's back was still turned to me, Ed started to talk.

"You've all read it?" he asked, asking the question again, louder, when he wasn't satisfied with our answers.

"Read every stinking word," Robyn muttered under her breath.

Ed sat up on the edge of the mixing desk. "It's important to remember," he said, "that Nicole is nothing to do with us any more."

I knew what expression would be on Robyn's and Brooke's faces without even looking.

"She's chosen to go to the press," Ed continued, "and tell them what she thinks is her side of the story." He looked at us all. "What you all have to remember as well is that Be4 are strong. United. Flying high. The fans?" he shrugged. "They'll have forgotten who she is already. As far as they're concerned, Be4 is you lot, not her."

"And the fans will think, thanks to her, that everything's been bollocks from day one," Robyn said. "All our interviews when we said we were best friends, when all we talked about was how tight we all were. So who's to say now they won't think this current set up"—she rolled a hand around the room—"isn't a load of bollocks too?"

"We *were* tight." I stepped in. "Everything we told the fans was true." My voice caught. "We were solid. Best mates, living the dream together." I stopped. "And when she went away? You all know no one was more gutted than I was. No one felt more guilt-ridden about what happened to her. But what could I do? I had no idea where she was. None of us did, so she's got no fucking right to say we didn't support her, or that…" I stopped again, my voice sounding small. The words hurting my closed throat.

All eyes were on me. I was crying, my words tumbling and bubbling out through a cascade of tears and I'd had no idea.

Unsurprisingly, it was Alex who came to me. I'd seen her watching me, listening to me. I'd seen it on her face that she was with me. In a heartbeat she was by my side, her arms tight around me.

"It's okay," she whispered into my hair. "It's all going to be okay."

❖

Nothing was going to be okay ever again. At least, that's what I thought. The press wouldn't leave us alone, constantly wanting our thoughts, our versions of events. The Internet, too, throbbed with a new salacious article practically every hour, on the hour, not helped by Nicole feeding the beast by giving it endless fresh titbits about her new, fabulous life now she was out of rehab.

I sat in the gloom of my room and listened to Alex's song for the fourth time in a row, then immediately pressed repeat. I needed to hear her voice, because that made me feel as though she was close to me, even though I knew she was across the other side of London. The words burrowed into my head, formed shapes, spoke to me. No one had ever written me a song before, and in my eyes that made Alex perfect, and lovely, and everything I would ever want in a person. But what had I done? Instead of thanking her, instead of going to her and telling her I felt exactly the same way about her as she obviously did about me, I'd stayed away.

And then Nicole had intervened. All the time she'd been in rehab she'd been the invisible barrier that kept me away from Alex, and now she was out, it seemed to me she was still doing the same thing.

I had no idea why Nicole had gone to the papers. For the money? Possibly. To hurt me? I didn't even want to think about that, because I couldn't believe Nicole could stoop so low. So I chose to believe she'd done it for the money, so she could start again with a financial cushion to fall back on.

I pressed repeat and let Alex's velvety voice soak into my consciousness.

I just hoped it was a very big cushion. Nicole would be needing it.

"You're still in pieces, aren't you?"

Alex's voice was like an oasis of calm in amongst all the mess. Why she still wanted anything to do with me, after the way I'd treated her, was anyone's guess. But I was glad she did.

"It's the betrayal." I shook my head slowly. "The mud-slinging. The lies."

We were tucked away in the corner of the studio, alone, getting ready for a final recording of "Perspectives." Work, apparently, still went on, and the irony that we were recording a song I'd written about Nicole was lost on neither Alex nor me.

"Nicole obviously feels the need to tell her side of the story."

"From her perspective, you mean?" I asked sarcastically.

Neither of us smiled.

Alex lounged back in her chair and crossed her legs. "You should go and see her," she said, and I'm sure I wasn't mistaken when I saw the brief flicker of anguish that passed her features as she said it.

"Maybe I should." I lowered my head. I was tired. Exhausted from the anxiety of it all. "I'm sorry." I spoke to the floor.

"What for?"

"Everything." I raised my head again and looked at her. "For being so horrid to you."

"Stop." Alex uncrossed her legs, reached over, and took my hands in hers. "You're just having a fight with yourself at the moment."

I gazed at her. She had so many beautiful layers.

"Remember the words of my song?" she asked.

"Your beautiful song." My throat tightened. "I never got a chance to say—"

Alex shushed me. "Do you remember the words?" she asked again.

"Every one."

"Then you'll know." She smiled. "I can wait."

Those layers just kept on coming.

Chapter Twenty-eight

It's true that music has the ability to calm a person. "Perspectives" was three-quarters of the way to being finished, and even though the smell of Nicole's betrayal still hung in the air of the studio that day, we were determined it wasn't going to ruin everything for us.

Ed had been right when he'd said his little speech before. We were united and we wouldn't be beaten. The song was mine and Alex's, and right now it needed my full attention—not Nicole, not her stories, not the press hanging around outside being constantly sent away by security, only to reappear time and again.

I sat in the studio, my guitar in my hands, and waited for Alex to join me to record our guitar parts. Our mixing engineer had already edited and arranged the first rough instrumental mix, which would be played back to us while we played. It already sounded awesome, and I knew the final version was going to sound just as I imagined it would do when I wrote the song.

When Alex arrived in the booth, her guitar strung, as always, around her shoulders, she brought in with her a sense of the normal. When I looked up at her and into her eyes, it was as though the past twenty-four hours had never happened, and suddenly everything that Nicole had done was immaterial. It was a relief. As if I could breathe easily for the first time in what had seemed like days.

Alex settled herself on the stool next to me and plugged her guitar into the fuzzbox next to her. When she was satisfied with the quality of the sound, she bent her head to catch my eye and asked, "Everything seem a bit better now?"

I nodded and opened my mouth to answer, but before I could, Ed's voice sounded in my headphones.

"Going for a take."

The melody Alex and I produced sounded beautiful. My guitar became an extension of me, just like it always did, and as I relaxed into the rhythm, I know I played better than I possibly ever had done before. As I strummed and plucked, I looked over to Alex and saw the serenity on her face too. While I watched her, she caught my gaze, and in that moment I felt we were as one.

I smiled across to her.

Maybe she'd been right.

Maybe everything really was going to be okay.

"I'm going to see her." I snapped my guitar case shut.

"Nicole?" Robyn was lounging in an easy chair in the studio. "You think that's wise?"

"Yes, Nicole." I sighed. Adrenaline had paled into tiredness. "And yes, I think it's the right thing to do."

"When did you decide that?"

"I spoke to Alex," I said, lifting my guitar. "She made me see sense."

"Alex?" Robyn asked.

I stole a look to Alex, still packing her guitar away.

"She told me to go and see her," I said, remembering the look of pain on her face as she'd said it. "If I'm to move forward," I continued, "I need to get rid of the past." I slipped another look to Alex. "Because the past is stopping me right now."

The realization arrived swift and heavy.

It was time to start thinking about me for a change.

Nicole's apartment seemed like the most logical place to meet up. About the same size as mine, hers was the same side of the

Thames but nearer the West End than my place. Less cosy too, I'd always thought. My apartment was my home; Nicole's always struck me as just being the place where she happened to occasionally sleep.

She buzzed me up, and the time spent coming up to the sixth floor seemed to stretch out forever as my body and mind hummed with nervous energy.

I wished I didn't feel so apprehensive. I'd understood my trepidation when I'd seen her in Croft House, but that meeting was entirely different to this one. Then, I'd been awash with guilt; now, I was abuzz with nervous energy because I knew I wanted answers and I wasn't sure Nicole was going to give me any.

Her door was already open when I got to it. I pushed it open, called out, then waited. It looked exactly the same as it had when I'd last been in it, nearly four months before. Nicole had always loved pop art, so there were a multitude of bold and bright Andy Warhol prints lining the walls, none of which were to my taste. Nicole appeared, looking every inch as refreshed and at ease as she had in her pictures that had appeared in the papers, and my resentment towards her rose.

"You're here." Nicole smiled. If she was as apprehensive as me, she hid it well. "Tube okay getting here?"

"Fine."

I accepted her offer to come in, and stood in her hallway, the Warhols staring down at me from all angles. Her apartment was spotless, but then again I figured she'd not spent much time in it just lately. I looked around me, into the lounge, and saw her guitar propped up against the arm of her sofa.

"You've been playing." I nodded towards the guitar.

"It's all I've been doing just lately," Nicole said, her gaze following mine, "playing. It kept me sane in…you know. Drink?" She started walking into her kitchen before I could answer, so I followed her.

"OJ. Thanks." I rested a hip against the counter.

It was all too friendly, and that threw me. I'd spent the Tube journey over thinking how our meeting would pan out, how furious I'd be with her the minute I saw her. Every time snippets of her interview came back to me, and I thought about her betrayal, my fury would jump up another level, and an argument would form in my mind. Now I was here, though, I just didn't know what to say to her.

She passed me my juice and wandered into her lounge, which I took as my cue to follow her. Instead of sitting down, she walked to the window and stared out. She didn't have a drink; her arms, were wrapped tight around herself, her body stiff. I didn't know if I should sit down or join her at the window, so I chose the latter.

"I always thought the view from this window was a bit crap," Nicole said, without looking at me. "Just roofs and that. But it's actually not too bad, is it?"

I looked out of the window across the rooftops. She was right. It *was* a crap view. Actually, it was no view at all.

I took a sip of my drink. "I didn't come here to talk about the view, Nic."

"I know."

"Do you have any idea what you've done?" I asked.

She turned and slowly looked at me.

"What *I've* done?" she repeated.

I ignored that.

"Why did you do it?" I asked.

"Sell my story?"

"Why?" I heard the hardness in my voice.

Nicole shrugged, which really annoyed me. "To tell my side of things," she said, "so everyone could see it wasn't all the sweetness and light you lot were telling everyone it was."

"Wait," I said, turning to look at her, "you were the one that spoiled everything. Not us. Everything was fine until you decided it was more fun to mess with dope than it was to be with us."

"Because it was," Nicole replied bluntly. "It was certainly more fun than being with you, anyway."

Her words stung like a slap. I swallowed.

"You could have ruined everything," I said. My voice had lost its hardness. "You could have ruined Be4 thanks to the drugs, and now you could still ruin us, thanks to you wanting to tell everyone that we were vile to you, when you know the truth is we were anything but that." I shook my head. "I mean, what part of you thought it was okay to talk about betrayal when you're doing precisely that right now?"

"Don't make me out to be the bad guy in all this," Nicole said.

"But that's just what you are," I replied, "isn't it?" I drew in a deep breath. "And it's unfair to say we never came to see you. I was told to stay away by Ed."

That, at least, caused a reaction to pass across Nicole's face.

"And you do everything Ed tells you, don't you?" she replied.

"Not always." I briefly cut my glance away, then back to her. "I understood why we had to keep quiet," I said. "It's a shame you couldn't have kept quite as quiet as we did."

"I felt abandoned!" Nicole threw her arms out. "Booted out, ostracized. What is it they say? *Not wanted on voyage.* Do you have any idea how that made me feel, shacked up in that place?"

I had no answer.

"Ed took me there personally," Nicole said. "Croft House. Said he'd come and see me again in a few days so we could talk about the future. That gave me a pinprick of hope." She nodded. "I'd get my head sorted, Be4 would take a small break while I was doing that. Maybe write some stuff. You lot would come and see me so I could have some input on it." She chewed at her lip. "He never came back. Next thing I knew, some reject from a lamebrained TV show has been shuffled in, and suddenly you're all over the Internet and TV."

"Don't call her a reject." A flame ignited inside me. "Alex isn't, and never has been, a reject."

I saw Alex in my mind's eye. It was midafternoon, and I wondered where she was, and what she was doing. I saw her sitting, her guitar in her hands, a pencil tucked behind her ear, that look of adorable concentration she got on her face when she was writing music, and felt my chest ache.

"You all replaced me like that," Nicole said, clicking her fingers. "All of you." She hesitated. "So when the press come calling, asking me for my thoughts, what do you suppose I'm going to say?"

"You could have told them the truth." The flame inside me blazed hotter. "You could have told them it was your way of punishing me."

"What was?"

"The drugs," I said. "You could have told them it was me that sent you into rehab."

"That would have been a lie." Nicole's voice was almost inaudible.

"What?"

"I was bored, okay?" She snapped her head round to me. "We were on the verge of something massive, but we weren't moving quickly enough. Weren't the success I knew we could be."

"But you told me—"

"I know what I said," Nicole said, "and for a while I *did* blame you. But then I met Freya, and she made me see that—"

"Ah, Freya," I cut in. "The girl in the interview."

"She told me it was too easy for me to blame others for my mistakes," Nicole said, "when really I only had myself to blame."

"Sounds like this Freya girl talks more sense than you do." I glared at Nicole. "So you and Freya are, what…?" I asked.

"Dating."

A ton weight lifted from my shoulders.

"She made me see things differently," Nicole said. "Made me see that everything happens for a reason."

"You didn't mention her before," I said. "When I visited."

"Because she's none of your business," Nicole said. "Nothing I do is any of your business any more."

"Except you running to the press to sell your story," I said. "Pity Freya couldn't stop you doing that, isn't it?"

Nicole was pathetic. I wandered away from her and over to her small piano, tucked away in the corner of her room. "At least you're seeing someone," I said. I picked up some sheet music and stared at it rather than looking at her. "And, trust me, Nic, that's the best thing I've heard in ages." I meant it.

A silence cut between us then because I figured I had nothing more to say than that, and I guessed Nicole had said everything she'd wanted to say to me. She was never going to apologize for going to the press, just like she was never going to elaborate over Freya.

When the silence became too much, I figured I was finally done with her and made to go, but Nicole put out a hand to me.

"Remember how we used to sit here?" she asked. "Wasting our days away just writing and playing whatever music entered our heads?"

Of course I remembered. I remembered so many times how we'd sat at that piano, one of us with a guitar in our hands, and just chilled. We'd never felt the need to speak; instead we'd slouch together in a comfortable silence, usually a bottle of something cold somewhere to hand, one of us scribbling down music, the other playing the piano or jamming.

Mostly we'd play music, but sometimes we'd put our instruments down and just talk and talk and talk. About the future. A song we'd been struggling to write. An upcoming gig. How Ed had pissed us off. Who'd go for pizza that night, because each of us was convinced it was the other's turn, and then in the end we'd text Robyn and Brooke, invite them over, and ask them to bring pizza with them instead. That's how we rolled back then. Silliness, companionship, bickering, laughter, and music.

When I thought about it now, it all seemed so simple.

Except now, it was all dead.

"I have something else to tell you," Nicole said, a faint smile on her face.

"Go on."

"Freya and I are going to California together," she continued. "Next week. Her parents have a house somewhere out on the coast there."

"You're leaving?" A pinprick of something—regret? relief?—needled my skin.

"Freya knows a record producer over there," Nicole said. "I wrote so much music while I was in Croft House, and she thinks he could really be interested."

I opened my mouth to answer, but before I could, Nicole said, "I'm on the up, Tally. I'm clean and I'm writing again, and I have a girl who loves me and who's prepared to take a chance on me." She looked at me. "It's a shame you weren't prepared to do the same."

I stared back at her, seeing, for the first time that day, a light in her eyes. It was a light that had been missing since before she went into rehab, and I could only assume it had been Freya who had lit it again for her.

"I'm in love, and you know what? It hasn't affected my music," Nicole said. "Fancy that." She stared at me. "You know what else?"

I shook my head.

"Your rejection of me didn't finish me."

That hurt.

"I didn't mean to reject you," I said. "I just didn't know what I wanted back then."

Did I know now?

"But I *did* know what I wanted," Nicole said, "just like I do now." She shot me a look. "If you and I'd had just one tiny piece of what Freya and I have now, you'd have seen how good it is to be in love with someone who loves you back wholeheartedly."

"I've got my music." But even I knew my words sounded hollow. The truth was, I knew I had with Alex everything Nicole and I had once had: the silliness, the laughter, and the friendship. Had I killed that too?

"Music isn't everything," Nicole said. "Because who's lonely now? You, not me."

While Nicole carried on talking, all the disparate thoughts that had been swirling around in my head, like leaves picked up by the wind, suddenly came together and settled into a neat pile. In an instant I understood, and finally everything made sense. I knew I wanted me and Alex to be alive, not dead before it had even had a chance to take off. She wanted it, and I wanted it, but I was the one who was killing it. I was an idiot. I'd been so busy wasting time worrying about what might or might not happen, when it was clear Nicole had moved on. She was happy and didn't resent me, and suddenly all the guilt that had been festering inside me for months rose up and away from me like a wisp of smoke and disappeared into the London sky.

"I have to go." I hastily put my glass down and fumbled in my pocket for my phone. "If I'm too late I'll never forgive myself."

"Too late for what?"

I turned and looked at Nicole.

"To have a chance at happiness," I said.

Chapter Twenty-nine

Alex wasn't answering her phone. I hurried down the steps of Piccadilly Tube station, Nicole already faint in my mind. I sidestepped and elbowed my way past the hordes of people snaking their way up the steps and wished everyone would just disappear and leave me with a clear path down to my train. It was quieter once I was underground; rush hour was still over an hour away, so the smattering of people on my platform mainly consisted of tourists and a few groups of schoolkids heading home.

I stood on my platform and gazed up at the board. Which way to go? Did I chance it and go to Camden? Or did I head to the studio out further east and hope she was there? Then what? I hadn't given much thought as to what I would do after that, but I nevertheless rang Alex again, resisting the temptation to hurl my phone onto the tracks when, for the fourth time, it went straight to voicemail.

My mind was racing and, along with it, my heart. I'd been so stupid, pushing Alex away all this time. Nicole was healed; Nicole was moving forward while I was stagnating, thinking I could never be happy with anyone. Alex made me happy; Alex had made me feel whole, but it had still never been enough.

Voicemail. Again.

Alex needed to hear that everything about her was enough for me before it was too late. Before she, like Nicole, moved on.

A train pulled into the platform with a metallic shriek of brakes and a warm blast of air. I looked up; this one would take me straight to the studio. I looked up at the announcement board again; the next train to Camden was still another fifteen minutes away. Pacing the platform as it slowed to a stop and the doors finally opened, I rang Robyn.

"Where are you?" My pacing increased as passengers started to file out of the carriages.

"Studio. You?"

"Piccadilly."

Did I get on this train or wait for the Camden one? My heart hammered faster as a group of kids shouldered past me and started getting on.

"Have you seen Alex today?"

The last kid got on.

"Yeah." I heard Robyn stifle a yawn. "She's right next to me."

I jumped on the train just as the doors closed shut behind me.

❖

The walk from the station to the studio never usually took this long, I was sure of it. Maybe constantly rehearsing in your head what you're going to say to someone when you saw them made time move slower than normal. Nervous legs walked heavier and slower, that's for sure. Apprehension did strange things to a person.

Everything was normal in the studio when I arrived. Except everything was now different. For me, anyway. Alex was leaning against a window frame, watching Robyn and Nate at the mixing desk, while Ed and Grant sat together in another corner, heads bowed over what, from where I was standing, looked like an iPad. I couldn't see Brooke. But then, I only had eyes for Alex right at that moment.

As I entered the room, Alex looked over. My eyes locked on hers, my heart hammering so loudly in my ears I was sure everyone would be able to hear it as I walked across the studio floor to her, suddenly feeling as though my feet were too big, and my legs too heavy. I didn't really hear Robyn's greeting as I passed her, I didn't see anyone else in the room but Alex.

She didn't take her eyes off me as I approached her. I held out my hand, grateful and relieved when she took it. Without a word, I took her by the hand and pulled her past the others, their faces a hazy blur, and walked with her back out of the room.

It was now or never.

❖

I didn't think I'd ever felt nerves like it. My hands felt clammy, my throat dry. Why was it never like this in the movies? Why did everyone always look so cool and confident in all the crappy romances I'd ever seen, when I was a shaking, messy, bag of nerves?

I pulled Alex with me back down the corridor, with no idea where to go, or what to say to her when we eventually got wherever it was I was blindly heading. I slowed, worried that Alex would think I'd gone mad, then muttered something to her about needing to find some place quiet.

"In here." Now it was Alex's turn to pull me. She leant her head close to a door, knocked quickly, then, flitting me the cutest nervous smile I'd ever seen, opened the door and peered round it. "It's empty," she said back over her shoulder to me.

I followed her in, closing the door behind me, then pushed back against it. It was dim in the room, the only light coming from a small window across from us. It looked like a meeting room or something: whiteboard, long table. Lots of chairs. I had no idea the studio even had a meeting room, and for some stupid reason I found myself saying that to Alex. Lamebrain that I am.

Fortunately, Alex smiled. I figured she could sense my nerves from where she was. I also figured that couldn't be too difficult.

"I tried ringing you." My voice sounded small. Painful in my throat. "Before."

"I switched it off," Alex said. "It rang during the recording the other day and Ed got pissy. Remember?"

Did I? No.

"He told me to shut it off."

"Right."

The room opened up between us. I felt exposed and vulnerable, and wished Alex wasn't standing quite so far away from me.

"Did you go and see her?" Alex asked.

"Nicole?" Of course Nicole.

Alex nodded.

"I just came from hers now," I said.

"Okay." She nodded again. Silence followed, then, "So did you tell her just what you thought about her," Alex asked, "or…?"

"We talked," I said. "A lot." I drew in a deep breath. "It helped, I think." I looked at her. "It made me think about a lot of things."

"Such as?" Alex's voice was so quiet I could barely hear it.

"Such as me and you." I looked over to Alex. She was looking down and biting at her bottom lip and it was all suddenly way too much. I wanted to feel her in my arms, to remember how good she felt against me. Thinking that if I didn't do it now, I might never do it, I pushed away from the door and walked slowly over to her.

"I had the biggest wake-up call there, ever," I said, "and I know it's taken me forever, and I'm really sorry about that, but…"

"But?"

"I love you," I said, the words making me feel bright and alive. I was in love with Alex and suddenly everything made sense. This was the feeling everyone else talked about. She needed to know it; she needed to hear just how I felt about her. "And it's taken me way too long to say it to you."

"You…love me?" Alex asked slowly.

"I'm sorry," I said. "I should have told you that ages ago, and I'm really sorry I didn't, and—"

"That's a lot of sorries." Alex smiled, and her face was so open and expectant, I felt my chest bursting with longing.

"I have a lot of sorries to say to you."

"You don't." Alex stepped forward, closing the gap between us. "You don't have to apologize for anything." She captured my hand, making everything feel better in an instant.

"I've been denying it for so long," I said, looking at her hand in mine. "How I feel about you."

"And now?"

"I can't deny it any more." My breath was shallow, and I felt as though I had to force my lungs open to breathe. "I thought being with you would ruin our friendship," I said, "but not being with you would ruin my life."

The certainty of my words made me feel so good, like the weight I felt I'd been carrying around with me for weeks had finally lifted.

"I love you," I said again, the belief sounding clear in my voice, "and I want to be with you. I've wasted far too much time already, worrying about what might or might not happen." I held her gaze. "Just tell me I'm not too late," I said. "If I thought that I'd blown it with you, then I—"

The smile on Alex's face stopped me saying any more. She stepped closer, her mouth achingly close to mine, her breath fluttering sweetly against my skin, making my stomach feel light. My eyes met hers and held them, almost as if I needed reassurance from her that this was what she still wanted too.

"You're not too late."

I could feel her breath on my lips as she moved closer, ever closer, until my lips touched hers.

We kissed tentatively at first, a small fluttering meeting of lips, as we each held back, unsure if the other was going to pull away. When I knew it was what we both wanted, our kiss deepened and I was instantly lost in her, knowing there was no one else in the world at that moment but me and her.

"I thought I'd lost you." I rested my head against hers, feeling the gentle brush of her hair against my skin. "I'd have never forgiven myself if I'd let you get away."

"I love you, Tal," Alex said. "I would have waited forever for you."

"I've been so stupid," I said, "thinking that I couldn't be with you, when that's all I've wanted for a long time." I lifted my eyes to hers. "To be with you."

"We can make this work," Alex said, smoothing the hair from my eyes, "because we both want it to." She lightly kissed my forehead. "We can make anything happen."

"But for now," I said, sighing, "I suppose we ought to go back into the studio."

"Not yet." Alex wrapped her arms tighter around me and I nestled my head against her. "I like the way you feel in my arms too much to let you go again, just yet," she murmured into my hair.

"Do you think they'll be wondering where we are?" I asked, slipping a look back to the door.

"Who cares?" Alex said. "Now I've got you, they can wait a while longer." She cupped my face and kissed me again, her lips warm and sweet against mine. I pushed my body into hers, intensifying our kiss, a deep ache settling in the pit of my stomach as I felt the brief sweep of her tongue against mine.

Finally, reluctantly, we knew we had to stop.

"You've no idea how much I love you, Alex," I said, my heart overflowing, "and if I have to tell you that every day for the rest of our lives, I will."

"The rest of our lives, hey?" Alex smiled.

I took her face in my hands and kissed her slowly one more time. "Forever." I smiled.

I took her hand and led her to the door, but I didn't let go.

I knew I'd never let go of her ever again.

Epilogue

The lights bore down on my face, blinding me. The roar from the crowd almost drowned out the feed in my earpiece, but I could still hear my vocals clear enough, could hear the rasp of my guitar, feel the electric pulse of it through my fingers.

It was while we were in New York, halfway through our promotional tour of the US, that Alex and I put a joint statement video out on YouTube, telling our fans we were a couple. Within thirty seconds, the video had gone viral. Another thirty seconds later our delighted fans had nicknamed us Talex, and Twitter was awash with our own personal hashtag. Within the hour, hundreds of offers had flooded in—from London to LA to Sydney—for Be4 to perform, and for Alex and me to give exclusive interviews about us.

Sometimes I thought I'd have to pinch myself to make sure none of it was a dream. As I looked over to Alex on the stage next to me, Brooke and Robyn slightly further away, I knew it was anything but a dream. I unhooked my mic from its stand and lifted it to my mouth, singing to Alex as she too brought her mic up and sang, directly to me. The words of our new song, "With You," had never meant so much to me, and I knew I was singing the song to her alone. The crowd and the noise and the heat and lights were forgotten, and then it was just me and her onstage, singing to one another. I saw in her eyes all the love that I knew was in my eyes too, and as I sang the words to the ballad we'd written for one another, I'd never been happier.

I threw a look out to the crowd, to the army of faces swelling and bobbing in front of me in rhythm to the music. I read the posters being held high in the air, the sheets with messages for me and Alex scrawled on them:

Talex 4ever…

NYC ♥Alex and Tally!

Talex: cutest couple ever xxx

As the song reached its end, I threaded my arms around Alex, pulled her close to me, and buried my face in her, smiling into her hair at the knowledge that she was mine and she loved me as much as I loved her. With the crowd still chanting our names, a pulsating, humming drone of thirty thousand voices, I reached up and slowly kissed her, the noise of the crowd roaring their approval ringing in my ears.

"I think they like us." I had to shout above the roar.

"Talex forever, huh?" Alex grinned.

I kissed her again as the intro to the next song sounded.

"Talex forever," I whispered back to her.

About the Author

KE Payne was born in Bath, the English city, not the tub, and after leaving school she worked for the British government for fifteen years, which probably sounds a lot more exciting than it really was.

Fed up with spending her days moving paperwork around her desk and making models of the Taj Mahal out of paperclips, she packed it all in to go to university in Bristol and graduated as a mature student in 2006 with a degree in linguistics and history.

After graduating, she worked at a university in the Midlands for a while, again moving all that paperwork around, before finally leaving to embark on her dream career as a writer.

She moved to the idyllic English countryside in 2007 where she now lives and works happily surrounded by dogs and guinea pigs.

KE can be contacted at kepayne@tiscali.co.uk

Website: www.kepayne.co.uk/

Soliloquy Titles From Bold Strokes Books

Before by KE Payne. When Tally falls in love with her band's new recruit, she has a tough decision to make. What does she want more—Alex or the band? (978-1-62639-677-7)

Banished Sons Of Poseidon by Andrew J. Peters. Escaped to an underworld of magical wonders and warring, aboriginal peoples, an outlaw priest named Dam must undertake a desperate mission to bring the survivors of Atlantis home. (978-1-62639-441-4)

Breaking Up Point by Brian McNamara. Brendan and Mark may have managed to keep their relationship a secret, but what will happen when they find themselves miles apart as Brendan embarks on his college journey? (978-1-62639-430-8)

The Orion Mask by Greg Herren. After his father's death, Heath comes to Louisiana to meet his mother's family and learn the truth about her death—but some secrets can prove deadly. (978-1-62639-355-4)

The First Twenty by Jennifer Lavoie. Peyton is out for revenge after her father is murdered by Scavengers, but after meeting Nixie, she's torn between helping the girl she loves and the community that raised her. (978-1-62639-414-8)

Taking the Stand by Juliann Rich. There's a time for justice, then there's a time for taking the stand. And Jonathan Cooper knows exactly what time it is. (978-1-62639-408-7)

Dark Rites by Jeremy Jordan King. When friends start experimenting with dark magic to gain power, Margarite must embrace her natural gifts to save them. (978-1-62639-245-8)

Driving Lessons by Annameekee Hesik. Dive into Abbey Brooks's sophomore year as she attempts to figure out the amazing, but sometimes complicated, life of a you-know-who girl at Gila High School. (978-1-62639-228-1)

Asher's Shot by Elizabeth Wheeler. Asher Price's candid photographs capture the truth, but when his success requires exposing an enemy, Asher discovers his only shot at happiness involves revealing secrets of his own. (978-1-62639-229-8)

The Melody of Light by M.L. Rice. After surviving abuse and loss, will Riley Gordon be able to navigate her first year of college and accept true love and family? (78-1-62639-219-9)

Maxine Wore Black by Nora Olsen. Jayla will do anything for Maxine, the girl of her dreams, but after becoming ensnared in Maxine's dark secrets, she'll have to choose between love and her own life. (978-1-62639-208-3)

Bottled Up Secret by Brian McNamara. When Brendan Madden befriends his gorgeous, athletic classmate, Mark, it doesn't take long for Brendan to fall head over heels for him—but will Mark reciprocate the feelings? (978-1-62639-209-0)

Searching for Grace by Juliann Rich. First it's a rumor. Then it's a fact. And then it's on. (978-1-62639-196-3)

Dark Tide by Greg Herren. A summer working as a lifeguard at a hotel on the Gulf Coast seems like a dream job…until Ricky Hackworth realizes the town is shielding some very dark—and deadly—secrets. (978-1-62639-197-0)

Everything Changes by Samantha Hale. Raven Walker's world is turned upside down the moment Morgan O'Shea walks into her life. (978-1-62639-303-5)

Fifty Yards and Holding by David Matthew-Barnes. The discovery of a secret relationship between Riley Brewer, the star of the high school baseball team, and Victor Alvarez, the leader of a violent street gang, escalates into a preventable tragedy. (978-1-62639-081-2)

Caught in the Crossfire by Juliann Rich. Two boys at Bible camp; one forbidden love. (978-1-62639-070-6)

Tristant and Elijah by Jennifer Lavoie. After Elijah finds a scandalous letter belonging to Tristant's great-uncle, the boys set out to discover the secret Uncle Glenn kept hidden his entire life and end up discovering who they are in the process. (978-1-62639-075-1)

Frenemy of the People by Nora Olsen. Clarissa and Lexie have despised each other for as long as they can remember, but when they both find themselves helping an unlikely contender for homecoming queen, they are catapulted into an unexpected romance. (978-1-62639-063-8)

The Balance by Neal Wooten. Love and survival come together in the distant future as Piri and Niko face off against the worst factions of mankind's evolution. (978-1-62639-055-3)

The Unwanted by Jeffrey Ricker. Jamie Thomas is plunged into danger when he discovers his mother is an Amazon who needs his help to save the tribe from a vengeful god. (978-1-62639-048-5)

Because of Her by KE Payne. When Tabby Morton is forced to move to London, she's convinced her life will never be the same again. But the beautiful and intriguing Eden Palmer is about to show her that this time, change is most definitely for the better. (978-1-62639-049-2)

Asher's Fault by Elizabeth Wheeler. Fourteen-year-old Asher Price sees the world in black and white, much like the photos he takes, but when his little brother drowns at the same moment Asher experiences his first same-sex kiss, he can no longer hide behind the lens of his camera and eventually discovers he isn't the only one with a secret. (978-1-60282-982-4)

The Seventh Pleiade by Andrew J. Peters. When Atlantis is besieged by violent storms, tremors, and a barbarian army, it will be up to a young gay prince to find a way for the kingdom's survival. (978-1-60282-960-2)

Meeting Chance by Jennifer Lavoie. When man's best friend turns on Aaron Cassidy, the teen keeps his distance until fate puts Chance in his hands. (978-1-60282-952-7)

Lake Thirteen by Greg Herren. A visit to an old cemetery seems like fun to a group of five teenagers, who soon learn that sometimes it's best to leave old ghosts alone. (978-1-60282-894-0)

The Road to Her by KE Payne. Sparks fly when actress Holly Croft, star of UK soap *Portobello Road*, meets her new on-screen love interest, the enigmatic and sexy Elise Manford. (978-1-60282-887-2)

Swans and Clons by Nora Olsen. In a future world where there are no males, sixteen-year-old Rubric and her girlfriend Salmon Jo must fight to survive when everything they believed in turns out to be a lie. (978-1-60282-874-2)